BRIAN
THE SHAR

C000152369

BRIAN FLYNN was born in 1885 in Leyton, Essex. He won a scholarship to the City Of London School, and from there went into the civil service. In World War I he served as Special Constable on the Home Front, also teaching "Accountancy, Languages, Maths and Elocution to men, women, boys and girls" in the evenings, and acting in his spare time.

It was a seaside family holiday that inspired Brian Flynn to turn his hand to writing in the mid-twenties. Finding most mystery novels of the time "mediocre in the extreme", he decided to compose his own. Edith, the author's wife, encouraged its completion, and after a protracted period finding a publisher, it was eventually released in 1927 by John Hamilton in the UK and Macrae Smith in the U.S. as *The Billiard-Room Mystery*.

The author died in 1958. In all, he wrote and published 57 mysteries, the vast majority featuring the super-sleuth Antony Bathurst.

BRIAN FLYNN

THE SHARP QUILLET

With an introduction by
Steve Barge

DEAN STREET PRESS

Published by Dean Street Press 2022

Copyright © 1947 Brian Flynn

Introduction © 2022 Steve Barge

All Rights Reserved

The right of Brian Flynn to be identified as the Author of the Work has
been asserted by his estate in accordance with the Copyright, Designs
and Patents Act 1988.

First published in 1947 by John Long

Cover by DSP

ISBN 978 1 915393 36 4

www.deanstreetpress.co.uk

INTRODUCTION

"I let my books write themselves. That is to say, having once constructed my own plot, I sit down to write and permit the puppets to do their own dancing."

DURING the war, Brian Flynn was trying some experiments with his crime writing. His earlier books are all traditional mystery novels, all with a strong whodunit element to them, but starting with *Black Edged* in 1939, Brian seemed to want to branch out in his writing style. *Black Edged* (1939) tells the tale of the pursuit of a known killer from both sides of the chase. While there is a twist in the tale, this is far from a traditional mystery, and Brian returned to the inverted format once again with *Such Bright Disguises* (1941). There was also an increasing darkness in some of his villains – the plot of *They Never Came Back* (1940), the story of disappearing boxers, has a sadistic antagonist and *The Grim Maiden* (1942) was a straight thriller with a similarly twisted adversary. However, following this, perhaps due in part to a family tragedy during the Second World War, there was a notable change in Brian's writing style. The style of the books from *The Sharp Quillet* (1947) onwards switched back to a far more traditional whodunnit format, while he also adopted a pseudonym in attempt to try something new.

The three Charles Wogan books – *The Hangman's Hands* (1947), *The Horror At Warden Hall* (1948) and *Cyanide For The Chorister* (1950) – are an interesting diversion for Brian, as while they feature a new sleuth, they aren't particularly different structurally to the Anthony Bathurst books. You could make a case that they were an attempt to go back to a sleuth who mirrored Sherlock Holmes, as Bathurst at this point seems to have moved away from the Great Detective, notably through the lack of a Watson character. The early Bathurst books mostly had the sleuth with a sidekick, a different character in most books, often narrating the books, but as the series progresses, we see Bathurst operating more and more by himself, with his thoughts being the focus of the text. The Charles Wogans, on the other hand, are all narrated by Piers Deverson, relating his adventures with Sebastian Stole who was, as per the cover of *The*

Hangman's Hands (1947), *"A Detective Who Might Have Been A King"* – he was the Crown Prince of Calorania who had to flee the palace during an uprising.

While the short Wogan series is distinct from the Bathurst mysteries, they have a lot in common. Both were published by John Long for the library market, both have a sleuth who takes on his first case because it seems like something interesting to do and both have a potentially odd speaking habit. While Bathurst is willing to pepper his speech with classical idioms and obscure quotations, Stole, being the ex-Prince of the European country of Calorania, has a habit of mangling the English language. To give an example, when a character refers to his forbears, Stole replies that *"I have heard of them, and also of Goldilocks."* I leave it to the reader to decide whether this is funny or painful, but be warned, should you decide to try and track these books down, this is only one example and some of them are even worse.

Stole has some differences from Bathurst, notably that he seems to have unlimited wealth despite fleeing Calorania in the middle of the night – he inveigles himself into his first investigation by buying the house where the murder was committed! By the third book, however, it seems as if Brian realised that there were only surface differences between Stole and Bathurst and returned to writing books exclusively about his original sleuth. This didn't however stop a literary agent, when interviewed by Bathurst in *Men For Pieces* (1949), praising the new author Charles Wogan . . .

At this stage in his investigative career, Bathurst is clearly significantly older than when he first appeared in *The Billiard Room Mystery* (1927). There, he was a Bright Young Thing, displaying his sporting prowess and diving headfirst into a murder investigation simply because he thought it would be entertaining. At the start of *The Case of Elymas the Sorcerer* (1945), we see him recovering from "muscular rheumatism", taking the sea-air at the village of St Mead (not St Mary Mead), before the local constabulary drag him into the investigation of a local murder.

The book itself is very typical of Brian's work. First, the initial mystery has a strange element about it, namely that someone has stripped the body, left it in a field and, for some reason, shaved the body's moustache off. Soon a second body is found, along with a mentally-challenged young man whispering about "gold". In common with a number of Brian's books, such as *The Mystery of The Peacock's Eye* (1928) and *The Running Nun* (1952), the reason for the title only becomes apparent very late in the day – this is not a story about magicians and wizards. One other title, which I won't name for obvious reasons, is actually a clue to what is going on in that book.

Following this, we come to *Conspiracy at Angel* (1947), a book that may well have been responsible for delaying the rediscovery of Brian's work. When Jacques Barzun and Wendell Hertig Taylor wrote *A Catalogue Of Crime* (1971), a reference book intended to cover as many crime writers as possible, they included Brian Flynn – they omitted E. & M.A. Radford, Ianthe Jerrold and Molly Thynne to name but a few great "lost" crime writers – but their opinion of Brian's work was based entirely on this one atypical novel. That opinion was *"Straight tripe and savorless. It is doubtful, on the evidence, if any of the thirty-two others by this author would be different."* This proves, at least, that Barzun and Taylor didn't look beyond the "Also By The Author" page when researching Flynn, and, more seriously, were guilty of making sweeping judgments based on little evidence. To be fair to them, they did have a lot of books to read . . .

It is likely that, post-war, Brian was looking for source material for a book and dug out a play script that he wrote for the Trevalyan Dramatic Club. *Blue Murder* was staged in East Ham Town Hall on 23rd February 1937, with Brian, his daughter and his future son-in-law all taking part. It was perhaps an odd choice, as while it is a crime story, it was also a farce. A lot of the plot of the criminal conspiracy is lifted directly into the novel, but whereas in the play, things go wrong due to the incompetence of a "silly young ass" who gets involved, it is the intervention of Anthony Bathurst in this case that puts paid to the criminal scheme. A fair amount of the farce structure is maintained, in particular in the opening section, and as such, this is a fairly unusual outing for Bathurst. There's also a fascinating snapshot of history when the criminal scheme is revealed. I won't go into details for obvious reasons, but I doubt many readers' knowledge of some specific 1940's technology will be enough to guess what the villains are up to.

Following *Conspiracy at Angel* – and possibly because of it – Brian's work comes full circle with the next few books, returning to the more traditional whodunit of the early Bathurst outings. *The Sharp Quillet* (1947) brings in a classic mystery staple, namely curare, as someone is murdered by a poisoned dart. This is no blow-pipe murder, but an actual dartboard dart – and the victim was taking part in a horse race at the time. The reader may think that the horse race, an annual event for members of the Inns of Court to take place in, is an invention of Brian's, but it did exist. Indeed, it still does, run by The Pegasus Club. This is the only one of Brian's novels to mention the Second World War overtly, with the prologue of the book, set ten years previously, involving an air-raid.

Exit Sir John (1947) – not to be confused with Clemence Dane and Helen Simpson's *Enter Sir John* (1928) – concerns the death of Sir John Wynward at Christmas. All signs point to natural causes, but it is far from the perfect murder (if indeed it is murder) due to the deaths of his chauffeur and his solicitor. For reasons that I cannot fathom, *The Sharp Quillet* and *Exit Sir John* of all of Brian's work, are the most obtainable in their original form. I have seen a number of copies for sale, complete with dustjacket, whereas for most of his other books, there have been, on average, less than one copy for sale over the past five years. I have no explanation for this, but they are both good examples of Brian's work, as is the following title *The Swinging Death* (1949).

A much more elusive title, *The Swinging Death* has a very typical Brian Flynn set-up, along with the third naked body in five books. Rather than being left in a field like the two in *The Case of Elymas the Sorcerer*, this one is hanging from a church porch. Why Dr Julian Field got off his train at the wrong stop, and how he went from there to being murdered in the church, falls to Bathurst to explain, along with why half of Field's clothes are in the church font – and the other half are in the font of a different church?

Brian's books are always full of his love for sport, but *The Swinging Death* shows where Brian's specific interests lie. While rugby has always been Bathurst's winter sport, there is a delightful scene in this book where Chief Inspector MacMorran vehemently champions football (or soccer if you really must) as being the superior sport. One can almost hear Brian's own voice finally being able to talk about a sport that Anthony Bathurst would not give much consideration to.

Brian was pleased with *The Swinging Death*, writing in *Crime Book Magazine* in 1949 that "I hope that I am not being unduly optimistic if I place *The Swinging Death* certainly among the best of my humbler contributions to mystery fiction. I hope that those who come to read it will find themselves in agreement with me in this assessment." It is certainly a sign that over halfway through his writing career, Brian was still going strong and I too hope that you agree with him on this.

Steve Barge

PROLOGUE
ARTHUR ROTHERHAM PEMBERTON

THE court was crowded. The trial of Arthur Rotherham Pemberton for murder was drawing to its end. The atmosphere that prevailed in the court was surely indicative that the final stages of the trial had been reached. The closing speeches for the prosecution and for the defence by Sir Graham Preston, K.C., and Keith Salt, K.C., respectively had been listened to by the twelve members of the jury with careful and intelligent attention and Mr. Justice Wilbraham was nearing the conclusion of his summing-up.

He had pointed out with exquisite fairness and scrupulous exactitude the various points which were the main strength of the case for the Crown, and with no less meticulous precision he had delineated the many shades of doubt which might be said to favour the accused and to fortify the alibi which had been put forward as the principal plank upon which rested the case for the defence.

Gradually and with infinite nicety, Mr. Justice Wilbraham inevitably came to his concluding sentences. He had spoken for just on fifty minutes. His voice was lowered just a little . . . the members of the jury leant forward slightly in their seats, the better to hear. . . . "and those are, I think, the salient points for your consideration. It is now incumbent upon me to ask you to retire and to perform the duty which has been entrusted to you through the exigencies of the law. It is for you to find a true verdict, a true and proper verdict, according to the weight of the evidence that has been put before you. . . . I must say, with scrupulous fairness by both learned counsel . . . and of course regardless of what the consequences of that verdict you shall give, may prove to be. Ladies and gentlemen of the jury, you will now retire and consider your verdict."

The various members of the jury rose from their seats and filed slowly to their place of consideration. Without exception, their faces were grave and charged heavily with the burden of responsibility. More than one of them left the court-room with their eyes fixed on the ground. A warder moved quickly forward and touched

Pemberton on the shoulder. Pemberton, a young man in the early twenties, fair and good-looking, rose and went the way directed to him. A nervous . . . almost hysterical unrest disturbed the court . . . the words of what had occurred came to the public waiting outside . . . "the jury has retired." The prevalent opinion in the precincts and corridors of the court was "six to four on acquittal."

The members of the jury came to the apartment duly appointed for this, their penultimate duty. They seated themselves on chairs provided for them. The foreman of their own appointment began to speak to them. His name was Brooks. Norman Brooks. By calling he was an insurance official. The names of the eleven people to whom he spoke were, in alphabetical order, Luke Allan (a fishmonger), William Cox (a house and estate agent), Charles Dutton (chemist and druggist), Edward Kitchingman (coal-merchant), Thomas Langdon (nurseryman), Mrs. Agnes Macdonald (confectioner), Mrs. Jane Nuttall (bookseller), Edgar Owen (solicitor's clerk), Cecil Pepper (teacher of shorthand), Mrs. Julia Rudd (retired—no occupation), and James Wintringham (bank clerk).

"First of all," said Brooks the foreman, "let's try to clear the air a little and find out exactly how we stand. I think that's the best procedure we can possibly adopt. All those of you in favour of a verdict of 'guilty'—please put up your hands."

For a moment or so, there was no response. Then, hesitantly almost, five hands went up. The foreman seemed a little surprised.

"Five for 'guilty'," he said. It seemed for a brief moment that he had a mind to comment, but whether this were so or not he refrained from making any observation on their expressed opinion. "Now for the other side of the question," he said, "all those of you in favour of a verdict of 'not guilty'—please show your hands."

Again there was noticeable the same interval of hesitancy before the request was obeyed. "One—two—three," the foreman counted. "That means," he went on, "that three of you haven't voted. Is that clear?"

Kitchingman, the coal-merchant, took it upon himself to answer. "That's quite right, Mr. Brooks. You're correct. I'm one of them. And the other two are Mrs. Macdonald and Mr. Pepper. We've just had a word or two, one with the other—and we feel that we'd like to discuss matters a little more fully before we give a definite opinion one way or the other."

He swallowed rather nervously and then looked round at the other members of the assembled company.

"That's quite all right," answered Brooks, "that's just how I felt about it. It's exactly what I wanted to find out. Now I suggest that we all sit round and talk matters over . . . generally. We all heard what the judge said. I looked upon it almost in the light of an instruction. 'We've got to make up our minds according to the weight of evidence.' They were the words he used. And if you'll permit me to put the point at the commencement of this discussion I think our chief difficulty is going to be our respective opinions of the worth . . . or the weight . . . of Pemberton's alibi. It's supported by the bus-conductor, the ticket-collector at East Dulwich station, and in a much lesser degree by the Pemberton neighbour, Mrs. Woodman. You remember, the woman who chattered so in the witness-box. But personally I thought that her evidence was considerably shaken by Sir Graham Preston when he cross-examined. Apart from the fact that it was obvious she was a natural wind-bag who never stopped talking. Now let's talk over this alibi problem. You, Mr. Dutton, put up your hand just now for 'guilty.' Let's hear your views. Then we'll take the others in turn—listen to each one very carefully—and see if, in time, we can't argue the thing out and achieve, in that way, some measure of unity and agreement. Now is that acceptable to all of you?"

Brooks stopped and looked round. There came a murmur of assent. "Good," he said . . . "now, Mr. Dutton—you first."

Dutton, a thin, stringy-necked man with a sallow complexion, began to speak. "My view of the so-called alibi is this. . . ."

One hour and forty-three minutes later, Brooks sent up the necessary message that the members of the jury were prepared to return to the court and declare their verdict. Almost at once, the atmosphere within the court was transformed. Excited buzzes of conversation took sudden life and the news travelled like fire that the jury had finished its deliberations and was about to come back.

Mr. Justice Wilbraham entered in due course. The Clerk of the Court and the Judge's chaplain accompanied him. Norman Brooks, as he led in his eleven arbiters of human destiny, saw the ominous square of black silk ready to hand. The members of the jury took their seats. Brooks saw the Clerk rise and noted the unusual movement of his shoulders. The hush that descended upon the court had the suddenness of a sharp, physical shock. Brooks heard the Clerk's voice ring through the court.

"Ladies and gentlemen of the jury. Are you agreed upon your verdict?"

Brooks became suddenly nervous and coughed a little before he spoke. "We are."

"Do you find the prisoner at the bar, Arthur Rotherham Pemberton, guilty or not guilty?"

Brooks had a strange feeling come to him that he must pause before he answered the pregnant question. He squared his shoulders.

"Guilty," he said, quite quietly and with an entire absence of drama.

The court became deathly still. The black silk square was placed on the head of Mr. Justice Wilbraham. He leant forward just a little towards the prisoner. In a voice charged with feeling and deep emotion he said: "Arthur Rotherham Pemberton, you have heard the verdict which the jury has returned against you. They have arrived at that verdict. . . ."

At half-past eight on that same evening, the twelve jurors who had returned a verdict of 'guilty' against Arthur Rotherham Pemberton, sat down to dinner in the Sceptre Room of the Epicurus restaurant in Oxford Street. Norman Brooks, as befitted one who had been elected as their foreman, was in the chair. The dinner, of course, was restricted to either soup or *hors-d'oeuvres*, a main dish (pigeon) and a sweet. The gathering had been arranged by them some days previously to celebrate their release from judicial captivity and it had been strictly understood that at the dinner, no member was to be permitted to allude in the very slightest degree to the recent trial, in conversation. As Langdon, the nurseryman, had said at the time, "the whole affair will be over and done with and a thing of the past—let us remember that and allow it to remain so. And I'm sure we shall enjoy the dinner a great deal more that way than if we keep on chowing things over."

On this point they had reached unanimous agreement. As the dinner was nearing its completion, however, Brooks couldn't help his thoughts straying to the condemned man. The pact that no reference was to be made that evening to the trial in any shape or form, had been scrupulously honoured by all of them. But thoughts cannot be harnessed. They come unbidden and unsummoned. Sometimes they may be fugitive, at other times they may become tyrannous and despotic. Try as he would, Brooks was unable to rid himself of the picture of Pemberton in the condemned cell.

'I'm eating,' thought Norman Brooks to himself, 'a reasonably good trifle—under conditions as they are—I wonder what that poor devil's getting his teeth into. Condemned to death at twenty-three years of age! My God, what an appalling tragedy! Taken out and hanged in about three weeks from now. Fancy having to die at that age. What indescribable agony for his poor family.'

Thus were the thoughts that flooded the brain of Norman Brooks as he sat silent in his chair at the head of the table. 'And yet' (his thoughts continued) 'when you realize the grand young fellows of the Navy, the Air Force, the Army . . . and of all the other auxiliary services who have given their lives . . . who have lain and suffered in prison camps . . . with little food and under conditions of terrible privation and frightful torture . . . that realization puts a matter of this kind into its right and proper perspective . . . so why should I—or anybody else, come to that—worry myself or himself unduly as to the fate of this young murderer, Pemberton? After all, he's only deliberately asked for what he's got.'

Owen, the solicitor's clerk, happened to look up at that precise moment and saw Brooks shake his head in a conclusion, as it were, of his own argument. Owen then began to wonder what it was that had been specially exercising Brooks and then by some species of mental telepathy, perhaps, his own thoughts began to work in his brain on the same lines that had been present in the mind of Brooks.

But as it happened, by means of the Destiny which shapes our ends, neither Owen nor Brooks, neither Allan nor Cox, neither

Dutton nor Kitchingman, neither Langdon nor Pepper, neither Mrs. Macdonald nor Mrs. Nuttall, neither Wintringham nor Mrs. Rudd, need have entertained the slightest apprehension as to the fate of Arthur Rotherham Pemberton, or as to what each juror's feelings would be on the morning nominated for the execution. For the unanswerable reason that exactly seventeen minutes after Owen had noticed Brooks's shake of the head and had followed on the same mental track, a rocket-bomb fell on the Epicurus restaurant and the Sceptre Room of the establishment received a direct hit. At the moment the missile fell, Mrs. Nuttall was on her feet, seconding the vote of thanks to Brooks as chairman.

It is recorded with sadness and regret that none of the Pemberton jury survived. Langdon, the nurseryman, lived for about an hour after he had been dug out by the members of the Heavy Rescue Squad, but died in hospital after recovering consciousness for but a few minutes. He had been pinned down by a heavy beam. His spine and both legs were broken.

It will be seen, therefore, that the twelve civilian arbiters of Pemberton's fate all preceded him to Paradise, Hades, Valhalla, Nirvana, the Elysian Fields—have it how you will!

The appeal by Arthur Rotherham Pemberton against the verdict of guilty which had been passed upon him was heard at the Court of Appeal approximately three weeks later. Before the Lord Chief Justice, Viscount Fifoot, sitting with Mr. Justice Flagon and Mr. Justice Madrigal. Keith Salt, K.C., counsel for the appellant, based his chief ground for appeal on misdirection to the jury on the part of the most efficient Justice Wilbraham. Mr. Justice Flagon made no less than five brilliant points in almost as many minutes and flayed Salt's argument with merciless severity.

Pemberton looked down from his curtained eyrie high up in the court and listened with a curiously churning fascination to the contest of words fighting the battle for his life. But Salt was engaged on a forlorn hope, almost from the start, and although he persisted tenaciously and to the best of his brilliant ability in the presentation of at least three arguments, the inevitable time came when the Lord Chief Justice announced Pemberton's fate for the second time

... "we are satisfied, therefore, that there was no misdirection ... that the case for the appellant has failed ... and that therefore the appeal is dismissed."

The father of the condemned man tried to rise from his seat as though he were about to protest. His face worked convulsively—but the other members of Pemberton's family pulled him back into silence.

Arthur Rotherham Pemberton was hanged by the neck until he was dead on April 17th, and his body was buried within the precincts of the prison. By a singular coincidence, the date was the anniversary of his birthday. He was twenty-four.

PART ONE
NICHOLAS FLAGON

CHAPTER 1

1

THE smoke-room and lounge of the 'Wheatsheaf' at Quiddington St. Philip in the county of Elmshire was unusually crowded for a weekday evening. On most Saturdays and on almost all Sundays, the 'Wheatsheaf' was filled to capacity, but on weekdays normally, the attendance was thin. But on the evening in question, the company approximated in number to that of a Sunday evening in the summer.

All the ordinary seats were taken and all the old-fashioned alcoves and antique settle-shaped seats tucked away in odd corners of the lounge, were in use as well. The old sets of harness which hung on the walls and with which the 'Wheatsheaf' generally abounded, gleamed in the homely glory of their burnished copper on this beautiful spring evening and paid tribute to that eternal friend of man, the horse.

In one of the far corridor-corners, a game of darts was in full play, and the noise of the darts as they found their way to the different parts of the board seemed thoroughly in keeping with the general atmosphere of the place. A chance observer, being suddenly called upon for an assessment of social value, would have placed the various members of the present 'Wheatsheaf' assembly into two distinct and sharply defined classes. There were, naturally, the local people, men of the countryside and farms, but there was also present on this particular evening a number of what some local people, had they been asked, would have described as 'the gentry.' The two social strains were not mixing to any great extent, but each looked good-humouredly and good temperedly upon the other and accepted complacently the fact of its presence and existence.

At about a quarter to eight the main door, situated on the Sword road, opened and two men came in. It was easy to see, immediately, that each belonged to 'the gentry.' The first of these two men to cross the threshold of the 'Wheatsheaf' was a man of considerable physical distinction. He was tall, well-built, with sharp features, raven black hair and a set of beautifully white teeth. His hands, too, showed evidence of care and attention, much in advance of the average. He was bare-headed and wore a stylishly-cut, loose-fitting belted overcoat into the pockets of which his hands, more often than not, were thrust deep. He suggested, very strongly, the *jeune premier* of stage and screen. His companion was also not without certain physical advantages. He was of medium height with dark-brown hair thinning on top, well-cut features, but his face was lean and rather hollow-cheeked—almost gaunt. His eyes, however, were sharp, and continually moving . . . on the alert . . . as it were . . . always . . . and giving the onlooker the impression that the owner of them didn't intend to be caught napping or unawares . . . at any time . . . by anybody.

The taller man manoeuvred his way to the bar with considerable skill and the agility fostered by long practice. His companion came a pace or two behind him. The taller man turned and said:

"What are you going to have, Harcourt?"

"A pint of draught Bass, if you can get it . . . and in a tankard for choice."

The landlord, who was giving a hand behind the bar himself, owing to the size of the 'house,' overheard Harcourt's remark.

"Doan't you worry, sir," he said with his country burr in strong evidence, "we got most things 'ere at the 'Wheatsheaf,' I'm pleased to say. We got both draught Bass and draught Worthington, most all the spirits you might see fit to call for, drop o' port, drop o' sherry, cherry brandy, and a real lovely drop of sloe gin."

"Good for you, landlord," said the tall man, "that's about the best news I've heard for many a long day. I'm a good mind to put it to music. How do you manage it?" The voice was cultured and the tones incisive.

A slow smile spread over the landlord's face. "I've 'ad to 'ave it—let me tell you. It wouldn't ha' done if I hadn't. Up to a few months ago, we 'ad over five thousand American troops stationed in this 'ere district and the powers that be saw that they were well supplied. One of the biggest aerodromes in the country's only about a mile distant."

"There you are, Fothergill," said Harcourt, "that's your answer. We've struck oil. I'm glad we arranged to put up here."

The landlord drew the beer. "We be tidy full to-night, gentlemen. But it ain't always like this. Some evenings in the week this room be almost empty. But this evening's different. There be a few 'undred people 'ere in the district for to-morrow's point-to-point meeting. I suppose I wouldn't be far out in thinkin' that's what's brought you two gentlemen?"

Fothergill laughed a pleasant laugh. "You wouldn't, landlord," he replied in his habitually easy way, "in fact you'd be dead right."

He took a tankard, handed it to Harcourt and then picked up his own. Motioning to Harcourt, he said: "There seem to be a couple of seats vacant in the secluded corner near the darts players. See where I mean? I noticed two people drink up and go out. What do you say, Ronnie?"

Harcourt nodded. "Suits me." He followed Fothergill to the two seats mentioned.

"The Bar Point-to-Point meeting at Quiddington St. Philip always attracts a pretty good gathering," said the latter, "you'll see legal luminaries to-morrow by the dozen. And quite a few, too, of the *hoi polloi*. Though, of course, in that direction, the pull's by no means so strong. That's what I wanted to talk to you about."

As he spoke, one of the darts players approached the man sitting on Fothergill's right-hand side.

"Care for a game, sir? Best of three legs? Locals versus the Visitors."

The man addressed smiled. Fothergill noticed that he had white hair. "Sorry," he said, "but I don't play." As he spoke, he held up his right wrist in an attempt at explanation. "I had the misfortune to break my wrist some years ago. More than I care to remember. Never been able to bend it properly since. But I like to watch a game, you know."

The local nodded. "Yes. I've noticed you sittin' 'ere, 'avin' a look at us for several evenin's now. All right, sir, I understand—no offence, I 'ope."

"Not a bit of it," laughed the white-haired man—"very sporting of you to ask me."

The local made off, to put his request to somebody else. The white-haired man who had been approached, turned to Fothergill.

"Decent fellows, these country chaps. All good fellowship and very little malice. Comes from old Mother Earth, I expect."

Fothergill nodded. "I quite agree with you. Good fellows to a man."

"And surprisingly skilful at this game of darts," went on the other man, "I've noticed quite half a dozen of them go round the board in no time. Or rather, 'round the clock,' as they describe it."

"You down for the Point-to-Point to-morrow?" asked Fothergill.

"In a way," replied the white-haired man. "What you'd call professionally. I'm covering it for my paper. I'm a journalist." He fumbled in his waistcoat pocket and produced a card. 'John Bentley, *Daily Fanfare*.'

Fothergill read it. "I say," he remarked, "that's interesting."

"We always feature the Bar Point-to-Point," explained Bentley. "In fact this is the third year running I've been on it for them. So I know Quiddington St. Philip pretty well, as you may guess. I do Bisley as well and Henley and the Public Schools Racquets at 'Queen's.' Wonderful pair, the present Winchester pair. The long and the short of it. Treat to watch, believe me." He took a lighter from his pocket and lit a cigarette. "Ever seen them? The Winchester pair?" he asked of Fothergill.

"No. Can't say that I have. But I know they're good. Pal of mine saw them beat Harrow. And speaking of darts, I'm no mug at the game myself. The same goes for my friend here, Harcourt. Oh, Harcourt—I forgot—this is John Bentley of the *Fanfare*. Ronald Harcourt!"

The two men concerned, nodded to each other as men will in those circumstances.

"If that's the case," remarked Bentley, "I'd like to see you take on some of these locals and give them a jolly good caning. They play a game sometimes they call 'cricket.' I like to watch it. The stakes are pretty low as a rule," Bentley laughed, "no more than 'a pint.' So you won't suffer unduly, should you happen to lose."

"We might see about it a little later—we're staying here—" returned Fothergill—"in the meantime you'll excuse us, won't you? Harcourt and I have a little business to discuss."

"Oh, certainly," conceded Bentley, "you carry on. I'll stroll over and get another beer. That'll be my final for the evening. I usually sink three pints of this country wallop, but I make it a hard-and-fast rule to stop at three."

"Excellent idea," replied Fothergill—"I must congratulate you on your strength of mind."

"My dear sir," replied Bentley—"my mind's much stronger than the beer." He collected his tankard and strolled over to the bar-counter.

"Nice voice that chap has," remarked Harcourt, "yours is good, Maurice, but I don't know that it possesses the tone-colour that Bentley's has."

Maurice Fothergill grinned at the dubious compliment. "I didn't bring you down here, Ronnie, to expatiate on elocutionary qualities. I brought you here for another purpose. Now you listen to me for a few minutes and don't interrupt."

"I take it, Maurice," said Harcourt, "that you're pretty deeply involved in something to-morrow. I know the signs and portents of old. Am I correct?"

Fothergill said: "You are, Ronnie."

"Which is it?" asked Harcourt.

"It's the three-mile event. Ridden by members of the Bar. That's what I wanted to tell you about. I made a bloody fool bet on it as long ago as last Christmas Day. At my brother's place, down at Sonnet Magna in Hampshire. There was a crowd of us there for the Christmas holiday. You've met my brother Paul, haven't you?"

"Oh, yes. You introduced him to me at Newmarket the afternoon Helleniqua won the Cambridgeshire. Quite a few years ago now. Struck me as no end of a decent bloke."

"Sauce," commented Fothergill—"still—as you say—old Paul's quite one of the best. Well—to get back to first principles. There was a pretty mixed bag down at Sonnet—including Nick Flagon."

"What—the—?"

"I know what you're going to say. And you're quite right. Yes—no less a person than 'Flagon J.' Despite his eminence and terrific success, he's relatively young. In fact he was up at Oriel with old Paul. Hence the association of contemporaries. They've been cronies for years. Well—ever since their Oriel days. Nick Flagon's only in the early forties now. Has the distinction of being one of the youngest 'silks' ever to be raised to a judgeship. I say—drink up and let's fill up again."

"My shout," said Harcourt. He collected the tankards, went to the counter and returned with replenishment. "Go on, Maurice."

Fothergill, thus prompted, went on with his story. "Paul always maintains that Nick Flagon intended to be a judge from his cradle days. He read Law, was called to the Bar and achieved his crowning ambition about a year ago. But what I really mean to tell you is this. Nick Flagon's a Leicestershire man by birth and tradition. Keen as mustard on hunting and anything to do with our noble friend, the horse. His father was M.F.H. His mother hunted with the Pytchley before she married and Nick himself has carried on the good work with terrific enthusiasm and undiminished ardour. And even now, he won't altogether say 'good-bye' to the saddle and spurs." Fothergill paused to drink his beer. "Now there you are, Ronnie," he said as he replaced his tankard. "I've filled in the preliminaries of the picture for you. Nick Flagon, Mr. Justice and intrepid horseman.

Mind as sharp as a stiletto. Always very fit, thank you, and as hard as a bag of nails."

Harcourt drank and wiped his forehead with his handkerchief. "What's all this leading up to? Is it a eulogy of Nicholas Flagon—or is it?"

"Don't be so damned impatient, Ronnie. Wait for it. I'm trying to tell you the story properly and with the appropriate perspective. The main point is this—Nick Flagon has won the big event, riding his own horse, mind you, at the Bar Point-to-Point at Quiddington St. Philip for two years running. Last year and the year before. On each occasion he's sailed home comfortably on a big raw-boned bay by name 'Bloody Assize.'" Fothergill grinned as he named the horse. "The bookies make a rare mouthful of it when they shout the odds—believe me. I always enjoy hearing them give tongue."

"I can well imagine it," contributed Harcourt—"but go on."

"Well—down at Sonnet Magna—it was on the Boxing Day as far as my memory goes—the weather was properly foul—Paul, Nick Flagon, Cynthia—that's Mrs. Paul—and I, were in the billiard-room playing a foursome and the conversation turned on Nick's riding exploits. Not via Flagon himself—oh, no. I'll say that about him—no roll! After a lot of talk, Flagon said: 'If I do the hat-trick at Quiddington St. Philip next April, it'll be a record.' Paul chipped in with: 'How do you fancy your chance, Nick,' and Flagon replied: 'Well, my particular headache is the horse. Poor old "Bloody Assize" has got a touch of ringbone and won't run. Cullis, my trainer, told me last week there wasn't a hope. So I shall have to find another mount. Still—never mind that—I'll have a good shot at the hat-trick all the same.' Then, like a prize fool, I jumped in and said: 'I'll lay you tens, Flagon, you don't do it,' and then, as slick as a knife cutting butter, Nick Flagon said: 'That's a bet, Fothergill, in hundreds,' so there you are. I couldn't possibly back out of the offer and to-morrow I stand to lose a cool thousand Jimmy o'Goblins. Pretty grim prospect—what? Situated as I am—with hardly a bean to bless myself."

Fothergill picked up his tankard and looked gloomily into the recesses thereof.

"You certainly didn't advertise your intelligence—I must say, Maurice," remarked Harcourt. "What's the strength of the opposition? Any idea?"

"Well, of course, with these comparatively obscure 'point-to-points,' you never can tell. There's an entry of nine. I've done a bit of ferreting round the last week or so, and as far as my information goes, the race is between three horses. There's Sir Walter Mayhew's 'Brewer's Dray,' Noel Ware's 'St. Bartholomew's Eve' and Nick Flagon's, which only goes to show."

"What's Flagon riding in the absence of 'Bloody Assize'?"

"An absolutely 'dark' animal. He's supposed to have picked it up in the autumn by private sale. In the Midlands somewhere. Claverdon, I believe."

"What's it called?"

"'Legal Tender.' It's well bred. The dam was sired by 'Son-in-Law,' so there's staying blood there right enough."

"What'll it start at?"

"Oh—round 'threes' I should think—knowing Flagon's reputation. Not the foggiest hope of hedging, if that's what you're hinting at."

"H'm! Not so good. Very definitely not so good. Frankly, Maurice, you're a bit in the dirt as I see it, and you must trust to the fickle jade to get you out. Still—I'm curious. What was your idea in inviting me down?"

Fothergill shrugged his shoulders uneasily. "Oh—I don't know exactly. I think that I felt I wanted a spot of company. You know the idea—a pal to turn to as you hear the bomb whistling down."

"I see. Thanks for the compliment. But there's always another way of looking at it. You may be worrying your guts all unnecessarily and to-morrow evening may find you a hundred quid to the good."

"Wish I could think so," said Fothergill.

"I rather fancy 'Brewer's Dray' myself," continued Harcourt optimistically.

"Why—in the name of conscience? What do you know about its—"

Harcourt shrugged his shoulders. "I like the name. Sheer poetry, if you ask me."

But Fothergill wasn't in the mood for flippancy. He shook his head despondently. "No, Ronnie, I'm in a foul mood about all of it.

Something in my bones tells me that the worst is going to happen and that there's nothing I can do to avert it. I've never felt quite so depressed about anything before in all my life. Ah, well—no use meeting trouble half-way."

He looked up and saw the darts players with Bentley watching them. "Think I'll have a game, Ronnie. Take my mind off things a bit. What do you say, old man? Will you join me?"

Harcourt shook his head in refusal. "You play, Maurice. Leave me out this evening. I'm very comfy here, the beer's good—so why on earth should I exert myself? I've always been a bloke to sport with Amaryllis in the shade."

"Right-o. I'll be seeing you." Fothergill drank up his beer and lounged over in the direction of the darts board. When he arrived, he looked round the company a little superciliously and made an announcement.

"I'll play any man here best two out of three for a thousand quid! Any takers?"

There came a roar of mocking laughter. The declaration appealed to the locals as a piece of supreme amusement.

"Ha-ha! Did ye 'ear tha-at, Tahm? Gennelman'll play any one of us for a thousand quid! I'll bet he will an' all. If you lost, Garge, it 'ud take yer best part of two thousand years to pay up—it would an' all."

Fothergill noticed, however, that a big burly fellow was being encouraged by several of his compatriots. "Go on, Mike—play the gennelman. Doan't be bashful, Mike—do'ee take his trowsis down for 'im for the honour of the old 'Wheatsheaf.' 'Ave a bit more confidence in yourself. Go on, Mike, doan't 'ang back."

The big fellow, thus encouraged by his fellows, came slowly forward. "I'll play you, sir—but not for your sta-akes. But I'll play you for a pint."

Fothergill smiled at him. "Good for you, Mike—whatever your name is. Three hundred and one up and start off with a double—eh? That suit you?"

"That'll sure-ly suit me,, sir," replied Mike as he picked up his three darts.

The game was soon over. Fothergill proved far too strong for his local opponent—although the latter played with unusual skill. Mike

Keegan walked ruefully to the counter, produced the necessary coins and bought beer. He brought a brimming pint-glass back to Fothergill. Then he lifted his own pint to his lips and blew off the froth.

"'Ere's luck to you, sir. You're a bit too strong for me. I'm not quite up to your form. Still—I'll do my best to shake you up a bit to-morrow evening. That's to say should you be 'ere, sir."

"Don't know that I shall be, Keegan. Probably not."

As Maurice Fothergill spoke, Bentley came over and joined them. "Good show—I must say. I had no idea just now when I got mentioning darts that I was talking to such an expert. And Keegan here's pretty good, you know. I usually sit in my corner and see him victorious over all corners. To-night's a most abnormal experience."

Fothergill said: "Thank you, Bentley." Then he turned to the group of locals. "Anybody else want a game? Name your own stakes."

There was no reply. Keegan said: "Suppose you're down for the races to-morrow, sir? That's my guess."

Fothergill said: "And your guess is a good one, Keegan. What do you know, anything?"

Keegan shook his head at the enquiry. "No, sir. Wish I did. Might pick up a bit for the summer holiday. But I shall go along there and 'ave a look at 'em." He drained his glass. "One thing I do 'ope though," he added, as he put the glass on a near-by table.

"Oh—and what's that, may I ask?" said Fothergill.

Keegan leered. "Why—that Mr. Bloody Flagon don't win again to-morrow. I'd like to see him break his blasted neck, I would!"

Fothergill looked at the speaker with surprise. "Well—well—well," he said half-jocularly. "Fancy that now. I gather from those remarks that you and his lordship aren't exactly 'buddies.' You surprise me."

It was evident at once that Keegan resented Fothergill's banter. He turned sour and surly. "That may amuse you, sir—but I tell you it doan't amuse me. Far from it. If I 'ad my way—"

Before Keegan could complete what he was about to say, Bentley intervened.

"Do you know," he said benevolently, "that's the first time I've ever heard a word against Mr. Justice Flagon. It is—honestly! And my journalistic work takes me all over London into all corners of it and into the various grades of society. Everywhere I go, I hear Mr. Justice Flagon described in the most glowing terms. He's the . . . er—"

Fothergill filled in for him. "I know! The bee's knees. Likewise, the cat's whiskers. Is that it?"

"He is that," confirmed Bentley. "Still, Keegan here, doubtless, knows his own business best."

"You're right, Guvnor," said Keegan with an ugly look on his face. "I do and we'll leave it at that, if it's all the sa-ame to you. I do know my own business best. And as it *is* my business—I'll keep it to myself."

Keegan lurched away to join his own kindred spirits.

2

The following morning broke beautifully fresh and sunny. April had decked herself in her most beautiful garb. Fothergill was down to breakfast in the coffee-room of the 'Wheatsheaf' and Harcourt followed him less than a quarter of an hour later.

"Tea or coffee, Ronnie?"

"Oh—I don't know. Don't care much. What are you having?"

"Tea, my lad. Every time. Prefer tea in the mornings. Like coffee for my 'elevenses' and during the evening. Come on, man, make up your mind."

Harcourt picked up the morning paper. "You please yourself. I'm going to have coffee."

Fothergill gave the order and turned again to his companion. "Thought any more of what I told you last night?"

"Which one? Taking things by and large, you told me a good many."

"Our last discussion before we hit the hay, old man. What motive has Michael Keegan, a horny-handed son of toil, and a quite nifty thrower of darts, to hate the guts of Mr. Justice Nicholas Flagon, the eminent pillar of Law, Order and Justice, so much so that he hopes he'll break his bloody neck—or words to that effect? I won't have it that Keegan cut Flagon out for the love of a lady and I shall equally refuse to hear that he did Flagon out of his house-colours at one of our more distinguished seats of learning."

Before Harcourt could reply, a maid entered with the breakfasts. "Cereal, Ronnie, bacon *and* an egg! Toast and marmalade. Shades of pre-war luxury. Trust 'em to do themselves well in the country. Come on, pull up your chair, get cracking and answer my question. Keegan-Flagon—murderous attempt—query?"

Harcourt helped himself from the coffee-pot. "You're quite certain, I suppose, that the merchant was in earnest deadly? It wasn't hot air? Not just talking for talking's sake?"

"My dear Ronnie, you may take it from me that at the very thought of Flagon, Keegan absolutely flew off the handle. And if ever I saw murder glinting in a bloke's eye I saw it in Keegan's when he mentioned Flagon's name. I should say the least Flagon can have done is to have seduced Keegan's only daughter. Fair hair, blue eyes and the sweetest voice in the serried ranks of the village choir. Brought to shame by a High Court judge!"

Harcourt crumbled a piece of bread, almost abstractedly. "It's an idea—certainly. Is Flagon that way inclined?"

"How do you mean?"

"Why—what you hinted at. Is he a woman-hunter?"

Fothergill burst into raucous laughter. He seemed in much better spirits than had been his on the previous evening.

"Good Lord—no. The last man in the world. Nick Flagon is, and always has been, a paragon of all the virtues. Another Tunstall, my boy, and then some."

"Can you be absolutely sure of that?" Harcourt persisted. "Well—there you are? Can one be sure of anything?"

"That's just what I mean," said Harcourt quietly, "that's the very point I'm trying to make and . . . er . . . bring out. How do we ever know the *real* man? No, Maurice, we're very much inclined to take people for granted and on trust. We accept a reputation as the world knows it, as it's carefully wrapped up and given to the world at an entirely superficial value. The result is that when a crash *does* come—and you'll admit that they do very often—everybody seems thoroughly astonished and murmurs weakly—'Just fancy! Bill Smith of all people! Who'd have thought it! I've known him since he was a small boy. He seemed *such* a splendid fellow.' And you can pick the bones out of that, Maurice."

Fothergill thought it all over and nodded. "There may be something in what you say, Ronnie, but take it from me it doesn't apply to Nicholas Flagon."

"Say you don't know," retorted Harcourt, "every man's got his price *and* his Achillean heel. I'm as positive of that as I am that I'm eating bacon and egg for breakfast. And nothing you or anybody else may say will convince me to the contrary."

"Obstinate little fellow, aren't you?"

Harcourt grinned at the pleasantry. "We'll change the subject, Maurice. Arguing won't get us anywhere. We'll change it. From Flagon, the possible libertine and seducer of maidens, to Flagon, the strong-armed rider of 'Legal Tender.' Why the pronounced rise in the Fothergill barometer this morning? The very noticeable rise?"

Fothergill rose from the breakfast table and walked to the window. His back was to Harcourt. He stood there a moment or so looking out on to the garden before replying. The April dew glinted on the grass in the clear hard spring sunshine with the brilliancy of diamonds. There was a lane within his vision, with many twists under overarching branches. The lane ran down a steep hill and made the open again by a big house of light grey stone with a pillared portico. It had an amazingly beautiful garden of green lawn and many spring flowers. Just beyond the house was an old Norman church with narrow graveyard and carefully-trimmed yew bushes. And then again beyond the church the lane dipped down to the river Quidder.

Fothergill could see all this as he stood there. He turned to Harcourt and pushed his hand through his hair.

"I don't know. It's hard to explain. But I think I always feel better and more optimistic generally in the mornings. For no real reason that I could advance to you. It's just me." He returned to the breakfast table. "Your cup's empty. Let me pour you out some more coffee."

Harcourt looked somewhat surprised at this unusual gesture on the part of Fothergill, but accepted the offer with equanimity.

"Thanks, old man. Very good of you."

Fothergill, when he had poured out Harcourt's coffee, walked back to his window-view. It seemed that Harcourt's allusion to them had dissipated the fund of good spirits with which he had commenced the day. As before, he stood there looking out, with his back to the breakfast-table. The April sunlight was now pouring into the room in a golden cascade. The garden outside was noisy with the song of birds. The wings of birds fluttered in the boughs of trees. The morning air was cool, fragrant and fresh. As Fothergill watched, a big burly man, whose face he couldn't see, but whose gait was reminiscent, came out of the gate of a thatched cottage in the distance and began to walk down towards the bank of the stream. He passed out of Fothergill's sight and then a question from Harcourt brought Fothergill from his reverie.

"How far are we here from the course?"

"A good couple of miles. Perhaps a trifle more. Most of the events start abreast of that big red-roofed farm I pointed out to you on the way down yesterday evening. It belongs to a farmer named Castle. His family have farmed in this district for generations."

"Where does Flagon's event finish? The three-mile?"

"Oh—way over by Newstead Green."

"Where do you intend to be? To watch the race?"

"Somewhere near the finish. Between the last jump and the winning-post. Flagon can lead anywhere else for me by as much as twenty lengths as long as he doesn't get his head in front there. There's only one winning-post, young-feller-me-lad—and don't you forget it."

"How do we get there?"

Maurice Fothergill pointed down to his feet. "Shanks's pony, Ronnie. What were you thinking of in the transport line—a Rolls Royce? Or a magic carpet?"

Harcourt remained imperturbable under Fothergill's banter. "I thought perhaps we might scrounge a couple of push-bikes."

"Some hopes," retorted Fothergill contemptuously, "you'll hoof it, my boy, and like it."

"Well," returned Harcourt, "the going should be pretty good. That's one thing. There's been no rain for at least a week. So we shouldn't have to trudge our way through mud, mud and more mud. Had that been the case, I should have politely but firmly refused to accompany you and spent the day in the Verne Museum of relics and curios."

"I've been thinking," said Fothergill, "if we go up by the road which skirts the wall of Lord Geddy's park, there's a sort of conical shaped hill right above Newstead Green. There's a kind of escarpment of grass bank which guards a hollow right at the top. Not a hollow so much perhaps, as a shallow sort of crater. If we got up there we could see all there is to see absolutely splendidly and without interference from a soul. A real bird's-eye view."

Harcourt grinned at Fothergill's description. "Is that the ideal—from your personal point of view?"

"I don't say it's the ideal exactly—but I can't pretend to be over-joyed when I'm jostled by dozens of people. Or are you one of those gregarious souls who revels in crowds?"

"Maurice, you're being guilty of exaggeration. You're not going to put into me that the event here to-day is going to attract huge crowds. Because I shall refuse to believe it."

"Perhaps not. Certainly not 'huge' crowds, as you put it. It won't suggest Wembley or Kempton Park on an Easter Monday. But there'll be quite a decent-sized crowd, believe me. You'll be surprised. At least there always has been when I've come down before. This particular strip of countryside takes the Bar Point-to-Point quite seriously, I assure you."

Harcourt still looked sceptical. "I'll believe it when I see it."

"All right, Didymus. Have it your own way, then. I'll call upon you at dinner to-night to eat your words."

Harcourt rose from the table and joined Fothergill by the window. "What are your plans for this morning, Maurice?"

"Well, I wanted to go into Verne. There's a 'bus runs there from here at two minutes past every hour. The next one's due at ten two. And—I want to 'phone to Cynthia—my charming sister-in-law."

"What time do you expect to be back?"

"I shall be back soon after midday, old son. What do you intend to do? Coming with me?"

Harcourt looked through the window at the sky. "Don't think I will—if you don't mind. Think I'll stay and potter about here.

Perhaps I'll even do a spot of exploring. What time's the first event on the card?"

"Half-past one. But don't worry, I shall be back in ample time for that. We'll have a spot of lunch and leave here about a quarter to one. I'll fix that with old Willmott, the landlord, before I catch my 'bus."

"O.K.," returned Harcourt, "I'll take a stroll then, and meet you here again soon after twelve o'clock. Till then, my gay cavalier, *au 'voir*."

Harcourt slipped out of the breakfast-room and Fothergill went to arrange the matter of lunch with the landlord, before he caught his omnibus into the neighbouring town of Verne.

3

When Maurice Fothergill got back to the 'Wheatsheaf' that afternoon he could see no sign of Harcourt. He looked at the time by his wrist-watch. It showed ten past twelve. Ah well—it might be that he himself was a trifle early and that Harcourt had perhaps travelled farther abroad than he had originally intended to. But when the half-hour struck on the big old-fashioned clock in the dining-room, Fothergill sought out Willmott, the landlord, and made enquiries as to whys and wherefores.

"Any idea where my friend Mr. Harcourt is? I expected him back soon after midday?"

Willmott, who was serving in the saloon-bar, looked blank, fingered his chin and shook his head.

"No-a, Mr. Fothergill. I doan't seem to 'ave seen 'im about 'ere for some time now. Now where would it be that I last set eyes on him? Was it in the billiard-room?"

Willmott looked rather vacantly at the glass of beer that he happened to be handling at the moment. "Well, now I come to think of it, it would have been just after ten o'clock this morning. Not long after you caught the 'bus to Verne. Mr. 'Arcourt was in the billiard-room. That would be it."

"And he hasn't been back since?"

Before Willmott could frame a reply, the barmaid, Doris, spoke up.

"I can tell you where your friend was going, sir, if that would be any help to you. Because he happened to mention it to me. He was going for 'a walk round the village.' That's what he said. Oh—and something else. That he'd be back in time for an early lunch. I remember him saying that as he went out through the door there."

"Thank you, Doris," returned Fothergill. "He must have walked farther than he intended, and misjudged the time. That's all I can think. I expect he'll be rolling up in a few moments or so."

"Will you be 'aving lunch now, sir," asked Willmott, "or will you wait awhile for your friend to come back?"

Fothergill looked at his watch again. "Yes. I'm afraid I must have lunch at once. I haven't any time to spare."

"Very good, sir. I'll see that it's sent in to you within a few minutes."

"Thank you, Willmott."

Fothergill, looking annoyed at Harcourt's unpunctuality, went back to the luncheon-room. He made a quick lunch and at ten minutes to one was ready to start off. There was, however, no sign of Harcourt. At one o'clock, Fothergill made his decision. He would have to go. As it was, he had half an hour only, before the first event. He told the landlord of his decision and made arrangements for Harcourt to follow on, after he had returned and had his lunch.

"Tell him," he said, to Willmott, "that our arrangements made this morning still stand, and that I shall expect to meet him on the hill where we said."

"Very good, sir. I'll see Mr. 'Arcourt and tell 'im what you've said directly 'e comes back."

Fothergill waved his hand to the old chap and set off down the road to the Bar Annual Point-to-Point meeting at Quiddington St. Philip. Fothergill walked fast.

4

As Fothergill had anticipated and informed Ronald Harcourt the Bar was well represented at the meeting. Prominent K.C.s, at least half a dozen judges, two Recorders, several Clerks of Assizes and quite a hundred smaller fry were to be seen in what did duty as the Members' Enclosure. And farther down in the different fields, there had gathered quite a good sprinkling of 'locals'—notabilities and otherwise.

Fothergill kept his eyes open and just before the opening event, he saw Nick Flagon drive up and get out of a powerful raing car. He thought that his lordship looked a trifle paler than usual, perhaps, but otherwise perfectly fit. Later on, Fothergill spotted the burly form of Michael Keegan in close conversation with a seedy-looking little man who looked like an old-time jockey who had seen better days. Flagon's event came third on the card and directly the second race finished and with half an hour's margin of time, Fothergill made for the road by Lord Geddy's park and started to walk towards the hill he had mentioned to Harcourt as overlooking Newstead Green. Before he started, he saw that 'Legal Tender' had opened favourite.

The afternoon was hot for mid-April and when he had been walking for ten minutes, Fothergill began to mop his forehead with his handkerchief. There had still been so sign of Harcourt, and Fothergill felt that something serious must have happened to him. Eventually, Fothergill came to the top of the hill. He took the time again. It was ten minutes to three. Harcourt was not there. There wasn't a soul near or even in sight. It was evident now to Fothergill that Harcourt would not see the finish of the three-mile event. Fothergill looked round for a moment or two and then decided to have a look at the other side of the hill. There was just the possibility perhaps . . . He walked down and in this way was travelling away from Newstead Green and in the direction of the starting-post. There was still no sign, however, of Ronnie Harcourt.

CHAPTER II

1

Mr. Justice Flagon, fit as a fiddle for a man of his forty odd years, had 'Legal Tender' nicely balanced right from the start. He was, as Fothergill had indicated to Harcourt on the evening previous, a born horseman. He had balance, excellent judgment of pace and beautiful hands. And he had no doubts as to his mount's staying powers. By 'Robin Goodfellow' out of a 'Son-in-Law' mare, he knew that the big, long-striding gelding he was riding would get every yard of the distance. And in addition he was a clever jumper.

He kept 'Legal Tender,' therefore, tucked in very handily behind the field, took good stock of his two principal rivals, 'St. Bartholomew's Eve' and 'Brewer's Dray,' the only opponents which he regarded seriously and made his effort at precisely the right moment.

'Legal Tender' took the last jump cleanly and confidently, challenged at the distance and then started to forge ahead. Flagon was riding both confidently and comfortably. But about three hundred yards from the winning-post, with the race absolutely in his pocket, Flagon suddenly rolled from the saddle and 'Legal Tender' galloped on, gallant but riderless. A mere handful of spectators saw the incident and for some minutes Flagon lay on the green grass uncared for and untended. 'Brewer's Dray,' urged on by an enthusiastic rider, passed his prostrate form and ran out an easy winner by a margin of something like a dozen lengths.

The general impression along the course was that Flagon had fainted. But inasmuch as he failed entirely to respond to the usual ministrations for the fainting, his body was placed on a hurdle, removed to the side of the course and a doctor sent for. A small crowd had by now gathered round the hurdle and under a line of elms as the doctor's arrival was awaited. Maurice Fothergill was one of them.

When the doctor came galloping up on a borrowed horse (he had been compelled to come nearly three miles, it must be remembered), Fothergill, wondering why he hadn't come by car, got a little nearer to the hurdle in case he could be of any assistance. Doctor Harradine knelt down by the hurdle and busied himself there, professionally, for some minutes. From where Fothergill was standing, he had a good view of Harradine's face. To Fothergill's way of thinking, the doctor's face grew graver and graver every moment. Harradine tested the heart of the prone man and then carefully ran his fingers round Flagon's skull.

'Suspects a double fracture,' said Fothergill to himself.

After a time, Harradine looked up from where he was kneeling and spoke to Sir Claude de Monterey, one of the stewards who had come running up breathlessly a few minutes before. Fothergill noticed that Sir Claude's official rosette had become displaced from his coat and was hanging all awry from his lapel. But Fothergill heard what Harradine said to the steward. The words were plain. Fothergill had no difficulty whatever in distinguishing them.

"He's dead, Sir Claude. Dead as mutton. But how he died or what killed him—at the moment I haven't the foggiest idea."

De Monterey knelt down by the doctor.

2

Fothergill contrived to hang round in the crowd for some little time. Every now and then he scanned the faces of those who were looking on or who had come up, wondering and curious, to see if Harcourt had managed to put in an appearance. But to no avail. Harcourt was still missing.

When a further twenty minutes had elapsed, an inspector of police arrived on the scene accompanied by a constable, had a few minutes' conversation with Doctor Harradine and then promptly dismissed the gaping crowd towards the furthering of their individual occupations such as they might be.

Fothergill, very loth to leave the arena, had perforce to obey the inspector's orders, as conveyed to him by the constable, and started reluctantly to make his way back. His feelings were in active conflict. He would have found it difficult, had he been challenged, to describe them. Many emotions were in active contest within his brain. There were several things, too, which he found himself unable properly to understand.

Now that the gaping crowd had been cleared away, the Verne inspector, by name Catchpole, began to interrogate Doctor Harradine more closely. Then he turned to de Monterey.

"You say he suddenly fell off the horse, sir? Am I to understand that?"

Sir Claude nodded. "That's so, Inspector. I had the glasses on him. Flagon had the race well won with about a couple of furlongs to go when he just rolled out of the saddle. Just there it was." Sir Claude pointed over the hedge rather vaguely and uncertainly.

Doctor Harradine had his eyes closely fixed on the body. Sir Claude's eyes followed the doctor's. The face of the dead Flagon had now set in *risus sardonicus*. A fixed grin was the dominant feature of the face and the steely-blue eyes stared as though they had but recently encountered the most fearsome of sights. Harradine went across and knelt again by the body. He put his hand on Flagon's arm and then did a similar thing on the dead man's legs. When he took his hand away, he peered appreciatively at the drawn contracted muscles of the face and nodded to himself two or three times. Straightening himself again, he motioned to de Monterey and Inspector Catchpole to come nearer.

"I'm getting warmer," he said, "this is death from some powerful vegetable alkaloid. From some strychnine-like substance which produces symptoms akin to tetanus. The muscles of the dead man are as hard and unyielding as a board."

Catchpole searched Harradine's face with his clear unemotional eyes. "If that's so, Doctor Harradine, then it looks to me uncommonly like a case of murder. What do you think yourself?"

Harradine looked a little scared at Catchpole's statement and Sir Claude de Monterey, powerful and erect, whitened under his outdoor tan. Harradine began to explain.

"When I examined the body first of all—only for a moment or so, you must understand, Inspector—it seemed to me that something had caused the inspiratory muscles to fail to act. But even then I never considered—"

Catchpole intervened with a question. "How long would—well, let me put it like this, Doctor. I take it from what you've said, that you suspect poison of some kind?"

"Er—yes, Inspector, I suppose I do—now you put it like that. Although I hadn't—at the beginning—dreamt of such a thing."

Catchpole, who was nobody's fool, fingered his chin reflectively. "Something here I don't understand, Doctor. I confess it's got me puzzled. But how could a man who'd been poisoned ride as far as this man did? Don't forget he'd covered nearly three miles. It just doesn't add up, to my way of thinking."

Harradine was cautious in his reply. He shrugged his shoulders. "Depends how and when the poison was administered. Obviously."

Catchpole nodded. "Exactly, Doctor. If it didn't seem too damned absurd, I should have said that the poison was administered in some way during the time the man was riding. But that would seem a manifest impossibility. Now, Doctor Harradine, what do you say to that?"

"I don't see how—" Harradine broke off. But then spoke again almost immediately. "I must reserve my opinion, I'm afraid, Inspector, until I've had the opportunity to examine the body thoroughly, and apply the proper tests."

"I accept that, Doctor. Only fair to you."

At that moment a man came up and asked Catchpole for permission to speak to Sir Claude de Monterey. Catchpole gestured the concession. The man conferred with de Monterey for a few minutes until the latter disengaged himself and came back to Harradine and Catchpole.

"They've sent a message up to me," he announced. "The Stewards, I mean—that the rest of the meeting's been cancelled. To my mind—in the circumstances—a very right and proper decision."

For the first time he noticed that his official rosette was hanging inverted from the lapel of his coat. De Monterey flushed with annoyance and proceeded to straighten and replace it.

"So they've packed up, have they?" commented Catchpole—"Ah well—much the best thing as you say, Sir Claude. Get rid of the people for one thing. Besides—"

"Not, perhaps," contributed Harradine drily, "an entirely unmixed blessing."

Catchpole shot him a shrewd glance. "I'm going on to the course," he said. "Now does anyone of you happen to know which side of the course Mr. Flagon was riding? When he came down?"

"I think I can answer that," replied Harradine. "I was standing at the Brook Turn, just where Farmer Scudamore's meadow starts. Almost on a level with the last jump. Flagon was on this side. I mean the side we're standing now. That is to say he was galloping on the extreme right of the course. He was probably drawn one of the low numbers. But you can corroborate that by an enquiry of the starter, Sir Kenneth Peach."

"O.K.," said Catchpole. He walked along until he came to something like a break in the hedge, pushed his way through and walked on to the course. The grass was roughish in places but the surface, on the whole, comparatively good. Catchpole walked back until he drew abreast again of where the doctor and Sir Claude were standing. He called to them over the hedge. Harradine called back: "Hallo?"

"About here, wasn't it, where Flagon came down?"

"Just about," replied the doctor, "or as near as makes no odds. I was a good distance away, you know."

"Right-o," sang out Catchpole as he proceeded to walk across the grass.

One or two hoof marks showed the stretches where the going had been on the soft side, but otherwise there seemed nothing at all to excite comment. Catchpole was on the point of turning away and returning to the others when the luck changed. His sharp eves caught the glint of something where the sun was shining on it. Catchpole walked over to it. It was lying, as nearly as he could calculate, about a dozen yard behind the spot which Harradine had indicated as the place of Flagon's fall. Catchpole bent down and picked it up. It was a dart. An ordinary dart such as is handled daily and nightly by thousands of darts-players the length and breadth of England. But although it was ordinary in itself, there was yet something abnormal about it. It had an attachment. Tied round the middle of the haft was a tiny slip of paper, now grass-stained and creased. On it were printed, in small but well-shaped letters, five words. As far as Catchpole could make out they read thus: 'A nice sharp quillet? Ay!'

"Well," said Catchpole to himself. "I've never heard a common or garden dart called that before—but you live and learn."

He pursed his lips and walked back with his trophy, to where Doctor Harradine and Sir Claude de Monterey were standing. By the hurdle on which lay the dead body of Nicholas Flagon.

"What about this, Doctor Harradine?" he said curtly.

3

Harradine saw what the inspector was carrying. He looked at him curiously, the unspoken question in his eyes.

"Out on the grass there," said Catchpole, "about a dozen yards in the rear of where you think Flagon rolled off. May supply the explanation we've been seeking and that's been puzzling you."

Harradine held out his hand. Then he spotted something else. "Good heavens, Inspector," he cried, "handle that carefully—for the love of Mike."

"I know," replied Catchpole, "I've seen the wording tied on it. But I never knew they called these fellows 'quillets.' New one on me. Means a little quill or something, I suppose."

"I didn't mean that—I meant something else. Ah—I see what you're alluding to."

Harradine held the dart by the feathered end very gingerly and with an excess of care. Sir Claude de Monterey crowded round the two others, excited and interested.

"A nice sharp quillet," quoted Harradine, "dear me, how extraordinary."

"Tell me," said Sir Claude, "I must confess to a certain old-fashioned ignorance of these matters. But isn't that just an ordinary dart? You know what I mean. Such as . . . er . . . is used in the hostelries and . . . er . . . inns of this country? Looks like it to me."

"That is," said Catchpole. "That's a regulation metal dart such as is used for most matches and tournaments in clubs and pubs and places where they sing. I believe the trade-mark of this particular variety is 'Mongoose.' And—what's more—this is not a new dart. I'd stake my oath on that. It's been used before—several times, I should say—it's about 4¾ inches in length. The flight is renewable."

"I think," said Harradine slowly—he was choosing his words carefully—"that as divisional-surgeon, I'd better keep this for the time being. I feel that it's my duty to. I've seen something here that demands an immediate investigation on my part."

Catchpole looked a little doubtful. He pursed his lips. "All right, Doctor," he said eventually, "I'll leave it with you. As you point out, you're the divisional-surgeon. Till when, shall we say?" Harradine puckered his forehead. "Come round to my place at nine o'clock to-night. That should give me time enough for my purpose. That suit you?"

Catchpole nodded agreement. "That'll do for me, Doctor. Now I must make some more routine arrangements."

He walked over to the uniformed man and gave him certain instructions, after which he returned to Harradine and de Monterey.

"In the meantime, gentlemen, I'll wish you a very good afternoon. There's one thing—Quiddington St. Philip will be in the headlines to-morrow morning. And not only to-morrow at that."

4

The light from Harradine's surgery lamp was reflected on Catchpole's features as the latter stood outside the doctor's premises at nine o'clock that evening. Harradine blinked at him.

"Oh come in, Inspector. I thought it must be you."

Catchpole went in. "Sit down," said Harradine, "cigarettes on the mantelpiece. Like a drink?"

"Wouldn't mind, Doctor."

Harradine nodded towards a tray suitably furnished: "Help yourself. There's beer or something short if you prefer it that way."

"Beer for me, please." Catchpole helped himself to a beer. "Thank you, Doctor. I'm looking towards you." Catchpole drank. Harradine said: "Glad you've come."

Catchpole said: "Any luck?"

Harradine said: "H'm, depends on what you call luck. Look on that table."

Catchpole looked. On a side-table lay the dart—the dart he had come to hear about. Harradine picked it up by the flight and held it up to the light.

"Come here, will you, Inspector?"

Catchpole went and stood at Harradine's side under the light. "See the point?" asked the doctor. "I mean the point of the dart."

Catchpole stared at it. "Do you mean a slight discoloration?"

"Ah-ha! That's just what I do mean. That's been caused by a gummy substance applied to the point of the dart. And unless I'm hopelessly mistaken, Catchpole, that gummy substance is a very powerful poison of the curare or 'woorari' type. It's a dark-coloured extract obtainable from certain trees of the Strychnos family. Used by the South American Indians for arming the points of their arrows. Its action, Catchpole, depends upon an alkaloid which it contains, called curarine. Also—there's another rather interesting feature about it—and that's this. Given by the mouth it's almost devoid of action. By a strange dispensation of Nature, the kidneys excrete the poison as rapidly as it is absorbed. Remarkable, that, isn't it? But when injected under the skin, it paralyses the nerve endings in muscle. A person poisoned in that way would lie motionless until death ensues as a result of stoppage of the breathing which would be caused by failure of the inspiratory muscles to act."

"I see," said Catchpole slowly.

Harradine said: "I thought you would."

Catchpole said: "But that's only a start, isn't it? Where do we go from here?"

"Where do you think? That's *your* headache."

Catchpole took up his glass again, drank from it and set it down rather heavily. "I think that our steps should be directed to the mortuary. I'd like to hear the final score before I go to bed to-night. This is the biggest case I've ever had—or am ever likely to have—come to that. And I don't want it to go hay-wire."

"That's just exactly what I think," said the divisional-surgeon. "I'll get the car out and we'll run round to the mortuary together." The inspector rose. "I'm your man, Doctor."

5

Harradine pulled down the blinds of the mortuary and walked over to the slab where lay the body of the late Mr. Justice Flagon.

"Now, Inspector," he said, "in a way—you know as much of what's happened as I do. If there's a wound on the body, which side do you expect to find it? Bearing in mind what I've just told you?" Catchpole thought over the question.

"There's no catch in it," said Harradine, "just plain horse-sense." Catchpole looked up. "Sorry," said Harradine, "the play on words was an accident—it wasn't intended, I assure you."

"Probably," said the inspector, answering the original question, "on the right-hand side of the body—yes—on the right-hand side."

"High up or low down?"

"Er . . . high up."

Harradine nodded. "Good. I'm glad you've answered as you have. Because it shows me that your thoughts are travelling in the same direction as my own and you're beginning to get a picture of what may have occurred. Now let's have a look and see what really did happen."

The doctor pushed the slab round to the middle of the room and switched on the big powerful electric light directly over the top of it. The town of Verne prides itself on the way in which its municipal authorities have kept pace with the march of progress. The two men bent over the body. The examination was but brief. Suddenly, Harradine gave a sharp exclamation.

"There you are, Catchpole! There it is—see it? By the right ear there."

Catchpole craned his head forward. Harradine pointed to a place at the top of Flagon's neck—just behind the right ear and just under the inferior maxilla.

Catchpole spoke. "There's just a little—"

"That's the puncture there, Catchpole, very tiny but quite distinct," interrupted Harradine. "That's where the dart entered and fell out again, naturally, as Flagon toppled out of the saddle and the horse went galloping on. But it had sufficient impetus in its flight to penetrate the skin and the damage done was sufficient to kill him."

Catchpole grunted non-committally. "Tell me, then, Doctor," he said eventually, "this is all very well as far as it goes—but how do you think the murder was committed? Because I must confess that I—"

Harradine cut in again. "Do you want me to answer your question in detail—or just merely to give you broad outlines? Because frankly, I can't do the first. But I can—within limits—the second. There's little doubt, as I see it, that Flagon was killed by a dart thrown with amazing skill and dexterity from somewhere near where he and his horse were. As to how, etc.—" Harradine shrugged his shoulders: "Sorry, no can do."

"During the race, you mean, Doctor—not before?"

"Oh, undoubtedly during the race! Anything else is unthinkable. Death from the particular poison used would take place in a few seconds."

Catchpole lit a cigarette and offered the packet to the doctor. "In that case then, Doctor, it narrows the murder down, doesn't it? I mean it narrows it down as to the guilty party. Because it comes to this. The judge was killed by either a spectator standing very close to Flagon as he rode past or by another person riding in the race. You wouldn't fault that reasoning of mine, would you?"

Harradine thought for a moment before he answered: "No, I—think that I must accept that as eminently sound."

"Well then," went on Catchpole, "it seems to me that it's pretty big odds on it being the nearest rider that did the job. No spectator could have done it."

"Why not?" queried the doctor.

Catchpole spread out his hands to emphasize what he was about to say. "Well—I don't know how it strikes you, Doctor, but to me it almost borders on the impossible for a spectator to have done it. In the first place, leaving out the difficulty of the whole business, he would have been seen; which fact would have given him away at once."

Harradine pursed his lips. "I don't know that I altogether agree with you, Inspector. Don't overlook the possibility of him having been hidden somewhere."

Catchpole said: "Hidden where?"

Harradine said: "In the hedge, possibly."

Catchpole pounced on the divisional-surgeon as a terrier would on a rat. "I'll tear that idea to pieces, Doctor Harradine, without the least trouble; (a) Where and how could he have obtained the freedom of arm movement necessary to throw a dart with the degree of accuracy which *must* have been demanded to kill his man, crouched in a hedge, and (b) how did he get away—that is to say—crawl out of the hedge—without being seen—directly the murder had been committed? A hedge gets in your way—it's obstructive everywhere. Don't forget, the moment Flagon fell from the saddle, every eye was glued on that particular spot and thereabouts. No, Doctor, your hedge theory won't hold water with me for a moment."

"I must hedge from my hedge, eh? But I don't know that I'm anything like as certain about that as you are. Well, perhaps I shall be able to think of an alternative theory. I'll put on my best thinking-cap and do a spot of meditation."

Catchpole leant forward towards the doctor. "Now, I'll tell *you* something, Doctor! We'll trade our respective information fifty-fifty. From what my constable told me *and* showed me, and from what I saw myself, I'm inclined to the opinion that the murderer got away from the place on a bicycle. Had you thought of that?"

Harradine seemed a trifle disconcerted. "What makes you think that likely?" he asked.

"Why, this. On the grass, just in the lee of the hedge on the side Flagon fell, the blurred marks of a bicycle tyre were just visible. I looked for something of the kind and found them. They ran for about a hundred yards. Then they disappeared—and the disappearance is just before you come to that lane which curls round to Newstead Green."

"The marks of the bicycle were going in the same direction as the horses?"

"That's so. *Towards* the winning-post."

"Oh, but I say, Catchpole! You're coming it a bit, aren't you? You won't have my hedge and you calmly present me with a bicycle and the murderer escaping by riding it. What about *him* being seen?" Harradine chuckled. "Not bad that—I must say."

Catchpole shook his head. "Wait a moment, Doctor, before you scoff. A man, crouched down over the handle-bars, in the lee of the hedge as I said, and with only about a hundred yards to go before he turns off down a side lane, *might* get away with it, because all eyes by that time would be on the dead rider."

"Equally so," retorted Harradine, "could a man *running* by the side of a hedge! No—*not* equally so—definitely *more* so. The condition would be in his favour. And you can put *that* in your pipe and smoke it, Catchpole!"

"I don't know that I agree," returned the inspector phlegmatically. "There's the time factor for one thing. The man on the cycle would do the job much more quickly than the man running."

"Just a matter of a minute or so—and no more."

"Anyhow, I'm sticking to my ideas. You can stick to yours."

"O.K.," said Harradine, "I won't quarrel with that. I'm beginning to concern myself with another aspect of the case."

"What's that?"

"Motive, Catchpole, motive. Why should a man of such distinction as Flagon undoubtedly was, be murdered like this in an obscure country district?"

"One of two possibilities," answered Catchpole laconically, "as it appears to me—either gain or revenge. Find the person who benefited by his death to satisfy either of the possibilities I quoted, and you've laid your hands on the murderer."

"You think so."

"I do, Doctor. And what's more, when it's all cleared up, you'll find that I'm right. You see." Catchpole rose. "Now that I know where I am, I must get things moving," he added. "And I'll take this, I think." He stretched out his hand to take the dart from the table.

"Not yet," said Harradine, "if you don't mind. I want to test that point again and make more sure of the poison."

"Oh, yes. I forgot that. I'm running on too far ahead. I shall have to attend to the other matters. I must try to trace the dart—where it came from, I mean, and I must get the Press to work. I don't believe in hush-hush methods and never did. Especially with a man like Justice Flagon involved."

As he spoke there came a tap on the door of the mortuary. Catchpole looked at Harradine with raised eyebrows.

"Now who the blazes is that at this time of night and in this place of all places? Bit peculiar, Doctor, don't you think?"

"We'll investigate," replied Harradine. He made his way to the door. Catchpole listened attentively.

CHAPTER III

1

A SLENDERLY-built, white-haired man stood at the door.

"Yes?" inquired Harradine, rather curtly, "who are you and what do you want?"

"I wonder if I could come in for a moment, Doctor?" said the white-haired man, "perhaps I could explain myself better if I did."

"Well," Harradine hesitated, "I'm afraid not. It's rather irregular, you know—"

The white-haired man fumbled for a moment and then put a card in the divisional-surgeon's hands. "There you are, Doctor, you'll see who I am from that."

Harradine looked at the card. 'John Bentley, *Daily Fanfare*.'

He was about to reply when he thought of what Catchpole had been saying to him when the man had knocked.

"I see," he said slowly, "all right. Come in for a moment, Mr. Bentley. But you'll have to have a word with Inspector Catchpole—I don't know how he'll react to it."

Bentley sidled in. "Thank you, Doctor. You leave things to me."

Harradine took him along to Catchpole. "Here you are, Inspector," he said, "Mr. John Bentley of the *Daily Fanfare*. Can you use him? Or shall I tell him to clear out?"

Catchpole grinned. Before he could say anything, Bentley spoke.

"I'll be very frank, gentlemen. I know that this is an intrusion on my part. And candidly, I haven't come here to inquire after your health. With me, it's a matter of business. Business, pure and simple. Neither more nor less. I'll admit that before we go any further. But I was covering the Bar Point-to-Point meeting for my paper, the *Fanfare*. That fact explains my being in Verne this evening. This is the third year in succession that I've covered it. It's one of my specialities—a job of this kind. I do Bisley, Public Schools Racquets, and I have covered Henley Regatta. You get the idea, I'm sure. Well—" Bentley stopped and gestured with his hands. "I was near the stewards' enclosure this afternoon when the news came along to us that Mr. Justice Flagon had met with an accident. That was bad news, of course. Very sad indeed. From all points of view. Everybody regretted it. I think everybody liked Flagon. He was unusually respected and one of the most popular judges in the country. But there you are—"

Bentley stopped. Catchpole gave him no help. He waited for Bentley to go on.

"Well," continued the reporter, "I'll be frank, as I said at the start. You know what it is yourselves. You weren't born yesterday. Rumours spread—and people will talk. Very often, the wrong people, who talk at the wrong time, in the wrong place and in the wrong way."

Bentley stopped for the second time, but again neither Catchpole nor Doctor Harradine came to his assistance.

"Well," Bentley went on again, "I believe in getting one's cards on the table. There's a strong rumour going round Verne and Quiddington this evening that foul play's suspected. There you are, gentlemen—" Bentley looked round: "Now I've got it off my chest. I've said what I came to say."

The frown was still on Catchpole's face. "Well—I've listened to you, Mr. Bentley, but what I'd like to know is this. Where do you come in?"

Bentley made the same gesture with his hands that he had made before. "I thought I'd made that clear, gentlemen. Just as a matter of business. I'm a newspaper-man. This gives me a chance of a little scoop. On the other hand, I can help *you*, perhaps. You know the *Fanfare*'s circulation. You don't want me to tell you how many Londoners alone will have the *Fanfare* on their breakfast-plate to-morrow morning. And, as I indicated, you can help me. That's all. Now I've put all my cards on the table as I said I would. If, of course, there's nothing doing, I can say 'good evening, gentlemen' and that's that, and none of us is any the worse for our little encounter. We can part with no regrets on either side."

Bentley paused and looked round a little helplessly. There was a silence which lasted for a moment or so. Catchpole's features relaxed a trifle and his frown subsided. He looked at Harradine, but the divisional-surgeon adroitly evaded his gaze. What Bentley had said about the *Fanfare* and its circulation was substantially true. Catchpole knew that full well and he realized that he might perhaps go a long way farther and fare worse. After all, the Press would have to come in on it sooner or later . . . but—! Bentley waited for the—to him—momentous decision.

"I see," said the inspector. "Well, you've been frank, as you say. I appreciate that—and I can see your point of view. I'll play ball with you. I'll give you something to get on with. Flagon was murdered. Doctor Harradine here has established that fact, entirely to my satisfaction."

Bentley received the announcement placidly. "So rumour, for once, was not a lying jade. But how was the murder committed, Inspector? That's the part where I can't possibly—"

Catchpole cut in. "Flagon was poisoned. Beyond that bare statement of fact, I'm not prepared, at the moment, to go."

Catchpole shut his mouth like a trap. Bentley waited. Harradine watched them both. Eventually, it was Bentley who broke the silence.

"Do I get any more, Inspector?"

Catchpole said: "For the time being, no." He scowled at nothing in particular. "Oh, yes. There's one thing you can tell the gaping public—the open-mouthed readers of the *Daily Fanfare*—tell 'em that the police have the matter well in hand and are hopeful of making an arrest within the next twenty-four hours. That's always a good card to play. Makes the murderer 'jittery,' which is all to the good, and gives the police a better chance. There you are, Bentley of the *Daily Fanfare*, there's the bones of your scoop. Get busy on that little lot. And—er—come and see me again in, say . . . twenty-four hours. That suit you?"

Bentley took out his note-book and made certain entries in it. He fastened it and replaced it in his pocket.

"Where?" he asked simply.

"Er—at Doctor Harradine's surgery. In the Quiddington road. Where you called in all probability before you came here."

"Thank you," replied the reporter. "So that's the way it goes, is it?" He ignored Catchpole's last sentence.

"That's the way it goes," repeated Inspector Catchpole.

2

With a grumble which he made no attempt to conceal, Inspector Catchpole put the copy of the *Daily Fanfare* which he had been reading on the desk in front of him. Then he looked with interest at the visiting-card which had just been brought in to him. 'Keith Salt, K.C.' "Show the gentleman in," he said to the constable.

Salt came in. Catchpole saw a man in front of him, as unlike the traditional King's Counsel as anyone could very well be. Salt was a big, burly, sunburnt man, muscular and agile. A thick crop of busby brown hair was upon his head. He was clean-shaven, had the blue eyes of a sailor, seemed loose-limbed, lissom and athletic, and, as he stood there in front of the Verne inspector, was value for every inch of his six feet two and every ounce of his fifteen stone seven pounds. "Sit down . . . sir," said Catchpole—habit asserting itself. Salt's voice was full but incisive for all that. "I understand, Inspector Catchpole—I've made the proper inquiries, of course—that you're in charge of the Flagon case."

"That is so, sir."

"Good. Then I haven't wasted my time, because it's about that that I've come to you. I have some information that I feel should be placed in your hands without delay. When you called at the 'Saracen's Head,' this morning, I regret to say that I was out. Otherwise I should have handed it to you then and there."

"You are staying at the 'Saracen's Head'?"

"Yes, Inspector. The late Mr. Justice Flagon and I booked rooms there for the Bar Point-to-Point. We always stay there when we come to Verne."

"You and he were friends?"

"More than that—if such a thing's possible, Inspector. We were bosom pals. I can't put it more clearly than that. I was even more than his *fidus Achates*."

"I wasn't told that," protested Catchpole, "when I made my round of enquiries at the 'Saracen's Head.'"

"You should have been. Because the fact is undoubtedly well-known. But I usually find, Inspector, that most people become a bit tight-lipped when the police come buzzing round with a nose full of suspicion. That's the explanation, in all probability."

"I see. Well—what's the information you wish to give me, sir?" Salt stretched out his long legs from the chair he was sitting in. "On the morning of the meeting, Nicholas Flagon received an anonymous letter."

Catchpole sat bolt upright. This was almost the very last thing he had expected to hear.

"How do you know this, may I ask?"

"For the very good reason, Inspector, that he passed it on to me at the breakfast table that morning and asked me my opinion of it."

"You've brought it with you, sir?"

"I have. You shall have it. I knew where Nick had left it, because he told me that morning, and when this dreadful thing happened I began to look at matters a little differently. So I made up my mind to get it and bring it straight along to you as the inspector in charge of the case."

Salt took out his wallet, extracted a letter therefrom and passed it over to Catchpole. The envelope was addressed in a somewhat illiterate handwriting to "Judge Flaggon," c/o 'Saracen's Head,' Longhorsley St., Verne."

Catchpole took out the letter enclosed in it. It read as follows. "Just a line to inform you that you ride to-morrow for the last time, you barstard! Why? Because you'll break your blasted neck and ride to hell. From one who knows."

Catchpole read the letter twice before he commented. "Rather different from the usual run of these things. Don't you think so, sir?"

"How do you mean?"

"Well—it's hardly a threat—is it? Just a definite statement that a certain thing will happen. There's no 'if you so and so' then 'so and so will take place'—is there?"

"No. I suppose not." Salt fingered his chin. "I see what you mean. I hadn't looked at it quite like that." Catchpole examined the envelope.

"Postmark Verne 7.30 p.m. Posted the night before the race meeting. Commonplace type of envelope—same remark goes for the paper. H'm. No address, of course, and no date shown on the actual letter itself. H'm. Not much to go on there." Catchpole looked across at the K.C. as he finished his comments. "I'll keep this, sir. The writer, whoever he is it turns out to be, evidently knew something. What was the late judge's real reaction to it? I'd like to know that. And I'd like you to answer, as carefully as you know how."

Salt nodded. "I understand—and I can. I'm absolutely positive that Nick Flagon took the whole thing as a practical joke and, after he'd read it and chucked it over on my breakfast plate, scarcely gave it another thought. That's my sincere and honest opinion, based on what I heard and saw. And I knew Nick Flagon better than his own arm ever did."

"Where did he put it, Mr. Salt, after you handed it back to him?"

"Between the leaves of a book he was reading—and he left the book in his bedroom. I saw him do it and I knew where he'd left the book. That's how I was able to go straight up there and collar the letter when I wanted it. I knew it was there."

"H'm. He wasn't perturbed at all by the letter—you say?"

Salt smiled. "Not in the slightest degree."

"What importance do you attach to it yourself, sir?"

"What importance *can* I attach to it? It's all . . . er . . . beyond me. I'm afraid that I treated it much in the same vein as Flagon did."

"Did you attend the Point-to-Point meeting?"

"Rather. That's the one reason I was staying in Quiddington St. Philip."

An idea came to Catchpole. He translated it into a question directly it was born.

"Were you riding in any of the events, Mr. Salt?"

The K.C. smiled a pitying smile. "At my weight, Inspector? Pity the poor animal that had to carry me. He's not been foaled yet. I'm a sixteen-stone man. Or just on."

Catchpole could have kicked himself for putting such a question. "Of course," he murmured apologetically. "I'm sorry. I should have thought before I spoke."

Salt bowed his head in acceptance of the apology. Catchpole thought for a minute or two and then went off on another tack.

"You know of no enemies, I suppose, that Justice Flagon might have had?"

"No. None at all. Neither did *he*, I should say—from his reception of that letter. Had he possessed anybody in the actual nature of a real enemy—that threatening letter, surely, would have brought that person to his mind? That's feasible, isn't it?"

"Yes. One would think so. I agree with you."

"By the way," said Salt, "now that we're on the subject, what was the real cause of Flagon's death? One hears so many rumours."

"He died of poison," replied Catchpole shortly.

Salt looked surprised. "Poisoned? Well—that's an eye-opener, I must say. You've taken my breath away. But how on earth was it administered, Inspector?"

"That point, at the moment, sir, is not quite clear. Frankly, the authorities are puzzled."

"H'm. I see. Investigations still proceeding—eh? Ah well—in that case I will refrain from asking any more questions."

"When did you last see the dead judge, Mr. Salt?"

"Immediately after the event which preceded the race that Nick was riding in and which he was so keen to win. I saw him and spoke to him before he went away to saddle up."

"He was . . . er . . . all right when you spoke to him? Nothing abnormal about him? As far as you could see?"

"He was as right as rain, Inspector," replied Salt emphatically, "and which is more, his riding up to the moment he fell off the horse proves the truth of my last remark. He had ridden a strong, confident and well-judged race. Nick had the race at his mercy when the tragedy came."

"Yes. So I believe. That's the general consensus of opinion. You say he spoke to you before the race? What did he say? His exact words—if you can possibly recall them."

Salt smiled a little but was ready to answer. "'You can back me, Keith, till the cows come home and barring accidents I shall win "pulling up."' They were Nick Flagon's last words to me. I've often thought of them since," he concluded with a tinge of bitterness, "'barring accidents'. And the accident came."

"Very sad. Very sad indeed. I haven't had time yet, Mr. Salt, to contact any of the late judge's relatives. But I intend to make—"

Salt interrupted him. "You're awkwardly placed there, Inspector. As far as I know, you won't find any. From the blood-relation point of view, he was alone in the world. He was a bachelor and an only child. Both his parents are dead. Been dead some years. He came of a Leicestershire family—hence his intense love of horses. I was very close to him, Inspector, in almost every human respect, as I indicated just now, and I've never heard him speak of any relations that are living at the present day. There may be, of course, an inevitable uncle or aunt, plus a possible concomitant cousin tucked away in some obscure corner of the globe, but as far as I'm personally concerned—I never remember hearing Nick Flagon refer to any of them."

"Is that so? Well—it's as well to know. Your information will save me wasting time on a round of futile and fruitless inquiries. I'm glad you told me."

Salt rose. At his full height, he towered over Catchpole's desk and made the inspector feel inordinately small. Salt picked up his hat. "Well—good morning, Inspector, and thanks for the interview."

"Thank you, sir—for the valuable information you've brought me."

"I shall be at the 'Saracen's Head' for a day or two should you require me for anything else. Give me a ring if you do. Don't hesitate."

"I will, sir."

Salt waved his hand to Catchpole and made his exit. He did bestride the narrow room like a Colossus. And Catchpole, entirely unmindful of the fact, was no more than peeping between his legs.

3

Maurice Fothergill returned to the 'Wheatsheaf' late in the afternoon that Flagon had died. Not only had he seen Catchpole and Doctor Harradine arrive, but he had also overheard several expressions of both opinion and fact from Sir Claude de Monterey. But the police had moved him from his 'ring-side' seat and after that occurred the time had come when he realized that he couldn't very well linger in the vicinity any longer, so, a prey to a wild conflict of emotions, he had made his way back to the inn where he was staying.

When he got there, he found Harcourt sitting in a big easy-chair in the smoke-lounge. Fothergill treated him to a peculiar look.

"Well," he said—"you're a nice bloke—I must say! I really must hand it to you. The perfect companion."

Harcourt waved him away. He looked sick and very definitely sorry for himself.

"I'm sorry, Maurice," he said, "to let you down as I did—but I wasn't to blame. As a matter of fact, old man, I've been damned ill."

"Ill? How do you mean—ill? What's been the trouble?"

"Don't ask me. But I must have eaten something which upset me. I'll tell you what happened to me. I went out for a stroll after breakfast, as you know, intending to be back in good time for that early lunch of ours. When I'd walked for about an hour—done three to four miles, I suppose, I came over damned ill. It was gastric—no doubt about that. I vomited like a dog, had a terrific pain in the guts and generally was all in. I sat down on some grass for a time and was then visited by another delightful business. Violent diarrhoea. All I could do was to crawl in a field under a hedge to relieve myself. My dear chap—it was an absolutely ghastly business. I've never felt anything like it in my life. I lay there for some time—couldn't move. Prostrate!"

Harcourt paused as Fothergill looked at him somewhat incredulously. "After a time," he went on, "I must have dozed off to sleep, I suppose. When I woke up it was half-past three. I had the shock of my life. I was feeling a shade better, then, so I crawled home as best I could—and here I am. Oh—and by the way, 'congratters' on the escape."

Fothergill eyed him sharply. "How did you know?"

Harcourt jerked his head towards the bar. "Old Willmott told me. The place is literally humming with the news. Flagon fell off his horse or something. Streak of ruddy luck for you, old son—if ever there were one."

"Flagon's dead," said Fothergill quietly—"it's as bad as that."

"Dead," exclaimed Harcourt, "that's different from what the landlord said. He'd heard that he was unconscious. Had a fainting attack or something. What was it then—fractured skull?"

"I don't know, Ronnie. There's no reliable news yet. But they called a doctor, naturally, and I heard the vet say this—or words to this effect: 'What killed him I haven't the foggiest idea.' Pretty fine kettle of fish, isn't it?"

"But surely—" Harcourt spoke petulantly—"they must know how a man dies! A doctor! Otherwise it doesn't make sense."

"I'm telling you all I know," returned Fothergill. He looked at Harcourt again. The man certainly looked as though he had recently undergone a tough experience. His face was drawn and round his eyes were lines of pain.

"Leave Flagon out of it for a moment," continued Fothergill, "this illness of yours—I can't understand that—either. What upset you? You and I have eaten the same grub—more or less—since we've been staying here. I wonder, Ronnie—if it could have been the beer?"

"What beer?"

"The beer we had last night."

"Good Lord. How much did I have? Can't a fellow sink three pints of wallop without it upsetting him? Have a heart. Anybody would think to hear you talk that I was a Son of Temperance."

Harcourt shifted bad-temperedly in his chair and propped his chin on his hand. But Fothergill was both ready and inclined to argue.

"Very likely he can. I should be the last person to say he couldn't. But sometimes strange wallop does upset a chap. Another thing. Depends on the state of the tummy when the wallop's lowered."

"You drank much more than I did—you always do," persisted Harcourt dully, "so how could it have been the beer?"

"Might be a chill," suggested Fothergill almost hopefully.

"Oh—stop chewing the fat over it, for the love of Mike. It's my ruddy funeral. I've had to put up with it all—you haven't." He curled himself up in the big chair again. "Tell me more about Flagon and the Flagon tragedy. Tell me how it all happened. I'm darned curious." Fothergill described what had taken place as he himself had witnessed it. Harcourt listened to the narrative with rapt attention. "Just rolled off the horse, you say?"

Fothergill nodded. "Just rolled off the horse and lay there on the grass. The horse galloped on—riderless. I tell you it was a horrible and rather unnerving experience."

"Must have been," retorted Harcourt sourly, "for you! Your tears must have flowed by the bucketful. A thousand quid—eh?" He changed to a more serious tone. "Damned funny business though— all the same."

"You've said it," returned Fothergill. There was a pause.

"And while all this was happening, Maurice, where exactly were you?"

"Where I had arranged to meet you, of course. Up on the top of the hill towards Newstead Green that overlooks the finish. I told you this morning it was the best place to see from. I got up to the top at about ten minutes to three. As a matter of fact, I actually took the time. My main worry then was concerning *your* whereabouts. For the life of me, I couldn't make out what had become of you."

"I was sleeping in a field—little realizing the tragedy that was being enacted a short distance away. All the same—I've heard your story and I should say that there's only one possible solution. And that's an eminently simple one. Flagon died a natural death. That any other idea is all hooey. Probably suffered from unsuspected heart trouble. Like plenty of other people. Had an attack, brought on by the excitement of the race, just toppled off his horse and died."

"There's one big snag in all that," said Fothergill quietly.

"What's that—may I ask?"

"Why—this. If Flagon had died in that way, the doctor would have discovered it at once. At least—that's what I'd think."

"He mightn't be able to tell—you can't always say from a cursory examination."

"Well—that's my opinion, and I'm sticking to it." Harcourt shot him a searching glance. "How, then, do *you* think he died? If you won't have my heart-failure theory, what are you going to put in its place? An act of God?"

Harcourt grinned sardonically. With unnatural pallor, he reminded Fothergill of a death's head. Fothergill turned.

"No—not an Act of God, Ronnie. Although I appreciate the delicate nature of your sarcasm. No—I honestly think Flagon was the victim of foul play. Though how it was pulled off—I'm like that doctor chap—I haven't the foggiest."

"Can't see it. The idea's fantastic. According to you, there wasn't a soul near him—barring the rider of the horse behind. And I don't see what the hell he could have done."

"I admit all that, my dear chap. But I'm not budging from my opinion. I'm not satisfied. I still feel that there was dirty work somewhere."

"In that case, then," concluded Harcourt, "it'll be a question of waiting for the morning papers. Till then, my dear Maurice, we'll possess our souls in blistering impatience. They get here about half-past nine, I believe. The newspapers, I mean, not our immortal souls."

4

Harradine tossed the dart over to Catchpole. "There isn't a doubt about it, Inspector. Woorari. I've tested it thoroughly and I'm completely satisfied."

Catchpole pushed his fingers through his hair. He felt that the case was becoming too big and too involved for him. He looked at the lethal dart and then somewhat foolishly, perhaps, said the first thing that came into his head.

"It's not a new dart, Doctor. I mean—it's been used before. Look at the state of the flight. You can see that the feathers aren't new."

Harradine looked at the feathers and nodded. "That's an idea, Catchpole." He stopped, but went on again almost immediately. "Seems to me you've a fair chance of tracing that dart, Inspector."

"Maybe. Maybe not. I'm not too confident. Depends on how cunningly this job's been worked out. The dart might have been brought from anywhere. From Verne or from Timbuctoo. Might be one of anybody's private possession. Afraid I can't see too much hope in your suggestion."

"You never know," replied Harradine hopefully, "and your experience of crime and criminals should tell you that even the most cunning murderer invariably makes an appalling mistake which delivers him into the hands of justice. You may be lucky."

"Oh yeah! I've had photographs taken from all angles—in fact, I think I've done everything that can be reasonably expected of me. The Chief Constable agrees with that, but all the same I know he's not satisfied. I can see it in his eye. How can I expect him to be, knowing him as I do? He'll have the 'Yard' in, in my opinion, within the next twenty-four hours. Unless I make an arrest. An arrest! Some hopes!"

"Well—you've got more dope now for the Press. That *Fanfare* scoop-merchant's in luck. I'll say he is! Gives him the dish of a lifetime, I should imagine."

"I promised I'd see him again, didn't I? I'll keep the promise, Doctor. It won't do me any harm—and on the other hand—it may possibly help me."

"You made an appointment with him for the evening, if you remember. At my surgery. I suppose he'll turn up?"

"Bet your life he will. Cats don't run away when the cream's put out. Or the fish-heads. What's the time now?"

Harradine looked at his watch. "Just on eight. Wants a few minutes. I'm fit if you care to come along with me now."

"Right-o. May as well, I suppose. No point in staying on. I know what I came to know. Bring the dart."

The two men returned from the mortuary to Harradine's surgery, and shortly after they arrived, Bentley kept his appointment. When he entered, it was—as before—almost apologetically.

"Good evening, gentlemen. I hope that I've done the right thing in coming along as we arranged. I should hate to feel that I was becoming a nuisance to you."

Catchpole nodded to him curtly and told him to sit down. "I told you last night, Mr. Bentley, that Doctor Harradine had established, to my complete satisfaction, that Justice Flagon had been murdered. I said that the cause of death was poisoning. But beyond that, I refused to go. I can go further than that to-night. And I'll tell you this. The judge was killed by a poisoned dart, thrown at him in some way while he was riding. If you look on that table, you'll see the actual dart. I want you to put those facts in to-morrow's morning paper. But no more than that. Just those bare facts as I've given them to you. Not too late, is it?"

Bentley shook his head. It was evident that he was wildly excited at the prospect of this second scoop that had come his way within twenty-four hours. His eyes were round with incredulity.

"Am I ... er ... permitted to see the dart? Do you mind if I go across and look at it."

"You may look—but don't touch it. Don't muck it about."

Bentley got up and went across to the table. He stared with astonishment at the toy which the malignity of man had converted into a lethal weapon. Catchpole noticed a curious expression cross his face. Catchpole found his own curiosity aroused. He jumped up and went to the table and stood at Bentley's side.

"What is it?" he asked peremptorily.

For the moment, Bentley made no reply. He just stood there looking at the dart and shaking his head slowly from side to side.

"Well," demanded Catchpole again, "what's troubling you? Don't tell me you've seen that dart before."

Bentley answered him with carefully chosen words. "One dart, Inspector, from what little I know of them, is very like another. And yet—" He paused. Catchpole look him up instantly.

"And yet—what?"

"That dart lying on that table there, seems to me to be very like, in every way, a dart which was being used a night or so ago, at a pub not a hundred miles from here."

Catchpole frowned: "What pub?"

"The 'Wheatsheaf.' The best hotel in Quiddington."

"But taking your own words, man, one dart is very like another. You said it yourself. On what then are you basing your statement? That you think this is any particular dart."

Bentley was still ultra-careful in the terms of his reply. "I'm going on the feather—what's it called—the . . . er . . ."

"Flight," snapped Catchpole. "What about the flight? What's significant about it? It looks quite ordinary to my eye."

"I'll show you." Bentley pointed to it. "The end of the . . . er . . . flight is dark-coloured on one side. On the other side it's a light brown. See what I mean?"

Harradine came over and looked. "Yes," he said. "I see what he means."

"I'll tell you," went on Bentley, "how I came to notice it. I was in there the night before Flagon's affair. Only having a beer. Or perhaps a couple, if I felt like it. I don't play darts myself, but I was watching a game. One of the players made a bad shot and the dart hit the edge of the . . . er . . . target, ricocheted and fell at my feet. I stooped, picked it up and handed it back. It was very like the dart there on that table. There may be nothing in it, of course, but it might be worth trying—an enquiry at the 'Wheatsheaf.'"

"I hope it will show a better dividend than something you told me last night," said Catchpole with a hint of churlishness.

"What was that?" asked Bentley.

"You gave it as your opinion that everybody liked the late Justice Flagon. Somebody liked him so bloody much that he murdered him. So your psychology slipped up somewhere. But this 'Wheatsheaf' place of yours? I haven't been out there for some time now—I've been too busy ever since Christmas—do they get a crowd in there playing darts?"

"Only a 'regular' could answer that question accurately, Inspector. But there was a goodish muster in there the evening before last. I was quite surprised to see the crowd when I got there."

"H'm. How many would you say?"

"A dozen to twenty must have played at different times while I was there. They have two ... er ... targets."

Catchpole smiled to himself at the journalist's description of the board. "The last time I popped in there," said Harradine: "it was a Sunday evening just after Christmas. About the end of January perhaps. They had a roaring big fire in the lounge and I found the place most attractive—I don't mind confessing it. *Also*—a most distinguished company was playing darts—including Sir Claude de Monterey and Paula Secretan. The lady threw a nifty dart—believe me."

Catchpole looked amused at Harradine's statement. "I've heard a good deal about her, but I've never yet made her acquaintance. And my days of going up to town to do a show are over. Give me the 'flicks' every time. No waiting and a comfortable seat. And no intervals for changing scenery and hammering something or the other." He turned to Bentley. "You weren't aware, I suppose, that we had a celebrity residing in Quiddington?"

Bentley shook his head. "No."

"We have. Paula Secretan lives on the main road between Quiddington and Newstead Green on the way to Sword. Nice little place she's got there, too."

"I've seen her many times, of course. At the theatre. As a journalist I naturally get pushed about a good deal. And I admire her tremendously—as an artist. But I had no idea she lived in this locality."

"She do an' all," replied Catchpole humorously. He seemed in better spirits now than he had been when the interview started.

Harradine laughed. "It's a sight worth seeing—La Secretan playing darts. Superbly gowned always, backless of course, and with a gorgeous fur draped across one of her shoulders, she'll walk up to the line—cigarette invisibly attached, as it were, to her lips. She can make old de Monterey pay for the beer nineteen times out of every twenty."

Catchpole looked up interestedly. "De Monterey? Is he concerned then in that particular quarter?"

"It's looked like it for some time," returned Harradine, "he's been dancing attendance on her very zealously for over a year, I should say."

"H'm. That's worth knowing." Catchpole rose. "Well, Mr. Bentley—you've got the dope I promised you. I've kept my word. Use it to the best advantage. Both from your point of view and from mine. I've indicated how far you may go."

"Thank you, Inspector—I will. And good luck to you *re* the dart inquiry."

A sudden thought seemed to occur to Catchpole, "By the way, Bentley, have you ever heard in the course of your career, a dart referred to as a quillet?"

Bentley shook his head. "A quillet? No. I've never heard the word before—in any sense. How do you spell it?"

Catchpole told him.

"Never heard the word in my life," Bentley repeated, "Is it another name for a dart?"

"Apparently," replied Catchpole. "Still—don't fret about it. Forget it."

Bentley looked at him curiously but made no further comment. He turned to pick up his hat. "Good night, gentlemen," he said as he walked out of the surgery.

5

Willmott, the landlord and proprietor of the 'Wheatsheaf,' scratched the lobe of his ear and listened attentively to what Inspector Catchpole had to say.

"Darts? Oh—ay—we got plenty 'ere. Rare call for 'em we get—and no mistake. Everybody almost 'as a game nowadays. The gentry an' all! What was it you wanted to know about 'em, Inspector?"

"I want to have a look at your stock, Willmott, before you open up to-day."

"That's all right, Inspector. That be easy."

Willmott leaned over the counter and called back into the inner regions of the inn: "Doris! Coom 'ere, gal, will yer?"

Doris duly obliged, wiping her hands on her apron.

"Take the gentleman round to where the dart-boards are and show 'im our stock of darts, will yer?"

"Come this way, sir," said Doris.

Catchpole followed her. "There you are," she said, nodding her head towards various boxes lying on a ledge, "there are five dozen there. Twenty sets of three each. Do you want to look at each one of 'em? Or just see the boxes?"

Catchpole answered: "Look in each box and make sure there's the complete set in there, will you, my girl? You know what I mean—make sure there isn't one missing."

Doris opened the various boxes one by one and showed the contents of each to the Inspector. "They all look alike to me," he muttered.

"Same 'ere, mister," said Doris. Carefully, but steadily, Doris worked through the boxes that held the twenty sets. "None missin' 'ere, mister," she said with a touch of defiance, "all present and correct."

Willmott came from behind the counter and joined the other two. "Everything satisfactory, I hope, Inspector?"

"Depends on the point of view, old man," rejoined Catchpole. "I see. And what you were lookin' for, I suppose."

Willmott wagged a sapient head. "Yes. It's astonishin'!" he elaborated, "the number o' gentry what like a fling at my old dartboard. There's Sir Claude de Monterey himself from Sword Mount and his lady friend the actress—Miss Secretan. There's Mr. Hubert Vernon from the Hall and his missus—Colonel Fane and Major Stondon—Canon Galbraith and his young niece—and about a fortnight ago who d'yer think walked in the old 'Wheatsheaf' with a pal of his and 'ad a game? You'd never guess in a month o' Sundays." Willmott chuckled at the savour of his reminiscence.

Catchpole shook his head. He wished the landlord anywhere but where he was. Why couldn't he have stayed behind the counter and left the job to Doris? Also, he was annoyed that the tally of 'Wheat-sheaf' darts was apparently correct.

"I haven't the least idea," he answered rather shortly.

Willmott sank his voice to a whisper. "No less a person than the gentleman who had the fatal accident. That they're using the word 'murder' for. Which, for myself, I jest can't come to believe. Mr. Judge Flagon. Michael Keegan pointed him out to me. I'll lay that's a surprise for yer, Inspector!"

This last opinion was certainly true and Catchpole knew that it would be no earthly use for him to deny it.

"Is that so, Willmott? A fortnight ago—eh?"

"About a fortnight, sir. He'd come down to look at the Point-to-Point course. I wouldn't like to swear to the exact day. Yes—'e was in 'ere with his pal—a big feller with a first-class 'ead of 'air. And they 'ad a spell at the old dart-board. While they was a-playin' Sir Claude came in with his lady friend and that meant a rare lot of conviviality all round. To all appearances, they was all well-known to each other. At any rate they was all merry and bright together. We what was behind the bar couldn't 'elp remarkin' on it."

Inspector Catchpole began to realize that he was most definitely hearing things. "I had no idea, Willmott," he said slowly—and rather awkwardly, "that your house was frequented by such a number of distinguished people. What was the name of Judge Flagon's friend—did you happen to hear it in the course of their conversation?" Willmott rubbed the side of his nose with his finger. "No, Inspector Catchpole. Now you ask me—I can't say that I did. But I'll say this—'e was on rare good terms with 'is lordship—they was a-slappin' each other on the back pretty well all the time they was playin' darts. Treated 'im as a fair equal 'e did and no mistake. I'm rare sorry I can't remember 'is name seein' as 'ow you was a-wantin' to know it."

"Was he a good player—this friend of Judge Flagon's?"

"'E was that! One o' the best I've ever seen in this 'ouse."

"Don't you worry about remembering his name, Willmott—it's of little consequence to me," lied Catchpole valiantly. "I dare say I can find it out all right later on, if I want to."

Doris, by this time, had closed the dart-boxes again and replaced them on the ledge. "Would there be anything more that you be wantin', Inspector?" asked Willmott.

"No. I don't think so. Many thanks and good morning." Catchpole walked back. The case was a pain in the neck to him and showed no sign yet of becoming any different. He little knew, however, that before very long it was going to be a sick headache as well.

PART TWO
THEODORE MADRIGAL

CHAPTER I

1

SIR Austin Kemble, D.S.O., looked across his room at Anthony Lotherington Bathurst and smiled as attractively as he knew how. The post of Commissioner of Police is never exactly a bed of roses and at the present moment it had degenerated much nearer to the apple-pie condition of recumbency. No arrest had been made by the local police in connection with the murder of Mr. Justice Flagon and the chief-constable concerned had, albeit somewhat reluctantly, called in the assistance of Scotland Yard. Thus it will be seen that Catchpole's fears had been justified.

"I'm approaching you, my dear Bathurst," Sir Austin said to Anthony, "with a certain amount of . . . er . . . misgiving . . . and, er . . . diffidence."

Anthony grinned. He had heard that opening gambit more than once in the past and knew what was cooking. The Commissioner noticed the grin.

"Ah—but I am! In all sincerity. I know you intended going into Warwickshire for the late spring and early summer—and I'm damned sorry to chuck a spanner in the machinery—but frankly, I'm in a hole. And I should be eternally grateful, my dear Bathurst, if you'd give me a hand."

"What is it?" asked Anthony. "The case of the late Mr. Justice Flagon?"

The Commissioner nodded. "It is. And a more mysterious and . . . er . . . baffling affair has never fallen to my lot. You know most of the details, I suppose?"

"Very roughly, sir. And those merely from the dailies. But I'm aware of the main pattern of the affair. I made myself familiar with it. And I'm reluctantly compelled to point out that the scent, such as it may have been at the inception, is pretty well frozen stiff by now."

"I know. I know. None better. I told Colonel Stanborough that when he asked for us! It's always the same story with these local police wallahs. They ass about for days, get in each other's way, mess everything up and then send along the S.O.S. for us to haul them out of the dirt. It fairly sickens me."

"When exactly was the murder?"

Sir Austin consulted certain notes he had in front of him. "Five days ago now. Flagon's funeral's to-day."

"Where?"

"Oh, down there. In the village churchyard at Quiddington St. Philip. Near the spot where he was killed. It was a toss-up between burying him there or taking him up to Leicestershire. That's where the family came from. I don't know who or what decided the question. Convenience, in all probability. He was a fine fellow, Flagon! And he'll be sorely missed in legal circles. Did you ever happen to meet him?"

"No. I don't think I ever had that pleasure. My acquaintance was limited to hearing him on two or three occasions in the Court of Appeal. And I'll admit that I was impressed with his lucidity and soundness of judgment. I should say that but for this tragic business, no distinction that the Law holds would have been beyond his reach. But there you are." Anthony shrugged his shoulders, *"Dieu dispose."*

The commissioner nodded. "If you take it on, Bathurst, you can take MacMorran down with you, if you'd care to have him. He hasn't too much on at the moment. But that's a matter for you, of course. Please yourself."

"Oh, yes, I should like him. In fact I was going to ask for him, if you hadn't mentioned it."

"When will you go down?"

"Oh, directly after lunch. Must do. If I'm going to take the job on, it's essential that no more time is wasted."

"Very good, then. I'll arrange that Stanborough has somebody to meet you on arrival."

Anthony went across and picked up his hat and gloves.

"Tell MacMorran to meet me at Liverpool Street at two o'clock sharp, will you, please, Sir Austin? How far's this place actually, any idea?"

"It's about forty miles out, but there's an excellent train service, so I'm told. Pretty country, too. All round the Verner valley's quite delightful. One of the prettiest stretches in the whole of England. Book to Verne—there's no station at Quiddington St. Philip, and put up at the 'Saracen's Head.' Very decent place, you'll find. There's a bus runs in from Verne. To Quiddington, I mean. And there's nearly always one that meets the main-line trains. Still, they'll send a car in, no doubt. I'll fix that with Stanborough. By the way, we may as well look you up a train."

"Two-seventeen," said Anthony, "two stops, I fancy, Shakespeare and Darvill. I looked it up in the 'A.B.C.' after you 'phoned me this morning."

Sir Austin stared at him incredulously. "You looked it up, you say, this morning? But how in the world did you know what I wanted you for?"

Anthony stood in the doorway and waved to the Commissioner. "My dear Watson," he said gaily, "my very dear Watson, oh, tell MacMorran I'll meet him under the clock at two p.m. sharp."

2

Punctually at twenty-two minutes past three, Anthony Lotherington Bathurst and Chief Detective-Inspector Andrew MacMorran alighted from the train on to the platform of Verne station. As they passed the ticket-collector, a uniformed man came bustling forward to meet them.

"Good afternoon, gentlemen," he said with a marked country accent. "Sergeant Harrison at your service. Inspector Catchpole sends his apologies for not coming to meet you. He intended to, but unfortunately something turned up at the last moment and he was called away."

MacMorran seemed far from pleased at the information. "H'm. Bad job. What was it? The vicar's wife lost her terrier?"

The sergeant shot him a sharp glance. Although on the bucolic side, MacMorran's irony was not lost upon him.

"No, sir," he said semi-defensively, "from the inspector's manner I should say it was something highly important. Anyhow he rushed straight out, after telling me to meet you, without saying another word to anybody."

Anthony kept quiet during this verbal exchange. The country they were passing through was typical of the county. Trees, pasture-land sandwiched between woods, an occasional valley suggesting a green lake, farm-houses dotted at brief intervals, old cottages with long, low tile-roofs and lovely long winding lanes which crept placidly into the valleys which flanked the many ridges.

"Beautiful country, Sergeant," said Anthony, "remote, peaceful and nestling."

"Ay, sir, it is that," replied Harrison. "I like it, sir, I must confess, and I like to hear others say that they agree with my taste. It sort of pleases me, sir, to find people appreciatin' my own district."

"Look around, Andrew," said Anthony, "a little bit of old England. The real stuff at that. Nothing faked or phoney. And we're brought down here because of man's inhumanity to man. When you think that, it brings you up with a bit of a jerk, doesn't it? The flesh and blood, Andrew, which did in Adam fail."

He handed cigarettes round and shook his head again: "Makes you wonder."

"How far now, Sergeant?" asked MacMorran.

"Five minutes, sir, no more," replied Harrison laconically. He spread his big carpet-bag hands over his knees. Hands that snapped 'em up at silly point on the village green at Quiddington St. Philip. "Inspector thought you'd rather come straight here than stop in Verne. Leastways, so he told me. We've got a little old station in Quiddington that ain't too bad as things go. It's been adequate, up to now. But of course, this last business—" he broke off and made a helpless sort of gesture with his big hands.

The car turned a sharpish corner and Anthony could see that they had now entered what was probably the main street of the village of Quiddington St. Philip. On this particular afternoon, it was sleepy and sun-bathed. They passed a thatched and whitewashed smithy, clusters of tiny quaint lop-sided houses, a few nondescript shops, a general store, the 'Wheatsheaf' on the corner, the solid creeper-covered rectory, and pulled up with more noise than should have been necessary on the opposite corner.

"'Ere we are." He leant forward courteously and opened the door of the car for Anthony and MacMorran to get out. "Maybe," he said with an air of apology, "inspector's back by now. Whatever caused 'im to rush out, shouldn't take 'im all the afternoon."

"And maybe he's not," returned MacMorran, "anyway, if he's not I suppose we can wait for him."

They entered the tiny country police-station of Quiddington St. Philip. Simultaneously with their entrance, Catchpole came bustling out. Directly Anthony caught sight of his face, he knew that the business which had demanded Catchpole's recent attention had been no trivial matter, and that his seeming discourtesy had been dictated by circumstances over which he had no control.

3

Directly Catchpole spoke, Anthony knew that here was a singularly harassed man.

"Oh, come in, gentlemen," he said, "come in, please."

MacMorran led the way and introduced both himself and Anthony.

"I'm so sorry not to have met you," stammered Catchpole, "but we've run into another spot of bother. Came on us like a bolt from the blue. That's what took me away just as I was on the point of starting out for the railway station. Mr. Justice Madrigal was murdered this afternoon while attending the Flagon funeral."

After he had made the announcement, Catchpole slumped into the nearest chair. Anthony could see that the man was a bundle of nerves. MacMorran sat down and crossed his legs.

"Tell me," he said simply.

Catchpole started. "Just after three o'clock, I was telephoned for. The call was put through to Verne. They passed it through to me here. They knew, you see, I'd come along here. All I was told was that there had been another tragedy in the old churchyard at Quiddington St. Philip. This time the man dead was Mr. Justice Madrigal. Another judge, you observe. Of course, I had to go over there at once. That was why I asked Sergeant Harrison to deputize for me and meet you."

Catchpole paused and moistened his lips with his tongue. MacMorran waited for him to go on.

"I went straight over to the old churchyard at Quiddington St. Philip. As far as I can make out what happened was this. The service in the church had finished and the coffin was being carried to the grave. The interment was to be in the west corner of the churchyard. A very delightful spot, with trees and their overhanging branches all helping to make it particularly lovely. Well, the coffin reached the grave and just as the committal sentences were being spoken and the coffin being lowered, Justice Madrigal, who was standing by himself on the fringe of a knot of mourners, suddenly pitched forward on to his face. I suppose it must have been a second or two before anybody got to him, but when they did, he was dead."

Again Catchpole paused in his story. He took a handkerchief and wiped his forehead. "When I got there, some time later, of course," he resumed, "I found that Doctor Harradine, the divisional-surgeon, had already arrived and he at once told me that Madrigal had died in exactly the same manner as Justice Flagon. So I knew what to look for."

"What was that?" inquired MacMorran.

"This," replied Catchpole. "And it didn't take me long to find it." He took an envelope from his pocket and from the envelope he took a dart. "There you are, gentlemen," said Catchpole, "a dart killed Flagon and a similar dart has killed Madrigal. That's what Doctor Harradine says. A dart dipped in 'woorari' or 'woorara'—I'm not quite sure which he said. But it's a particularly virulent poison which acts something like strychnine does. That's what I've been up against. A killer who can place a dart neatly and accurately as this fellow can. If he goes on like this, nobody in the place'll feel safe. Oh, that reminds me. There's something else to show you."

Catchpole inverted the envelope and shook something from one of the corners into his hand. Anthony could see that there were two absurdly small slips of paper.

"On each occasion," said Catchpole, "a tiny piece of paper was attached to the dart. The slightly smaller piece was on Flagon's dart, the larger of the two pieces was tied round Madrigal's." Anthony and MacMorran got up from their seats and went to look more closely at the slips of paper. 'A nice sharp quillet! Ay!' and 'An even sharper quillet' were the printed words they read.

"I never knew," said Catchpole lugubriously, "that darts were called quillets before this job fell into my lap. And nobody else I've spoken to seems to have either."

Anthony looked at him curiously.

"No more did I," commented MacMorran.

"Has Doctor Harradine examined this?" asked Anthony, indicating the Madrigal dart.

Catchpole nodded. "Yes. Same procedure in all details—that's what he reports. Flagon and Madrigal both travelled the same road." MacMorran went back to his chair. He was too old a hand to panic and he was refusing, at this early stage in the case, to be hustled off his proper game. Anthony recognized the signs.

"Tell us," said MacMorran quietly, "everything. From the beginning."

Catchpole said: "I was going to."

MacMorran said: "Good. That's what I want."

Catchpole told the story of Flagon's fall, of his own finding of the dart, of his conferences with Doctor Harradine, of his negotiations with Bentley, of his visit to the 'Wheatsheaf' and of the interview that he had with Salt. Thus he came to the incident of the anonymous communication which had been received by Flagon on the morning of his death.

"Can we see that?" asked MacMorran, leaning forward. Catchpole produced the letter which Salt had left with him. MacMorran read it carefully and passed it over to Anthony.

"H'm," said the last-named, "uncompromising tone about it. Added to a touch of vaticination. Hardly threatening, though."

"That's exactly how it struck me," said Catchpole, "and I told Salt so when he brought it along to me."

"The murderer," continued Anthony in comment, "seems to have a passion for expressing himself on paper. Not only does he send a letter by the morning post, he also attaches a message to the weapon he uses for the kill. It would be interesting to know whether the late Justice Madrigal was also the recipient of a letter by this morning's post. I'd bet that he was. Considering all the circumstances. What do you say, Andrew?"

"Probably. They usually murder to pattern, these blokes, once they start on it. Especially when they pull off a success."

"Well, gentlemen," said Catchpole, "I think I've given you all the details, and there's a hell of a lot for us to do. What would you like to—"

Anthony interrupted him. "I agree, Inspector. We must get to work immediately. I was thinking the same thing."

"Where would you like to start? Have you any preferences?" asked Catchpole.

MacMorran came in with another question. "I presume that you've already cleared all the routine stuff?"

"Yes. I've seen to all that. The photographers have been down, and all the usual arrangements have been made. I saw to all that before I came back here to meet you."

MacMorran spoke to Anthony. "Where would you rather? Flagon or Madrigal? Course or churchyard?"

Anthony's reply was prompt and decisive. "Oh, the latter, undoubtedly. The fresh before the stale, every time."

"My sentiments entirely. Right-o, Inspector Catchpole. The churchyard at Quiddington St. Philip."

4

As has been previously stated, the churchyard that had seen the burial of Flagon, and the murder of Madrigal, was serene and beautiful.

Anthony appreciated the fact, directly the car came to the old lych-gate of entrance. The churchyard lay under the down. The April sun was shining as Anthony and the others got out of the car. Catchpole took them straight over to a grave of newly turned earth. Wreaths and scattered flowers in prodigal profusion lay round the sides. Nicholas Flagon's body was below.

Catchpole stopped between a pegged space. "This is where Justice Madrigal fell and died. Just, so I'm told, as the earth was rattling on to the coffin. Just as—one of the mourners put it to me—the vicar's white surpliced sleeve was stretched over the dark grave with the mould in his hand."

Anthony and MacMorran looked at the marked spot. Anthony at once turned and made a quick survey of the churchyard.

"How many mourners were present, Inspector? Did you hear?"

"Yes. I made it my business to ask that question. Over a hundred. Mostly, as you may guess, from London."

"And they would be all round the grave," added Catchpole.

"All except the murderer," contributed Anthony drily.

Catchpole gave him a quick glance. "Yes," he said after a slight interval. "I suppose you're right there. Yes, I agree that that would be so." Catchpole looked round the old churchyard as though in search of sudden inspiration.

"Next point that arises," said Anthony, "is where was the murderer—said murderer not being near the grave."

MacMorran was quick to see the point and to answer the question. "The churchyard was an excellent place for him," he said unemotionally. "Look at all those tombstones. Gave him cover almost everywhere. Look at that one over there, for example."

MacMorran gestured towards a grave over-topped with a square white-stone monument with high railings round it. The inspector amplified his point. "Grand cover there for him—while everybody else is craning his neck into Flagon's grave."

"By Jove, Andrew," said Anthony, "I shouldn't be surprised if you haven't hit the right nail on the head. Good work. Let's go over and see how the land lies."

He turned to Catchpole. "You stay here, Inspector, please, as near as you can judge to where Madrigal was standing when he was struck down."

Catchpole took up his position as Anthony had indicated. Anthony and MacMorran went over to the monument and stood behind it. Then Anthony leant his body round one side.

"About twenty yards, Andrew, but I don't know that I'm satisfied, old man." He shook his head as he spoke. "The chap would probably be forced to use his left hand from behind here, to hit Madrigal standing where Catchpole is. You see, he'd have to stand on the left-hand side of this affair, and, that being the case, his right hand and shoulder would be behind the edifice. If they weren't, he'd be inclined to expose himself. See what I mean?"

MacMorran grunted an affirmative. "Yes. I think you're right. But it doesn't eliminate by any means. The bloke might be left-handed, for all we know. Plenty of people are."

"Might be. But the chances are very much the other way. Just a minute, though. There's something I want to ask Catchpole. You stay here."

Anthony walked back to the local inspector. "I say, Inspector Catchpole, what was the weather like here when the funeral service was taking place? Can you remember?"

"It's been a proper April day to-day, right from early morning. Sun and shower, shower and sun. Off and on all the time. Six of one and half a dozen of the other. Actually, I believe it was fine at the time of the murder. But just before, it had been raining hard. What are you after, footprints?"

Anthony went back to MacMorran, still standing behind the tomb of his selection.

"Any traces of footprints behind there, Andrew? There's been plenty of rain down here to-day, so Catchpole says."

MacMorran examined the ground. "No, nothing that I could say was worth anything. You see, the ground's protected here by the monument. It's comparatively dry. The rain doesn't get to it like it does in other places. No, there's no help here."

"I still don't care for this left-hand position, Andrew. This is by no means the best place from which to hit Madrigal standing where he was. What about that line of trees and bushes over there? They rather take my eye."

Anthony pointed across the churchyard. MacMorran's eyes followed the indication. "What do you think, Andrew?"

"H'm, might be a likely spot, as you say. A word with Catchpole should settle it, however."

"Yes. Let's go back to him."

They walked back to where the local inspector was standing. "Inspector," said MacMorran, "where did the dart actually strike Justice Madrigal? It's a question I should have asked you before?"

"The puncture is at the back of the neck." Catchpole's hands went to his neck as though in illustration of his words.

"Which side?"

"Er—a little behind the right ear. Just here." Catchpole pointed to the identical position on his own neck.

"There you are," said Anthony, "and in my opinion, Andrew, it rules out your monument affair as the coign of vantage. Definitely. In fact, I like my line of bushes a lot better, having heard Inspector Catchpole on the situation of the puncture."

"Maybe you're right. Maybe not," replied MacMorran.

"Stand where you did before, Inspector, do you mind?" Catchpole nodded at Anthony's request and went back to take up his previous position. Anthony beckoned to MacMorran and they crossed over to the green line of trees and bushes which had arrested Anthony's attention. When they got there, Anthony demonstrated to the 'Yard' Inspector.

"From here, Andrew, say, and with a right-handed throw. What do you think yourself?"

"Or with a left," commented MacMorran drily, "come to that. There's nothing like that monument on this side to make the throw awkward."

"Yes," conceded Anthony, "or even with a left—I take your point."

He suddenly walked away in the opposite direction to where Catchpole was standing. MacMorran heard the sound of his receding footsteps. Anthony walked across a strip of grass and came to a path. The whim seized him and he followed it. A few minutes' walking brought him to a small wooden gate. He had found another entrance to the churchyard. The road on which it opened was little more than a lane. So far so good. It linked up with a theory he was just beginning to form. Anthony stood at the wooden gate for the space of a few seconds before he returned to MacMorran.

"I've been testing a theory, Andrew," he said on his return, "there's another entrance to the churchyard just at the back here. You see what I'm after. Anybody could have come in this way, instead of mingling with the crowd of mourners behind the *cortège*. He would have more than a sporting chance of not being noticed. And, what's more to the point, he could have made his exit equally unobtrusively. Come and have a look for yourself. It's only a short distance away."

MacMorran walked across the grass and accompanied Anthony as far as the gate. After a brief period of consideration, he nodded his acquiescence of Anthony's idea.

"It's quite likely," he said. "And it fits in. Anyhow, let's get back to Catchpole. He'll be thinking we've deserted him."

"What will he do then?" asked Anthony quizzically. "Cry 'all is lost'? *Nous sommes trahis*?"

"I don't know what Catchpole will do, but I know what we're going to do. Having had a look round here. We'll move on to the spot where Flagon died. Agreed?"

"Lead on, Andrew," replied Anthony, "we'll pile the wall up with our legal dead. And already, let me tell you, I'm beginning to entertain ideas."

"Don't be in too great a hurry," rejoined MacMorran, "from your point of view and mine, these are early days."

"Or in other words, my dear Andrew, *festina lente*, eh?"

5

Catchpole took them to the place where Nicholas Flagon rolled from his horse and died. It was still clearly marked and pegged. MacMorran expressed his official satisfaction at what he saw.

"Good!" Catchpole then took them back along the course.

"The nearest rider to Flagon was about here." He indicated the spot with his heel. Anthony judged distances.

"Where was the puncture on Flagon?" asked Anthony.

"In almost the identical place to that on Madrigal. If anything, I should say a little lower down. A trifle nearer the point of the jaw."

Anthony looked along the course to where Flagon had fallen. "Then, as Flagon was riding on the right-hand side of the course, it's long odds that the dart came from that side. I think that's absolutely sound, don't you?"

Hearing no disagreement, he walked back to the pegs. From there he took a quick survey of the adjoining country. But there were no bushes here such as he had seen in the churchyard of Quiddington St. Philip. With the exception of the hill towards Newstead Green, the country was flat grassland. There was something else, however, which he saw and which gave him pause. There was a line of trees close to the spot where Flagon had fallen. Anthony knew that they were elms, typical trees of the county in which he stood. They were in good full foliage, too, for the time of the year. He left the course and made his way over to them. Another idea had come to him. He counted the trees. There were eleven of them standing in a straight row. He walked along their line, looking carefully at each one of them. At the fifth elm, he halted. For it had something for which he had been looking. There was a thick strong branch on this tree, relatively low.

Anthony measured its distance from the ground. He estimated this at about six feet, no more. That branch made, and a position established on it, this tree was not a difficult climbing proposition by any means. He then walked round in front of the elm tree and studied its relative geography to the place of Flagon's fall. To his immense satisfaction, he saw that it was almost abreast of it. He beckoned to MacMorran and Catchpole. They came to him.

"I want to try an experiment. I'm going to climb that tree. I want to test something myself and I also want you to test something. In other words I need your assistance." Anthony took off his jacket. Reaching upward to the low branch he had spotted he pulled himself on to it. From there, he found it a comparatively simple matter to climb upward into the upper branches and thicker foliage of the tree. Within a few minutes, Anthony found himself able to take full advantage of a most comfortable and convenient tree-limb. It was a substantial branch on which, leaning forward to his full height, he could lie with both hands completely comfortable and almost free to do as he willed. Moreover his view of the point-to-point course was practically unobstructed. From the standpoint of one part of the test he was making, the position was ideal.

With this thought in his mind, he called down to the others, "I'm well up in the tree now. Tell me, can you see me? Take the view from as many points as you can. Back, front and from each side."

MacMorran and Catchpole made the tests in accordance with Anthony's direction. Once or twice, he caught glimpses of them, as they made their respective ways round the fifth elm tree. All the time that this was going on, he was able to incline himself along the length of the branch without enduring any real physical discomfort.

After a time, he heard MacMorran calling to him. "Come down and we'll tell you."

It was the work of a moment for him to find the low bough again and jump to the ground to put on his coat.

"I could just see you when I stood at the rear of the tree," said MacMorran, "if I looked very carefully into it, and of course, with the knowledge that you were up there. Otherwise, from all the other points, I shouldn't have had the slightest idea that you were up there."

Anthony turned to Catchpole. "How about you, Inspector? Anything to add to that?"

"Well," returned the local inspector, "I say much the same as Inspector MacMorran here. By absolutely peering into the tree, I did manage to catch a glimpse of you two or three times, but there you are, I knew you were up there and was deliberately trying to see you, which makes all the difference. Frankly, I feel that you could have been there all the time and I could have been down here, and from what I could have seen of you I shouldn't have been a penny the wiser. That's my opinion."

Anthony rubbed his hands at Catchpole's reply. Taken in conjunction with Andrew MacMorran's, it suited his book remarkably well. He was more than reasonably satisfied. A theory which he had toyed with in the churchyard at Quiddington St. Philip was now taking definite shape in his mind. He attempted to develop it. He addressed himself to Catchpole.

"Now let's consider your bicycle evidence, Inspector. What you told us in the station first go off. Assuming that my theory is tenable, that the murderer threw his dart from that tree, and had a cycle handy somewhere near at hand, what was there to prevent him clambering down, after he had outed Flagon, jumping on the cycle and riding away in the lee of this hedge?"

"Nothing. I think you're right—probably."

"Good! Now just about where did those tyre impressions commence? Do you think you can show us with any degree of exactitude?"

Catchpole looked at the line of trees and then walked over to the hedge that ran along the side of the course.

"Yes," he answered, "they started quite close to the tree. To *the* tree."

"Excellent, Inspector Catchpole. Really excellent. And for how far did they run?"

"I can answer that also. And accurately. I measured the distance. They ran for a distance of about a hundred yards. Come here and I'll show you."

Catchpole methodically paced the strip of grass in the shadow of the hedge. Then he stopped and waited for what he knew would be the inevitable comment. Anthony looked at him with shrewd meaning and even MacMorran, the dour, exuded satisfaction. Each had seen the rough lane-track close to where the local inspector had halted.

"What do you think?" inquired the last-named.

"Same as you," returned MacMorran, "this is the road the murderer took to make his get-away. That's pretty obvious."

"Where does this lane lead to?" asked Anthony.

"It winds back to a little village, by the name of Newstead Green. About three miles away."

"What was the tyre, can you say?" inquired MacMorran.

Catchpole shook his head. "Couldn't get anything there. Not my fault. Don't think that. Did my best. But the impressions on the surface of the grass were far too blurred and indistinct."

Anthony grinned. "No patch showing on the rear tyre, eh, Inspector? As in all the best crime fiction? Nothing like that about it?"

"Nothing at all. You could just see that a tyre had been over the grass—and that was the lot."

"Never mind. We've definitely made progress. Far more, let me say, than I anticipated when we set out."

"What would you like to do now?" asked Catchpole.

Anthony's eyes sought MacMorran's. The latter looked at his watch significantly.

"I agree," said Anthony. "I'm with you all along the line, Andrew. I second your unspoken resolution that we adjourn for a light tea and a more substantial dinner. In the evening, I suggest that we sally forth again with Inspector Catchpole here and sample the local wine of Gambrinus. How does the full programme commend itself to you, Andrew?"

MacMorran furrowed his brows. "Where do we do your sampling act?"

"My dear Andrew—considering what Inspector Catchpole has told us this afternoon—where else than at the inn bearing the homely sign of the 'Wheatsheaf.'"

CHAPTER II

1

CHIEF Inspector MacMorran, Inspector Catchpole and Anthony Lotherington Bathurst entered the saloon-bar of the 'Wheatsheaf' almost exactly at half-past eight that evening. It may be recorded that present within the hostelry at the moment of their entrance were Maurice Fothergill, Ronald Harcourt, Michael Keegan and Keith Salt, K.C. They were not contained however in one company. Fothergill and Harcourt were seated next to one another in the saloon-bar, Salt was in a corner of the same bar brooding and unaccompanied, and Keegan, for some reason, was not playing darts as was his wont, but was seated on a wooden bench in the tap room silently contemplating a pint of 'wallop.'

MacMorran had intimated to Catchpole on the way to the 'Wheatsheaf' that he would like a private word or two with Willmott. Prompted thus, Catchpole pulled the landlord to one side and explained the circumstances. As Willmott listened, Catchpole thought that the man looked extremely worried. More than that even. Decidedly anxious with regard to something.

"All right, Inspector Catchpole," he said, "come into my private parlour. I'll be along there in a brace of shakes."

Catchpole motioned to the others and they followed Willmott into the room. As they went through, Maurice Fothergill noticed them and made appropriate remark on the incident to Harcourt. "The 'busies,' my dear Ronnie, are on the scent."

"Before you say anything, Inspector," said Willmott, "I've got summat to tell you. As a matter of fact, if you hadn't dropped in, I was comin' up to police-station to 'ave a little talk with you. It's been on my mind all day. But . . . er. . . ." he looked at MacMorran and Anthony and stopped.

"I see," said Catchpole, "so it's lucky for all of us that we've come along here this evening. Now let me start off to clear the decks and get everything straightforward for you. This gentleman is Chief Detective-Inspector MacMorran from Scotland Yard and this is Mr. Anthony Bathurst. You can guess what it is that brings them to these parts. And you can speak quite frankly in front of them, Willmott."

"Good evening, gentlemen. I woan't say I'm glad to see you—because I'm not. The less I 'ave to do with the police, the better I'm pleased. And I'm a rare one for the truth. And this na-asty business in Quiddington 'as fair got me down. It worries me no end. I don't like any of it and as far as I can see, it's going to make things ba-ad for nigh everybody."

The landlord looked up at the trio of men facing him and his thoughts seemed to take another direction.

"Would you gentlemen care for a little drop of something? Do-an't see why not. I am a man that likes things to be as congenial as possible?"

"I'd rather not," said Catchpole. "I'm on duty—in a way."

"So am I," put in MacMorran, "but I think I might relax a trifle down here in the country and accept Mr. Willmott's hospitality." He wheeled round to Anthony. "How about you, Mr. Bathurst?"

"Andrew," said Anthony, "I've never heard you to better advantage. A tray and drinks! Thank you, Mr. Willmott."

"If that's the case with you," conceded Catchpole, "perhaps I might—"

"Good man," said Anthony, "and now we're all old chinas together."

Willmott took the orders, went out and returned with the drinks.

"Now," said Catchpole, "these gentlemen came along here this evening with the idea of asking you a few questions. But I think they'd first of all like to hear what *you* have to say. I take it that it has a bearing on the murder?"

Willmott shook a solemn head. "It's not for me to say tha-at, Inspector. That'll be a matter for you to judge. Let the shoemaker stick to his last, say I. What I wanted to talk to you about was them da-arts of mine. Them what you looked at the other day."

Anthony and MacMorran reacted to the pregnant word immediately. They knew what Catchpole had told them concerning his previous visit to the 'Wheatsheaf' and his enquiry *re* the dart that had killed Flagon, and it had been this information which had mainly prompted their visit now. And here also was Willmott himself returning to the *motif*, entirely spontaneously.

"What did you wish to say to us?" demanded Catchpole.

"Why—just this, sirs. You know as 'ow you come along 'ere and asked me certain questions concernin' my da-arts? As to whether any of 'em were missin' like. And my Doris showed 'em all to you? And we all looked through 'em and said: 'no—there ain't any of 'em missin'? That's so, ain't it, Inspector?"

Catchpole looked startled at the turn Willmott had taken and MacMorran intensely interested. Anthony wondered what was coming next. Catchpole found words to reply.

"Yes. That's so, Willmott. I checked through all your boxes of darts with Doris, and according to her reckoning everything was in order. Well—what about it?"

Willmott spread out his hands at the inspector's question as though to explain that there must be extenuating circumstances.

"Well, Inspector Catchpole, I've got to tell you something more about tha-at. In a way, I've got to make a bit of a confession. It's like this. We 'ad some players in last night and I expect you know full well without me tellin' you that many of 'em always like to play with the same da-arts. Get attached to 'em like. 'My da-arts'—they always call 'em. Well, last night, one of our players, and 'e's pretty skilful with 'em come to that, comes up to me and says that 'is da-arts ain't there. They've gone, he says to me. And wha-at's more, 'e says there's some others what are much heavier, bin put back in the box in their place. So you see, Inspector, you can't very well hold me to blame for lettin' you think everything was satisfactory. All 'unky-dory as they say these days. We checked up on the numbers, you see, and the total was correct. I never gave so much as a thought to some 'avin' bin pinched, as it were, and others substitooted."

Willmott made another movement of resignation with his hands.

"May we see these darts—these replaced ones?" asked Mac-Morran.

"Why, of course, sir," replied Willmott. "I'll go and fetch them for you at once."

"Thank you, Willmott."

The landlord rose and made his exit. "The plot thickens," contributed Anthony as the door closed behind the old man.

"That's a fact," remarked MacMorran, "but I fancy the old boy's telling the truth, though. He struck me all the way through as being perfectly genuine. And, of course, you couldn't have expected him to be on the lookout for the darts having been changed. What do you think, Inspector?"

Catchpole nodded. "Oh, yes. I think old Willmott's a man to be trusted. He's genuine enough. Everybody in this quarter would give him that reputation. There's never been a whisper of anything against him. But here he comes."

Willmott came in again. He held three darts in his hand. "Here they are, gentlemen. These da-arts don't belong to me and never did. They're different entirely from ours. Much 'eavier than the standard da-art we use in the 'Wheatsheaf.'"

"Let's have a look at them, Willmott," said Catchpole.

The landlord handed over the three alien darts. MacMorran and Anthony gathered round to inspect them.

"Seem quite ordinary to me," said MacMorran as he balanced a dart on the palm of his hand.

"No, Andrew," said Anthony, "they're as our host says. I agree that they're heavier than the general run of darts."

"And there's another thing, sir," added Willmott, "the flight's not quite the same colour as the da-arts we use 'ere. Chance it, Mike Keegan, 'oo was the man what brought 'em to me, spotted the difference in 'em the moment 'e 'andled 'em."

"Oh," put in Catchpole, "it was Mike Keegan, was it, who detected them? As you say—he's a thundering good player."

"Tell me," said Anthony, "there's something that's rather puzzling me. If your darts were stolen and these substituted for them—and we're assuming for the sake of argument that yours may have been used for criminal purposes, how is it that Keegan or some other dart-player, didn't spot the change *before* last night? You see what I'm driving at, don't you?"

"I agree," said MacMorran, "the same point had already occurred to me."

"Yes—how do you explain that," supplemented Catchpole, "it's extremely important."

"I can explain that quite easily, gentlemen," said Willmott, "it happened on account of Mike Keegan himself. You see it's like this. With da-arts, it's a case of 'regulars' and 'occasional' as you might say. A 'regular' player such as Mike Keegan is 'as 'is own da-arts. That is to say as far as possible, 'e always uses the sa-ame da-arts. He gets to call 'em, as I said before, 'my da-arts.' An 'occasional,' on the other 'and, 'ull ta-ake any da-arts 'e can pick up to 'ave a ga-ame with. It's the sa-ame with tankards in a manner o' speakin'. That's why it was left for Keegan to spot the difference."

"But I still don't understand," said Anthony. "If your premises are correct, the theft of the original darts must have taken place some days ago. That's so, isn't it? Yet Keegan doesn't discover the change until last night. That's the part of it which baffles me. The 'regular' and 'occasional' position that you've just described I understand quite well."

Willmott had listened somewhat apprehensively as Anthony had been speaking, but when he heard the essential point that emerged his face brightened perceptibly.

"Oh—I see, sir, the point that you be gettin' at. There's no mystery as far as that goes. And no cause for you to be worried neither. For some reason best known to himself, no doubt, Mike Keegan ain't bin playin' da-arts in the 'Wheatsheaf' for some few da-ays now. He's bin layin' off. More than one of 'is cronies 'as remarked on it. But last night 'e said as 'ow 'e fancied a ga-ame. That's the fair and proper explanation of that."

"That certainly clears the point," said MacMorran, "perhaps for some reason best known to himself, the gentleman's been feeling a bit under the weather. Pretty good player, you said he was, didn't you?"

"Ay, sir. Mike Keegan, when 'e's in the right mood, can plant a da-art just where 'e pleases. Got the eye of an 'awk. Last year the *Noose o' the World* sent its special team down 'ere to play a ga-ame for one o' the local charities and Mike Keegan dusted their tails for 'em that night, I can tell you. They 'ad all their celebrities with 'em and all. Scored five tons that evenin' 'e did." Willmott chuckled at the reminiscence. "'E's the best player round these parts," he concluded on a note of happiness.

"H'm," remarked MacMorran, "interesting chap, this Mr. Keegan. Quite the local champion—eh? I should like to have a word with him on this dart matter. Does he live very far away?"

"As a matter of fact," replied Willmott, almost enthusiastically, "'e 'appens to be in the 'ouse now. I could put my 'and on 'im in a few seconds. Just before you came in, I drew 'im a pint o' bitter. Could I bring 'im in 'ere to speak to you? Would that be in order?"

"That's an idea, certainly," said MacMorran, "what do you say, Inspector Catchpole?"

"Well—I suppose it's all right if you say so. On what lines do you intend to question him?"

"Oh—just generally. On the matter of the darts. There's a good opening there. Why? What were you thinking of?"

"I just wondered. Some of these country yokels, you know, aren't easy to approach. They put the bars up in next to no time."

"We'll see about that. Here he comes."

Willmott, who had gone out immediately on MacMorran's acquiescence, came back to the room followed by a huge cart-horse of a man. His face was sun-tanned and weather-beaten and Anthony felt when he saw him that he had rarely seen such a powerful-looking customer.

"This is Mike Keegan, gentlemen," said Willmott by way of introduction. "These gentlemen would like a word with you, Mike, concernin' those da-arts of yours. You know—what you told me about last night. How there'd been some fiddlin' with 'em."

Keegan had entered with amiability on his features, but the instant he caught sight of Inspector Catchpole, the expression underwent a marked change.

"Gentlemen, you say! You mean 'rozzers' do-an't you, Bob Willmott? That ain't a fair call for a man what's enjoyin' a quiet pint o' beer, to bring 'im up against the police without sayin' a word in season like. It ain't fair play at all."

"That's all right, Keegan," said Catchpole, "this gentleman's Detective-Inspector MacMorran from Scotland Yard. All he wants to do is to ask you a few questions about those missing darts. You've no reason to be upset about it."

"Well, then, Inspector Catchpole, I ain't got nothin' to say. What I told old Bob Willmott 'ere, I told him in confidence. And I do-an't see why I should be called upon to repeat it. I ain't one to talk to the police. I never was and I ain't a-goin' to start now. I don't trust 'em and I hate their guts."

He paused and gazed truculently at the company. Willmott expressed his annoyance.

"What for do you want to make all this fuss, Mike Keegan? Seems to me you're like a great kid—cryin' out afore you're 'urt."

Keegan turned on the landlord almost ferociously. "And what I said goes for you too, Bob Willmott! Can t a man say something to you without yer goin' blabbin' to the police about it? I be surprised at you. Like an old woman that must always be givin' tongue. It do fair sicken me, it do. Any'ow I ain't talkin' and that's that. See?"

Keegan stood in the middle of the room, the picture of hostility and aggression. Catchpole looked at MacMorran in invitation for his cue. MacMorran came to a prompt decision and shook his head.

"All right, Inspector. For the time being, leave Mr. Keegan to his own resources. If I find it necessary, I'll interview him on another occasion."

Catchpole turned abruptly to Keegan. "You can go," he said curtly.

Keegan grinned at his temporary triumph. "You're tellin' me," he said offensively, "I know my rights if some other people do-an't. And there's no reason why a man should be trampled on by the police. Even though 'e do live in the country it do-an't mean 'e's ignorant of the law."

Keegan turned on his heel and lurched out. Catchpole shrugged his shoulders at the departure. "Well—that's that. Keegan's gone all tight-lipped. What do you make of it?"

He addressed his question generally, but as it happened, each one of his hearers answered it, in turn.

Willmott said: "That's Mike Keegan all over. Ignorant—although 'e says 'e ain't. Superstitious. One of the low Irish. Plenty o' lip as a rule, but when you want the man to speak, you can't get a blasted word out of 'im. Fair gets my goat, that sort o' conduct do." He spat skilfully into the fireplace in evidence of his disgust.

MacMorran said: "Don't quite know what to make of it. May be just natural perversity. On the contrary maybe there's something more behind it than that. Where was Keegan on the afternoon Flagon was put out? Was he close at hand? Worth an inquiry that— perhaps. On the other hand what possible motive can a man like Keegan have to murder two of His Majesty's judges? No—I'm afraid that recent exhibition was just pure cussedness on Keegan's part and nothing more."

Anthony said: "I think that Keegan either knows something or is afraid of something. And he may be the latter because of the former. It was the imminence of the police that caused him to act as he did. When he saw us facing him, he shied at the encounter. Otherwise, I think he would have refused to accompany Mr. Willmott here, in the first place. At least, that's how it struck me. And although he doesn't fill the bill from your 'motive' point of view, Andrew, he certainly fills it in two directions from mine."

MacMorran looked up at Anthony. "I get one of them. You mean he's a crack darts-player?"

"Ah-ha. Think of the testimonial our friend here gave him about a quarter of an hour ago. If I remember correctly, the phrase was 'Mike Keegan can plant a dart just where he pleases.' Isn't that the case, Mr. Willmott?"

"Ay, sir. They were my very words. And it's true. Uncommon seldom did Mike Keegan meet his match in my bar. That is, from any of the 'regulars.'"

"There you are, Andrew. In that direction he's certainly of the sort of man we're looking for. And my second satisfactory condition was this. Keegan looks to me just the fellow—how shall I put it—shall we say—to climb a tree. It would be interesting too, to find out whether he cycles. Do you happen to know, Mr. Willmott?"

"I couldn't say as to that, sir. I can't call to mind that I've ever seen 'im ridin' a bike. But a rare lot of them workmen do."

MacMorran leant forward towards the old landlord. "You said something a moment ago that interested me. With regard to Keegan's skill at darts. Actually—how many men in the district can beat him?"

"Nary a one, sir. When Mike Keegan loses, it's always a stranger that dusts 'is tail for 'im." Willmott emitted one of his sepulchral chuckles. "About a week ago, we 'ad one do it. Right in this 'ere bar. Rare pleased I was, too, to see it."

"Who was that?" asked Anthony quickly.

"A gentleman from London," replied Willmott, "what's stayin' in the 'ouse with a friend of 'is. Come down specially for the Bar Point-to-Point meeting. 'E gave Mr. Mike Keegan the 'idin' of 'is life t'other evening on one of my little dart-boards. You should 'a' seen the look on Mike Keegan's face when 'e coom up to order the pints o' beer what he'd lost on the ga-ame. It fair did me good to see it—so it did."

Anthony cut in quickly. "Is this gentleman you speak of still here?"

"Ay. He still be 'ere. And 'e's in the saloon-bar now. I see 'im there just now when I passed through. By name o' Fothergill. Rare smart 'and 'e be, with the da-arts, I can tell you that. Put Mike Keegan in his place."

Anthony looked at the two professionals. "I've been thinking," said MacMorran, "and it seems to me that there's something else, which very definitely lets Keegan out." He sucked contemplatively at his pipe. "Have you thought of it?" he added.

"I think I know what you mean," answered Anthony. "You mean the written attachments, don't you?"

"Exactly," returned MacMorran, "you'll never put into me that a man of Keegan's class and upbringing would call a dart a quillet. If you argued from now till Doomsday. What do you say yourself?"

"Perhaps not," said Anthony, "but I'll have more to say to you about that a little later on. When we're alone." He turned to Willmott. "Is Keegan a genuine local? That is to say a man who was born and bred here?"

"No," said Willmott, "as far as I know—'e's not. 'E came 'ere a matter of about five year ago. Where from I couldn't rightly say. I never 'eard."

"What's his job?"

"Only a farm labourer, sir. There be several biggish farms between Quiddington St. Philip and Sword. Works for Farmer Thornley."

"I see. Thank you, Mr. Willmott." Anthony turned and spoke to MacMorran. "This man, Fothergill, whom Willmott has told us about, interests me. A chat with him might be fruitful. He's on the spot. What do you say?"

MacMorran grinned. "I've no objection. But I'm bound to point out that Fothergill may be another Keegan. He may be chary of opening his mouth to the powers that be."

"What do you say to my idea, Inspector Catchpole?" inquired Anthony.

"I've no objection at all," replied Catchpole.

"All right then, we'll chance it. Do you mind if I do the talking this time?"

The two professionals agreed without demur. "O.K. then, Willmott. Would you be good enough to ask Mr. Fothergill if he'd oblige us with a few minutes' conversation? In here? Thanks very much."

The landlord went out to get Fothergill, but MacMorran thought, from the way he went, that he didn't seem too pleased about it. He showed nothing like the alacrity that he exhibited when he had gone for Keegan. But although MacMorran thought thus, neither he nor Anthony was prepared for Catchpole's reception of Fothergill when he entered the room.

"This is Mr. Fothergill, gentlemen," announced Willmott, "he tells me that 'e's quite willin' to—"

Before he could complete his sentence, a sharp exclamation from Catchpole halted him summarily.

"Excuse me for a moment," said the local inspector, "but haven't I had the pleasure of seeing you before?"

The intervention came so quickly that it completely put Willmott off his stroke, with the result that he failed to complete the usual introduction. Fothergill smiled easily at the Verne inspector.

"I don't know," he said with perfect aplomb, "have you? It's quite likely, I suppose. I've been staying in this district from some days now so you may have run across me on your rounds."

"I can't remember exactly," went on Catchpole, "but your face is distinctly familiar to me. I know that I've seen you before and very recently at that."

"Possibly," countered Fothergill, "in the saloon-bar of this excellent hostelry that we know as the 'Wheatsheaf.'"

"I don't think so," rejoined Catchpole slowly but with emphasis.

"Well," said Fothergill, "do I wait for the inspiration to come to you, or do you gentlemen desire to have a chat with me? Please make up your minds."

He took a seat with the utmost composure and crossed his legs. Before MacMorran was able to take a hand, Catchpole's face suddenly cleared. It was evident that he had collected the missing thread.

"I know," he said, "I knew it would come to me if I persisted. You were standing near Doctor Harradine and Sir Claude de Monterey by the dead body of the late Justice Flagon. I remember seeing you there, when I arrived at the spot."

Anthony, watching the scene intently, thought that Fothergill changed colour just a little at Catchpole's statement. His speech, however, gave no indication of any misgiving.

"That's quite true," he admitted. "Now you mention it, I fancy I remember you coming along. I must congratulate you, Inspector, on your memory for faces. You're one up on me. All I can remember of the affair is a lot of people crowding round, none of whom now seems anything like distinct to me."

Catchpole made an unintelligible reply. Then he glanced over towards Anthony. "I think, Mr. Bathurst, you wished to have a word with Mr. Fothergill?"

"Yes, Inspector," responded Anthony with a smile, "especially bearing in mind what Mr. Fothergill has just told us." He turned to Fothergill. "In view of what's just transpired, you saw Justice Flagon, I suppose, actually fall from his horse?"

"Yes. I saw the whole thing."

"Where were you exactly when that occurred?"

Fothergill considered the question. "I should think," he said slowly, "that I was within a couple of hundred yards."

Anthony smiled again. "Forgive me," he said, "but that isn't *quite* what I asked you. Perhaps I put the question somewhat vaguely. You've told me how *far* you were away. What I meant was where actually *were* you?"

"Oh—I see. I beg your pardon. Actually I had been on the hill near Newstead Green and was walking down the lane that comes out near the course."

MacMorran and Catchpole both realized the significance and importance of the reply.

"Is that so?" said Anthony, "and you were able to see the accident from there? I should have thought—"

"The hedge is quite low. I could see quite clearly."

"What did you do?"

"I ran towards the course and looked over that hedge. The hedge by the course, I mean. Not the hedge in the lane. On the side where Flagon fell."

"Did you see anybody else anywhere near?"

"Not immediately. After a time—two or three minutes, say—a number of people came running up."

"Did you see anybody with a bicycle?"

"No. Nobody. Why—should I have done?"

"I can't answer that, Mr. Fothergill. I wish I could. But I had a reason for asking you."

"Is that all you wanted?" asked Fothergill. "Because I've a friend in the—"

"Just a minute, if you don't mind, Mr. Fothergill. I should be tremendously obliged if you would help me. I'm Chief Inspector MacMorran of Scotland Yard."

"So I believe," replied Fothergill coolly. "Mr. Willmott told me before I came in. I'm not bound to answer you, am I?"

"No. Not at the moment. But I'm sure you won't mind in the circumstances."

"All right," said Fothergill pleasantly, "go ahead."

"Did you go to see the Point-to-Point meeting?"

"Yes. Naturally. Why else should I have been there? I came down here almost entirely for that purpose."

"Why were you in the lane then, where you say you were?" Fothergill smiled. "I guessed that was coming. The explanation is very simple. I had arranged to meet a friend on the hill by Newstead Green. It almost overlooks the winning-post and gives you a grand view of the finish. But he didn't turn up. I learned afterwards that he had been taken ill. When I felt for certain that he wasn't coming, I walked down."

"And you saw nobody in that lane or near that lane round about the time of Flagon's fall?"

"No. I said I didn't."

"Thank you. That's all I wanted to know. How about you. Inspector Catchpole? Any questions? No? You, Mr. Bathurst?" Anthony shook his head.

"That's all right then, Mr. Fothergill, and thank you very much for your most valuable assistance. How long will you be staying here, in case I should want to have another word with you?"

"Till the end of the week in all probability. I had intended to leave before this, as a matter of fact. But I won't bind myself." Fothergill rose and walked out.

"I thought," said Anthony to MacMorran, after the door had closed, "that in view of this new angle we have, I'd lie low with regard to the darts."

"I think you were wise. But I say—this Fothergill man gives you furiously to think, doesn't he? He fills the bill, to my mind, much better than our horny-handed son of toil, Michael Keegan. A crack darts player and bang in the picture when the balloon went up. Don't know what you think."

Anthony rubbed the ridge of his jaw. "There's one thing we mustn't forget, Andrew. When we investigate the question of motive. Besides Flagon, there has been Madrigal. Whatever motive there is it entangles both. We mustn't be short-sighted and take one without the other."

"I told Willmott to keep quiet about Madrigal," said Catchpole.

"And I 'ave, Inspector. I 'aven't breathed a word. So far the village is quiet about it. Most of 'em 'ave the idea that Justice Madrigal was took ill when 'e 'ad 'is attack—no wuss than a faint. But of course, the news'll soon get round in the morning."

Anthony gestured to MacMorran behind Willmott's back. The inspector rose in company with Catchpole.

"Well—we'll be getting along, I think. Thank you, Willmott, for all you've done—and mum's the word about everything here to-night."

"You can rely on me, sir. I know when to keep a still tongue in my 'ead."

The three men went out. "A pretty problem," said Anthony, "and a good job we booked to stay at Verne and not here. You can be *too* near the heart of things, you know. Cramps action! Anyhow, I propose we sleep on it until the morning."

"I agree," said MacMorran heartily. "Goodnight, Catchpole. We'll look you up again in the morning."

2

At breakfast the following morning Anthony, to MacMorran's surprise, was inclined to discuss the murders. This was most unusual and MacMorran knew it full well.

"You know, Andrew," said Anthony, "I've been thinking over our little problem and I find myself wondering whether our murderer is going to turn out one of the most cunning gentlemen whose path had crossed ours. If not *the* most cunning. I'll tell you what I mean."

"I'll be glad to hear-r it," said MacMorran, over his bacon and eggs. "Anything for a change."

"Well—I've been thinking on these lines. I lay awake a long time over it. You remember how I reminded you last night that the motive must involve both Flagon and Madrigal. Well—I've been trying to put myself in the murderer's place."

MacMorran grinned. "I hope I am never called upon to lay you by the heels."

Anthony waved an egg-spoon. "Skip that! Suppose I deliberately introduced the Madrigal aspect to put the police completely off the scent? Seems to me that the contingency is highly possible."

"Doubt it. Doubt it very much. Seems too far-fetched for me. Kill a second time for a mere whim? Not on your life!"

Anthony expressed indignation. "A whim you call it! I like that! Why, man—it might very well save our murderer's neck. That's quite conceivable. And you sit there wolfing prime Wiltshire and the produce of the best Buff Orpingtons and dismiss it as a mere whim! Andrew, you give me pain."

"All right. All right. But I disagree with you, just the same."

Anthony smiled. "Whatever I do, Andrew, and however I think, this 'motive' question always brings me back with a jerk. Jealousy, fear, greed, revenge, hate—where does one of these come in as applied to both Flagon *and* Madrigal? I don't get it."

"No—it's all on the nebulous side, I agree."

"We haven't been here twenty-four hours yet. And look what's turned up already. Shall I list them for you, Andrew? The effort's worth it."

Anthony proceeded to tick off the various items on his fingers with the end of the, as yet, unused marmalade spoon. "One—another murder of a Flagon colleague.—Two—a shrewd idea—something more than a theory in each case—as to how the murders were committed. You can't gainsay that. Three—similar ideas with regard to the respective get-aways. Four—stolen darts with substitutions. Five—the truculent Mr. Keegan. Six—the nonchalant Mr. Fothergill. Each of whom presents distinctly interesting possibilities. Don't you agree?"

"With every syllable of every word that you've just uttered. On the darts matter—by the way—I've arranged with Willmott and Catchpole that the former comes along to-day and has a 'dekko' at the two darts the murderer used. Won't do any harm to get confirmation."

"Good. I harbour little doubts, however. The lethal darts were removed from the 'Wheatsheaf' collection all right. The coincidence is much too strong to my mind to be ignored."

Anthony helped himself to a generous portion of marmalade. "Sing hey," he said jovially, "for the sweetmeat o' Bonnie Dundee." He paused, to go on, however, with the main business, almost immediately. "Coming back again to motive, Andrew. There's one point in connection with that, which we can check up on. As soon as possible. Greed! Avarice! Flagon's money, I mean. Where's it gone? He may have left much to be desired. Probably has, I should say. Yes—I know that I'm excluding the Madrigal angle for the time being—although I may be taking a grave risk in so doing. But Flagon's was the first murder. First things first. We must find out as soon as possible who clicks for the Flagon bequest. Rumour hath it that he was woefully short of kith and kin."

"I had a mind to do that this morning. I must get into touch with the solicitors. I'll do so as soon as I can."

"Good again. Let me know as soon as you hear anything, will you?"

"I'm also," continued MacMorran, "going to get Catchpole to investigate the movements of one or two people on the afternoon of the Flagon murder and then, if necessary, have a close look at their alibis."

"Namely?" questioned Anthony.

"Er—Fothergill . . . for one . . . Keegan and er . . . possibly Willmott."

"Willmott? My dear Andrew, I ask you!"

"That's all right," said MacMorran with dogged imperturbability, "so you can—but—you never know."

"My dear Andrew! Noticed his hands? If he'd thrown a dart at Flagon, he'd have much more likely killed Fothergill in the winding lane that leads from Newstead Green. Have a heart—or dart."

MacMorran pushed away his plate. "Carry on. I can take it."

"Andrew," said Anthony, suddenly discarding the bantering tone, "there's another point I wanted to discuss with you. It's just come back to me."

"What's that?"

"Do you remember something definitely important that Fothergill said when I was questioning him? As to the reason he was in the lane down which *we* think the murderer made his escape?"

"Yes. Very well. He stated that he went to the top of the hill to meet a friend who had arranged to be there. According to Fothergill there was an excellent view from there of the finish of the race which they both wanted to see. I presume he meant the race that Flagon was riding in. I think that may be taken for granted. Then he went on to say that his pal didn't turn up owing to sudden illness. So he walked down and into the lane. Is that correct?"

"One hundred per cent, Andrew. I don't know what I should do without you! But that's what I meant. What about this absent friend? Who didn't get to the top of the hill. And who therefore didn't march down again? If my memory serves me as correctly as yours has done, Willmott said earlier on that Fothergill was staying at the 'Wheatsheaf' *with a friend*. Yes?"

"Yes. I think you're right. The old fellow certainly did say that. What are you after?"

"Funny about that missing friend," commented Anthony contemplatively. "Wonder if it was the same bloke that's stopping there with Fothergill? Assuming—and it's a natural assumption—that Fothergill and he came to these 'ere parts to see the meeting (Fothergill did—he said so), why didn't they go off to the races together? Funny!"

"Can't see that there's much in that. The other chap may have had some business to attend to beforehand, and fixed up to meet Fothergill somewhere near the course when he had transacted it. Quite an ordinary procedure."

"Maybe you're right, Andrew. Anyhow, I'm keeping an open mind on it. Seems to me an interview with Comrade Fothergill's friend might show a small profit. He may still be down here. Fothergill is. They came together, I should say, so probably they'll depart together."

Anthony rose from the table. "An excellent breakfast, Andrew. Commend me to country pubs to satisfy the inner man. Not all of them, though. Did I ever tell you of my experience at 'The Greyhound,' Long Escreet? No? I must do so. Remind me sometime, will you? Hullo—what's this?"

A waiter had approached. Anthony saw him. "Were you wanting me?"

"I was asked to deliver this letter to you, sir. By hand. It is Mr. Anthony Bathurst, isn't it?"

"Quite right, waiter. And thank you."

Anthony turned to Inspector MacMorran. "Strange, Andrew. Very strange. Who knows that I'm rusticating at Verne? News, evidently, travels betimes in these parts. Interesting, at any rate." He opened the letter. It was addressed to 'Anthony Bathurst, Esq.' It ran as follows:

> The Old House,
> Quiddington St. Philip.
> *April 20th.*

My Dear Mr. Bathurst,

You will doubtless be more than surprised to receive this letter. And you will wonder how it is that I know that you are in Verne and also *why* you are there. But please subdue both your surprise and wonder and come to see me here, as soon as you possibly and conveniently can. Could you make it, say, eleven o'clock this morning and do me the honour of lunching with me afterwards? Please come! I have so much to say to you with regard to the death of Justice Flagon.

I remain,

> Yours most sincerely,
> Paula Secretan.

Anthony read the note twice and then tossed it over to Mac-Morran. "Andrew! Di-da-di-da-di-da! The pace quickens as the plot thickens. *The* Paula Secretan, you observe, of the 'Cornmarket,' the 'Hilarity' and the 'Vanity.' One of the biggest 'box-office' at the present moment. Not only does the lady know we're here, Andrew— and why we're here—but she also has much to tell us! Note the desire to impart information. The only fly in the ointment is that you've been excluded from the invitation and that I alone am asked to help dispose of the meagre rations."

"Suits me," returned Andrew. "This sort of thing is far more in your line than in mine. You'll go, of course?"

"I must, Andrew. The lady knows something—that's sticking out a mile. It would be criminally negligent on my part to treat it cavalierly. And she prefers us to the local Catchpole. I'll go along at once and 'phone my acceptance of the invitation. Verne 99, the notepaper informs me."

Anthony went along to the telephone and asked for the lady's number. When the answer came, it was conveyed to him in a deep rich contralto voice.

"I'm delighted, Mr. Bathurst, to receive such a quick reply. And thank you so much for coming along. I'll try to make the lunch moderately respectable. *Not* pigeons!"

Anthony replaced the receiver and went back to MacMorran. "O.K., Andrew. I've fixed it. The stage is set. And the lady seems eminently charming."

"Most of 'em do," grunted MacMorran, "when they want something."

3

Anthony arrived at 'The Old House' punctually at eleven o'clock. He was little prepared for the news which Miss Secretan had for him.

The larger part of the village of Quiddington St. Philip lay huddled, as it were, beyond the church. The surrounding country was pasture-land and woods. Old cottages turned up here and there—often in the most unexpected places. But 'The Old House' did stand at the top of a hill. It was authentically old, Anthony saw. A pair of yews were at the gate, the path was mossy and there was a timbered gable with a sweep of tiled roof. At the bottom of the hill, away in the distance on the other side, were a farm and its outlying buildings. Anthony walked up to the front door and used the old-fashioned wrought-iron knocker. He saw no sign of a bell. The maid who opened the door to him had been obviously instructed to expect him and she whisked him into the presence of Paula Secretan with commendable celerity.

Paula Secretan was standing in the morning-room to receive him. She had evidently just come in from outdoors. A dark-green scarf, gloves and mackintosh to match, lay over her arm. The lady was petite. But very wonderful! As Anthony entered, she was looking at a small watch inset in a ring which she was wearing on her left little finger. She had glorious dark-blue eyes and dark auburn hair. Her voice, as the telephone had previously told him, was rich and deep.

But her beauty was marred by something which sat heavily on her face and subdued, if only temporarily, her natural charm and vivacity. "You're punctual," she said. "I'm so pleased."

"I always endeavour to be, Miss Secretan. It's one of my vices."

"I might have known that, Mr. Bathurst. Cigarette?" She offered her case.

"Thanks."

"And I think"—she cocked her head alluringly—"sherry?"

"Thanks again."

"Good."

She moved across the room with lithe grace and rang a bell. She was small and slim and dynamic. Her closely-cut red-gold hair was swept back from her brow. Her wide blue eyes had an almost breathtaking beauty and in her face strength of character contrasted with her loveliness for the dominance. Her arms were white and superbly moulded. Anthony could only feel an almost ecstatic admiration for her.

The maid who had answered the door brought sherry and glasses. "Sit down, Mr. Bathurst," said Paula, "and when you've drunk your sherry, I want to talk to you."

Anthony drank. The wine was good. "I shall be happy to listen," he said.

"I'm not going to mystify you in any way," went on Miss Secretan, "and I'll tell you how I knew you were here. Because I expect you've been wondering. I saw you! I saw you in the company of that inspector from Verne and another man. Yesterday afternoon. You see—I knew you. That I suppose must be the *real* explanation. I saw you in court when Claude Merivale was on trial for the murder of his wife. You were pointed out to me by Sir Adrian Challenor who had taken me along to the court. So you see the explanation is absolutely simple. For when I saw you here, I knew that it simply *must* be in connexion with the death of Nicholas Flagon. Am I right?"

Anthony gestured. "I won't contradict you, Miss Secretan."

"I'm so pleased to think that I was right. Another sherry, Mr. Bathurst."

"Thank you—I will."

As he spoke, he noticed that her radiance came and went and that, more often than otherwise, her cheeks trembled and her eyes pleaded desperately. It came upon him with something of a shock, that this girl was facing horrible—and serious trouble at that. She poured out the second glass of sherry and handed it to him. He drank. As he did so, she sat down and looked straight at him. Her face was stubborn now with resolution and determination. It occurred to Anthony that she had screwed her courage to the sticking point.

"Well, Miss Secretan," said Anthony, "you have certain information for me, you say. I have come in accordance with your request. I am at your service."

For a brief moment she made no reply to him. Then she rose rather abruptly and came right over to him. She began to speak and her expression changed somewhat.

"Mr. Bathurst," she said, "I'm frightened. But that's not the only thing. Besides being frightened, I'm almost heart-broken." She paused. Anthony looked up at her. "Yes," she said quietly and reached out her hand to place it on his arm. "Yes. I am not talking idly. I have reason to be—believe me. Heart-broken, I mean. I loved Nicholas Flagon. Nicholas Flagon loved me. We were to have been married on Whitsun Eve."

To say that Anthony was surprised at this piece of news is to put matters mildly. "I am sorry, Miss Secretan," he said gravely, "more sorry than I can possibly express to you. Allow me to express my most sincere sympathy. I assure you that I hadn't the slightest idea of this."

"No. I know you hadn't. You couldn't have. Nobody had. It was a secret between us. Even our most intimate friends were unaware of it. That was Nick's wish, but our engagement would have been announced in a fortnight's time."

She struck her hands together and uttered a bitter cry. "Oh—why didn't I stop him riding in that wretched race! More than once I felt like so doing."

Anthony made no reply. The situation, as far as he was concerned, had developed in an entirely unexpected fashion. He looked at her. There was a strange look on her face. Her eyes were half closed as though she were attempting to shut out a vision of something appallingly horrible. Then she turned to him again with a white, tortured face and tightly clenched hands.

"And that isn't all, Mr. Bathurst. In a way, I almost wish it were. There's something else which I feel I must tell you." Her voice was hushed now. "I think you should know this—because it may have some bearing on the murder. It was Nick's intention to leave me everything he had."

"You mean—in his will?"

"Yes."

"And has he?"

She spread out her hands to him. "I don't know," she said, without a second of hesitation. "All I know is what we agreed on. He and I. I've left everything to him—and he was to leave everything he had to me."

"And you mean that you aren't certain if he had already carried out his part of the arrangement?"

"No." She clasped her hands in front of her and the fingers worked and twisted. "Oh—don't think I care about the money. It isn't that. I don't want it. I'm a well-to-do woman without touching a farthing of Nick's money. I want for nothing. It's the murder I'm thinking of. Has his money provided a motive for some mercenary beast to kill Nick? That's what I keep on thinking I can't help it."

"Miss Secretan," Anthony felt his way cautiously, "you have been very frank with me. I appreciate that—intensely. Will you forgive me if I ask you a question which may seem to be extremely personal? I wouldn't ask it, if I didn't consider it had an important bearing on the case. You understand?"

"I understand," she answered, with an inclination of the head. "Please answer this then. How long has your engagement been an accomplished fact. Is it, for example, of very recent genesis?"

"Oh—yes. Quite recent. Let me think." She broke off, to make the necessary mental calculation. "A fortnight yesterday, Mr. Bathurst."

"I see. So that it's eminently reasonable for us to suppose that your fiancé did *not* have the necessary time to make the arrangements you agreed on, with regard to his will?"

"Yes—I suppose you could say that."

"Although *you* have?"

She nodded and repeated his words. "Although *I* have. Yes!"

"You see," went on Anthony, "in the case of the late Justice Flagon, it may have entailed the alteration of an already existing will."

"I am not altogether sure on that point," she replied, "but I think from something Nick said to me one day that it did mean that."

"I see. That's exceedingly interesting."

Paula Secretan bowed her head at his expression of opinion. After all, this man to whom she spoke was a stranger to her. She knew nothing of the inner secret man which the outward trappings of success concealed from her. What was he thinking as he sat there? How could she obtain a real estimate of him? While she was thinking on these lines, Anthony looked up at her suddenly. His glance almost startled her. She was so close to the edge of things, under the intolerable strain which this tragedy in her life had brought to her, that she laughed harshly. But the sincerity in Anthony's manner and voice, when he spoke, steadied her considerably, so that she doubted him no longer. She went to her chair again and sat opposite to him. "Can you tell me, please, the name of your solicitors?"

"Of course. Why not? Messrs. Little, Pearce and Hills, Grays Inn Road."

"Thank you, Miss Secretan." Anthony noted the names. "And of the late Justice Flagon's?"

The answer came equally promptly. "Messrs. Sugden, Ward and Blake, Basinghall Street."

"Thank you, Miss Secretan. Now another question. It doesn't really matter if you can't answer this one. Do you happen to know the name of his executor?"

"Yes. I can answer that, too. His bankers are his executors. Messrs. Wynne, Floss and Company."

"Thank you again, Miss Secretan." Anthony put away his diary, in which he had noted the respective names. "Can you tell me," he said, "if from your knowledge, the judge had any enemies? That he knew about? I must approach the crime, you see, from every possible angle."

She shook her head. "I never heard him speak of anybody who owed him a grudge. Nick was liked and respected wherever he went. I—know that's a cliché—but nothing could be more true in this case."

"There is one thing, though. A judge, naturally, by reason of his position and the duty which he performs—"

She cut him abruptly. "I know what you're going to say. I know what you mean. But in Nick Flagon's case, I've never heard a whisper of anything of that kind. Neither from him nor from any other person."

"How long had you known him? That is to say—anything like intimately?"

"Just under a year. I met him for the first time at Eton. Last June. Sir Claude de Monterey, who lives near me here, took me down for the Winchester match. Nick Flagon was there. Sir Claude introduced me. Everybody thought that Nick was a confirmed bachelor. But he wasn't. At any rate after he had met me. He was the most charming person one could possibly meet."

Anthony felt that it was now due time for his next question. For he had gradually paved the way towards it. He put it therefore. "Did you attend the funeral, Miss Secretan?"

"No, Mr. Bathurst, of course not. How could I? If I had, I should have been categorized as a morbidly curious sightseer. But I saw it from my window here. The church is only a stone's throw distance. No, Mr. Bathurst, the only black that I can wear is next my heart. And I don't find *that* a trivial sorrow."

Anthony debated his next remark for a minute or so, before he made it.

"Have you heard anything about the funeral, Miss Secretan?"

She shook her head blankly. "No. Why do you ask? What should I have heard about it?"

"You have not heard, then, of an accident that occurred to one of the mourners?"

Her small vivacious face paled. "What do you mean?" she asked. There was now a definite catch in her voice.

"Just what I said, Miss Secretan. Neither more nor less."

"An accident? To one of the mourners? Who was it? Please tell me."

"Mr. Justice Madrigal."

She gasped as he spoke the name "Mr. Justice Madrigal?"

"Yes."

"What happened to him?"

"He died."

"Died?"

Anthony nodded. She saw that he was serious. Paula Secretan had learned her job as an actress in places where colours were plain and there was neither time nor plaudit for subtlety or nuance. Heroes were heroes and villains were villains indeed. She knew without any doubt that Anthony was not dissembling.

"Tell me," she said, "tell me what happened to Mr. Justice Madrigal."

"As you wish, although I would have spared you the details. As the body of Nicholas Flagon, in its coffin, was being lowered into the grave, Justice Madrigal was seen to pitch forward on to his face. The general impression, so I'm told, was that the judge had fainted. But when help reached him, it was discovered that things were very much worse. Madrigal was dead."

Paula put her hand to her mouth. "How?" she gasped, "was it his heart?"

"No, Miss Secretan. He had been murdered. And the manner of his death was exactly similar to that of Nicholas Flagon."

"I am glad," she said simply, "that I came away from the window as they carried Nick's coffin to the grave. I couldn't bear to watch any longer. Oh, now that you have told me this, I am glad that I did," she exclaimed passionately. Then she seemed to realize fully and for the first time, the enormity of what Anthony had just told her. "But why?" she exclaimed—"it doesn't make sense. Why kill both? I can't see any rhyme or reason in it."

She paused. It seemed, from her attitude, that she expected Anthony to supply the answers to the questions she herself had asked.

"I agree, Miss Secretan," he said. "I agree with you entirely. And there's more perhaps in it than that. Doesn't it effectively dispose of your theory? With regard to the conditions of Nicholas Flagon's will? We can't assume that there was a money entanglement in the case of Justice Madrigal."

"No. I see what you mean," she said dully. "This news of yours certainly does make a difference." Her face went blank. She sat mutely opposite to him. Her countenance reflected the mental agony she was enduring. She suddenly spoke again.

"Unless—" But she got no farther than the opening word of the sentence. Anthony intervened.

"Unless what, Miss Secretan?"

"Unless," she spoke slowly, "unless the second murder is a blind. You know—a feint—of some kind—to put the police off the scent."

"Miss Secretan," said Anthony admiringly, "I hand it to you for the idea. I think that you may have got something there. There are two people in this room who think alike."

"That pleases me," she said simply, "for if you and I think the same, I shall begin to believe that there's something in it."

"Good. Now for a little practical help. Will you take me, please, to the window from which you said you watched the first part of the funeral yesterday? It will give me a view of the churchyard different from that which I've already had."

"Yes. Of course. I see what you mean. Please come with me." He followed her upstairs to a reading-room which opened on to a broad balcony. Just across to the left lay the churchyard of Quiddington St. Philip. Standing on the balcony, one got an excellent view of it.

"Come out on the balcony," said Paula. "I had to watch from the window yesterday, because it was raining hard at the time. Much too hard to stand out there."

Anthony accompanied her on to the balcony. At the end of her garden, a flight of steps led down to a small bridge across the stream. Anthony watched the colours in the water changing as the sun caressed it. He could see the churchyard now in almost every

96 | BRIAN FLYNN

detail. But of course—he was forgetting for the moment—Paula Secretan had stood at the window—a few yards farther away than he was now.

"Come back into the room," he said, "and show me exactly where you stood. Then I shall be able to judge things better."

She demonstrated. The difference in the position and the marked disparity in their respective heights were potent factors with regard to the conditions of vision. All the same, there was no doubt that she could see a great deal. He had wished to satisfy himself as to that!

"Tell me, Miss Secretan," said Anthony, "as you watched yesterday, did you see anybody anywhere near that path? That one down there?"

He indicated the path which he had shown to MacMorran and which led to the small exit-gate at the back of the churchyard. Actually, the gate was visible to him now from where he stood and as he looked across from Paula Secretan's window. After a moment or so, he repeated the question.

"No," she said as though her mind had been far away when he had first asked her, "no, I saw nobody that I can remember. But why? Why do you ask?"

"For this reason. MacMorran, that's the name of the detective-inspector from Scotland Yard with whom you saw me yesterday, and I, formed the opinion when we went to the churchyard that the murderer might have used that path to get away. It leads to that little gate there through which he could easily have made his exit. But you are quite certain that you saw nobody?"

Paula shook her head. "No. I saw nobody there. But you must realize that my eyes were fixed on another part of the churchyard. As the men carrying the coffin left the church, after the first part of the burial service and came round that winding path there"—she pointed to where she meant—"I felt that I couldn't look any longer and I turned away."

"Was it raining then, can you remember?"

"I couldn't be sure. But it was raining when I first came up here to look. As I told you, that's why I stayed here and didn't go on to the balcony."

"I see. So you can't help me. I had hoped that you might have been able to."

"What age was Justice Madrigal, Mr. Bathurst?"

"I'm not altogether sure. But I believe he was an elderly man. Somewhere in the late sixties."

"Ah, well, he'd had the greater part of his life, then. Reckoning on man's allotted span. Different from Nicholas. Nicholas was over twenty years his junior. In the prime of life and on the threshold of a very distinguished career. His appeals to me as being the much greater tragedy of the two. Apart from my personal interest. Don't you think so yourself?"

"Yes. I suppose you're right, Miss Secretan. It's always more seemly for the old to be taken than the comparatively young. It fits better into the scheme of things."

She turned to him with passionate emphasis. "Mr. Bathurst," she said, "I'm going to put you on your mettle. I think that must have been the real reason why I asked you to come to see me. I know it was. I'll confess that it was. Find Nicholas Flagon's murderer for me! Leave no stone unturned until you have found him! And when you *have* found him send him to the gallows, have no mercy on him! You do that for me! And I'll do it for Nick! It's the very least I can do for him."

She stopped and then smiled. "And now what about coming into the dining-room for lunch."

Anthony followed Paula Secretan downstairs. The fire and passion in her outburst had been a revelation to him.

CHAPTER III

1

WHEN Anthony got back to the 'Saracen's Head' at Verne, he found MacMorran in.

"Any luck, Andrew?" he inquired.

"Nothing at the moment. But there's this. Madrigal came straight down here from town for the funeral. By train. I've spoken to Lady Madrigal on the 'phone. There are two points for you out of that. His solicitors are Messrs. Briggs and Mold of Macclesfield Place. That's the first point. *And*, on the morning of Flagon's funeral, he had an anonymous letter, same like Flagon. That's point number two."

"The devil he did," replied Anthony.

"Anyhow, we'll come back to that later on. I want to listen to you. What's your news from the lady?"

"Surprises, Andrew. I was entirely unprepared for what she told me. And I guarantee you will be, too. She was to have married the late Justice Flagon at Whitsuntide."

Andrew MacMorran sat bolt upright in his chair. "What?" he exclaimed.

"'Sright, Andrew! That is according to the lady. She should know! And I see no reason to doubt her. Do you?"

MacMorran stroked his chin reflectively. "No. Suppose I don't. Still—it's a startler. Didn't it give you a bit of a shock?"

"It sure did," mocked Anthony.

"Also," went on MacMorran, "it puts somewhat of a different complexion on things. Don't quite know where we are now. The engagement couldn't have been announced."

"It was to have been announced in a fortnight's time. According to the lady's version again. They've known each other for just under the year. Ten months to be exact. Agar's Plough was the place of introduction."

"Never heard of the place," returned MacMorran.

"There are also," continued Anthony, "certain interesting financial complications." He paused to reap the full effect of his words.

"Eh, what?" demanded MacMorran.

"Wills executed in each other's favour. At least, that was the mutual agreement. But the fair and exquisite Paula isn't sure whether Flagon had actually put his end of the agreement into effect. With regard to her part of it, she reports that all was in order. Apple-pie variety. Signed on the dotted line, etc."

"By George," said MacMorran, "do you see where this is leading?"

"Frankly, my dear Andrew, no. All foggy and highly nebulous to me. Still, glad of helping hand and sincere guidance from greater mind than my own. Expound, Andrew."

"Why, motive, of course. Here it is. All dressed up and definitely somewhere to go."

"Think so? Alas, my dear Andrew, I am compelled to join issue with you. I merely utter one word. One pregnant word. The key word is 'Madrigal.'"

MacMorran's face fell. "Good Lord. I'd forgotten that."

"I forgive you. One is inclined to omit it from one's calculations. 'L'affaire Madrigal.' I nearly walked into the same trap myself."

"Upsets everything, doesn't it?"

"Of course it does. I told you what it meant yesterday. We have to find the common factor which applies to both Flagon and Madrigal. After a great deal of consideration, I've definitely come round to that. Such common factor will supply the motive for the two murders. Until we find it, Andrew, our tendency will be to run round in circles. And the idea don't please me. Oh, there's something else for me to tell you. I have the names of Flagon's solicitors and also the name of the firm that represents Miss Secretan. Also Flagon's executors. Thought I might do the whole thing properly while I was at it. I'll let you have them. Here they are."

Anthony gave MacMorran the respective names. "Now what about the Madrigal anonymous letter?"

"I'm going up for that after tea. I'll see Lady Madrigal and spend the night in town. Get back here to-morrow morning. I want you to see Catchpole for me and also Harradine, the divisional-surgeon. Apart from those two jobs, your time's your own. You can put in a spot of independent investigation when and where you like."

"Thanks, Andrew. Thanks a million. Ruddy fine case altogether. Up to the moment I've found only one stray gleam of satisfying light."

"Bright and white?"

"No, Andrew. Green! The colour of Mother Nature in her restful mood. Elm trees in one case and a line of bushes in the other. They're my only clues which I consider of any real worth. Oh, and, of course, the sharp quillets." His eyes twinkled at the use of the phrase.

"That doesn't help me at all," remonstrated MacMorran, "on the contrary rather, up to now I haven't met a person who'd ever heard of the blasted word."

"Well, don't you think that fact ought to help us, Andrew? Pointing as it does to the unusual? Whereas one may be on familiar terms with a fillet or even a billet—a quillet must be regarded as an entirely different proposition. Anyhow, I'll follow my quillet where it leads afar as a mariner steers by his guiding star."

"Sez you," retorted MacMorran. "Chuck me over that timetable, will you? That's more in my line."

2

Anthony, having seen Catchpole and interviewed Doctor Harradine, in accordance with MacMorran's expressed desires, had dinner and then decided to drift over to the 'Wheatsheaf' for the evening. Not so much from the point of view of an official investigation, but merely to sink a couple or so in the saloon-bar, to watch points, and to snap up any unconsidered trifles that might be floating around. To mingle with the crowd near the bar had yielded him handsome dividends many times in the past. So he jumped on a 'bus in Verne about twenty-two minutes past eight and got off when they reached the outskirts of Quiddington St. Philip. He deliberately chose to walk the remaining half-mile to the 'Wheatsheaf.'

When he entered from the cool evening air to the warmth and comfort of the hostelry, he was somewhat surprised to find that the attendance was much larger than that of the previous evening. He saw no sign of Fothergill, but Keegan he could see on this occasion in the cheaper bar.

'Evidently,' said Anthony to himself, 'the gentleman divides his favours. To one thing constant never. Uses one bar one evening and the other the next.'

Anthony wasn't sorry not to find Fothergill and he avoided purposely that portion of the bar where Willmott reigned. As far as he knew, these two, with Keegan, were the only people who knew him and his business and who would be able, therefore, to recognize him.

Anthony ordered a beer and took his tankard to a side table. The inevitable game of darts was in progress, close to where he was sitting, but the standard of play was not over-high, and none of the local experts, apparently, was taking part in the game. According to Catchpole, though, and the account he had given them on the afternoon of their arrival, many local notabilities and personalities were in the habit of playing darts in the 'Wheatsheaf.' Possibly, this was an 'off' night, or on the other hand there was the possibility that some of them would turn up later on in the evening.

Anthony settled down to the enjoyment of his beer, and patiently waited for anything which might take it into its head to show up. He finished his beer at his leisure and walked up to the bar for a second one. As he did so, he was conscious of a little man watching him intently. He saw that the man had white hair. 'If he wants me,' he told himself, 'he'll come along and play his hand. So I'll return to my seat at the table, bide my time and see what happens.'

Anthony, therefore, collected his refilled tankard from the barmaid, and went back to his previous seat. As he had more than half-expected, the white-haired man watched him and gradually gravitated to an almost contiguous position. Anthony felt that a further move towards himself would undoubtedly be made sooner or later. He had disposed of about half of his second tankard of beer when a group of people who had been sitting near him suddenly broke up and three of them made their exit. Anthony waited for what he thought would be the inevitable move. He was right. The door had scarcely closed on the departing trio when the little white-haired man came along and appropriated the seat next to him. Anthony's interest began to grow. Things were promising. Say what you like about it, this 'Wheatsheaf' seemed to be very near the hub of things. His instinct to come here had been sound enough. He began to parade certain data in his mind.

Fothergill and his friends were staying here. Keegan played darts here. Flagon himself with his *fidus Achates*, Salt, visited here. And Sir Claude de Monterey had occasionally brought Paula Secretan here. Catchpole seemed to know Willmott pretty well and even Doctor Harradine, the divisional-surgeon whom he had interviewed a few hours ago, had admitted that he had called in at the place fairly frequently during the winter months that had just passed. Anthony still waited.

Eventually finesse gave way to direct action and there came the actual approach. The little white-haired man turned to him and smiled.

"I believe," he said a trifle timidly, "that I have the honour of addressing Mr. Anthony Bathurst."

Anthony returned smile for smile. "And I for my part," he rejoined, "find myself wondering how many people would regard it as such."

"A great many, I assure you," protested his companion, "and I expect while we're on the subject, you're wondering something else as well. You're wondering how it is that I come to know you. Well, this may explain matters."

He flicked a card over to Anthony, who picked it up from the table and read it. 'John Bentley, *Daily Fanfare.*'

"Press," murmured Anthony.

"Yes. Press, Mr. Bathurst. I've seen you too often both in court and in the company of Sir Austin Kemble and Chief Inspector MacMorran, not to recognize you when you're as close to me in this place as you are now."

Bentley leant over from his seat so that he was very close to Anthony. "The Flagon and Madrigal murders?" he whispered.

Anthony smiled again. "There might be another window open in this bar. Don't you agree with me? The atmosphere's getting definitely oppressive."

Bentley shook his head. "It's all right. You can play ball with me. You've nothing to worry about. Catchpole fed me on the first murder, it suited his book as well as it did mine and it didn't exercise my brain overmuch to add the Madrigal 'two' to the Flagon 'two' and make it a sensational 'four.' I've been at the Press game too long, Mr. Bathurst, not to smell a story."

"Really," said Anthony. He was considering things. Bentley's opening gambit had been unanticipated by him. But after all, it had run true to form. Wherever he went in this case, he encountered the surprising. From the moment he and MacMorran had met Catchpole. He decided to let Bentley go on talking.

"Yes," continued that gentleman, "Catchpole was good enough to let me use the *Fanfare* when the Flagon business hit the headlines.

Very nice, too! Suited me down to the ground, as you may well guess. Put me in clover." He dropped his voice again. "Anything doing?"

"How do you mean exactly?" asked Anthony.

"Any arrest imminent?"

Anthony shook his head. "Now, now, Mr. Bentley! Chief Detective-Inspector MacMorran's officially in charge of the case, a fact which you should also have guessed. Who am I to go on talking for talking's sake?"

"There's one thing, Mr. Bathurst, our murderer can throw a dart! *N'est-ce-pas?* Narrows the field, doesn't it?" Bentley put a volume of shrewdness into his whisper. "Pretty considerably, I should imagine."

"Well, there you are."

Bentley having said his say, looked round somewhat apprehensively. "I didn't tell Catchpole all I might have done," he volunteered, having evidently assured himself that the coast was clear.

"Wise fellow, in all probability," murmured Anthony, "always diplomatic not to empty sleeve entirely. Leaves one with ammunition for another day."

"Yes. But I might find time to tell you what I kept from Catchpole."

"Evening's young."

"Yes," went on Bentley, "I know of a man who not only chucks a champion dart but who also hated Flagon like the devil hates holy water. That's what I didn't tell Catchpole."

"Did he hate Madrigal in like measure? Appears to me he should have done to fulfil the complete equation."

The question seemed to throw Bentley out of his stride. But he quickly recovered. "So Madrigal's had it, too?"

"I fancied that you started this conversation on those lines? Was I mistaken? If so, my apologies."

Bentley coughed. "All right. I'll give you that one."

"But you haven't answered my last question. I must insist that you haven't. Did your vendetta-breathing dart player hate the Madrigal as you say he scorned the Flagon? Is the point taken?"

The white-haired man scratched his chin. *"Touché,"* he said at last, "that's another one to you. I confess it makes a big difference. I hadn't thought of it quite like that."

"Afraid it does. According to you, hatred of Flagon expressed to you by skilful dart player. Presumably frequents hostelry where you and I are now. Is it a likely proposition dislike of Flagon extends to equal dislike of Madrigal? Each, we must remember, was a dispenser of His Majesty's justice. Particular hater, therefore, not necessarily ruled out. You get my meaning?"

"Ye-es," said Bentley slowly. "You mean you're ready for my confidences."

"My dear sir, my very dear sir, you came to me with them and offered them on a plate. Don't put a closure on the feast."

Bentley shot Anthony a side-long look. "Perhaps you're right, Mr. Bathurst. Well, here's what I know. I came down here to do the Bar Point-to-Point for the *Fanfare*. It's an annual job of mine. The *Fanfare* makes a speciality of certain sporting events which are, as you might say, a trifle off the beaten track. I pop in here of an evening for a couple as a rule. It's the most comfortable house in the neighbourhood and the beer's really good. Well, I was in here a night or so before . . . er . . . Flagon died and I heard the crack local darts player fulminate on what he hoped would happen to Justice Flagon. Actually he wished him the very end which Fate eventually decreed for him. I heard it. In its full terms. That's what I didn't tell Catchpole."

"Why not?"

Bentley hesitated. "Er, I didn't want to be mixed up in the case. The association might have become, er, inconvenient. That's why I kept my mouth shut when I was with Catchpole."

"Why tell me, then? Why depart from previously prepared position? *Mes Beaux Yeux?* Am I to be flattered thus?"

"Er . . . not exactly. You see there's Madrigal gone now. Makes a lot of difference." Bentley now looked considerably discomfited.

"Don't quite see it. Still, your funeral. And the name of local fire-eater, presuming you are aware of same?"

"Yes. The man's a stranger to me, actually—but I know his name. Through hearing it in the bar here when he's been playing darts.

It's Keegan. Michael Keegan. Does it convey anything to you, Mr. Bathurst?"

"Oh, yes. Name not entirely unfamiliar. Been brought to my notice already."

"In connexion with the murder, or murders?"

"Can't disappoint you, Mr. Bentley. The answer's in the affirmative."

"So he's already suspect without my morsel of information? Is he likely to be arrested? Can you tell me that?"

"MacMorran's the name," replied Anthony. "I told you that before. For myself, must keep open mind. And moderately still tongue. Knowing what I know, can't say that Keegan fills the bill for me. Still, never know. The little more, and how much." Anthony shrugged his shoulders. Bentley nodded. "Can't see personally," added Anthony, "why Keegan should so conclusively withhold his love from both Flagon and Madrigal. Or even why anybody else should, for that matter."

"Bit of a problem," remarked Bentley, "I'm beginning to realize the difficulties you're up against."

"That's very nice of you. Tell me, Mr. Bentley." This time it was Anthony who leaned over. "Play darts yourself?"

"No. Wish I did. Like to watch a game, though. No, my wrist's 'wonky.' Broke it some years ago. In a cycling accident. Can't bend it. Or at least very little. Look."

Bentley held up his right wrist for Anthony's scrutiny. "I fell on it, you see, with all my weight on it. Broke two of the metacarpals."

"H'm," returned Anthony, "spot of bad luck for you."

"Might have been a good deal worse," said Bentley, "considering the distance I was chucked. Fishing-rod caught in my front wheel. So I suppose I mustn't grumble. Especially as I only had myself to blame."

"Very commendable of you. Best way to look at it. Count your blessings."

Bentley proffered his cigarette-case. "Cigarette, Mr. Bathurst?" Anthony took one. "Thank you."

Bentley extended his lighter. "Service," he said with an attempt at jocularity.

"Thank you again," said Anthony "Tell me," he said, "Flagon's funeral? Did you happen to attend, by any chance?"

"No. I had to return to town. Actually, I 'phoned to the *Fanfare*'s office for instructions. I should have liked to have gone to the funeral. Bearing in mind the sensational turn it took. But the powers that be ruled otherwise. I was disappointed."

"I'm sorry you weren't there. You might have given me the low-down on one or two points I'm in doubt about. Still—you weren't—and that's that."

"Yes—pity."

"What made you come back now?"

"Well, I tidied up the bits and pieces that the office wanted tidied up, and then I thought I saw daylight for about forty-eight hours. The wish may have been father to the thought. But anyhow, it was good enough for me to act on. So I followed my original inclination and blew down here again. I'm a newspaper man, you see, and that makes me on the look-out for any stray rumours that may be floating around. Lying jade or otherwise. They're my bread-and-butter. Nothing like being near the heart of things."

"No. I suppose not. And you regard the 'Wheatsheaf' as fulfilling that condition, eh?"

"Well, I wouldn't say the 'Wheatsheaf' exactly, but the village itself. Quiddington St. Philip. After all, it's where the murders took place, isn't it?"

As he spoke, Anthony stood up to brush some cigarette-ash from his coat sleeve. He looked across the bar and caught sight of Maurice Fothergill. Fothergill happened to be looking up at the same psychological moment and was unable to avoid catching Anthony's eye. Somewhat to Anthony's surprise, he waved his appreciation of his presence. Then he turned to speak to somebody at his side who had presumably addressed a remark to him. Seeing this incident occur, an idea struck Anthony. It might well be, he thought, that Fothergill's immediate companion was the man who had accompanied him to the 'Wheatsheaf' and who had been staying there with him. And who had also been stricken with illness, the afternoon of Flagon's murder. If this conjecture were correct, here was an opportunity that he had no intention of missing. He therefore excused himself to the journalist, Bentley, and strolled slowly over to where Fothergill and his companion were sitting.

3

When he got closer he saw that Fothergill's companion was a young man. A fellow indeed of about Fothergill's own age. As it happened, there was a vacant chair at the table where they were sitting. Anthony hooked it towards him, seated himself and said: "Good evening, Mr. Fothergill. Pleased to see you again. Not playing darts to-night?"

Fothergill shook his head. "No. Feel too tired. Content to sit here and watch. You do get like that sometimes, you know."

He noticed that Anthony was looking significantly at his neighbour and realized at the same time what was apparently expected of him.

"Oh—" he said. "Neglecting my duty. I forgot you hadn't met. This is Ronald Harcourt—er—Mr. Anthony Bathurst."

"Good evening," said Anthony.

"Good evening," returned Harcourt rather curtly.

"This gentleman," said Anthony, "is your friend who is staying here with you, I presume."

"Your guess is as good as it could be." Fothergill's tone was a shade surly.

"I take it," went on Anthony unabashed, "that you're thoroughly recovered from your recent indisposition, Mr. Harcourt? If I may be pardoned expressing an opinion, you look pretty fit at the moment." Harcourt seemed surprised. Fothergill spotted this and essayed explanation. "I told Inspector MacMorran how you turned up queer on the afternoon of the Bar Point-to-Point."

"Or rather," grinned Anthony, "that you didn't turn up. That is to say, where you were expected to."

Harcourt cut in. "Oh, yes. I get you now. You caught me on one leg for the moment. Yes, I went for a stroll on that particular morning before lunch, intending to return about midday, and while I was out I had a rather bad turn. Shook me up for the time."

"Bad luck. And you missed the racing? Annoying."

"Missed the racing! I'll say I did. Believe me, when I was lying in that field, I wasn't concerned about the racing or anything else in the world. I thought I was going to pass out, and more than once it would have been a relief to have done so. There I was, all by myself, stranded out there in the wilds and feeling like something the cat's brought in. Talk about a mess. Not a soul to turn to, I tell you I touched the depths that morning."

"What was it?" inquired Anthony, "a chill, or a fainting attack?"

"Neither," grinned Harcourt with a rueful savour of reminiscence, "tummy. Plain tummy. I had the grandfather of all ruddy awful guts' aches."

"Nasty experience. What was the cause of it—food poisoning of some kind?"

Harcourt shook his head at Anthony's suggestion. "I really don't know. I never actually discovered. The funny thing about it was that I'd had my previous meals here at the 'Wheatsheaf' and nobody else seemed in any way affected. Fothergill fed with me and nothing happened to him. Which makes it all the more inexplicable."

"That's quite possible," put in Fothergill, "very often, one small piece of food will become infected and the rest of it remain quite O.K. I was reading of a similar case the other day in the paper. Chap died of gastroenteritis. Nobody else who had had the same food as he had was in any way affected. A fly, crawling over grub, will often do it."

"There aren't any flies at this time of the year," commented Anthony, "later on in the summer perhaps. So we can hardly ascribe it to that cause. But what did you do when you felt as bad as you say?"

Harcourt laughed, but Anthony thought when he heard it, that the effort was forced and had little humour in it.

"I'm afraid I behaved in an atrociously undignified manner. I crawled through a gate into a field and lay there. Vomited like a dog, was seized with a violent attack of diarrhoea and eventually must have dozed off to sleep. When I woke up eventually and looked at my watch, the time was well on into the afternoon."

"Another thing," said Fothergill, "and as I suggested to you when you came back, the beer the evening before may have upset you. It often does. Especially if you aren't used to a particular brew. What I think took place was this. You'd been walking for some time, prob-ably got pretty hot, eased up a bit, caught a chill, and a tummy full of strange beer started to do its stuff. That, in my opinion, is by far the most likely explanation of your indisposition."

He spoke as though he was anxious to prove his point.

"Tripe," retorted Harcourt, "to hear you talk, one would imagine I'd never drunk a glass of beer in my life before. No, my boy, this was something out of the ordinary to put me out of mess like that I'm positive of it. Ptomaine or something."

Anthony had listened to Harcourt's story, and to the exchange of conversation which had followed it, with the greatest interest.

"Where was this field you lay in? Anywhere near the Point-to-Point course?"

Harcourt looked at Fothergill. It seemed to Anthony that he was inviting assistance. Fothergill gave no sign.

"Well," said Harcourt, "speaking for myself, I shouldn't think it was. But this is my first visit to the locality and I'm not too sure of my bearings. I've relied on Fothergill in the main to hold my hand and show me round. No, this field must have been somewhere between here and Sword. About three miles from here, judging by the time I'd been walking when I was taken ill. It was not in the Newstead Green direction at all. Where I should have been. You see, I intended to come back here for lunch and then accompany Fothergill to the Point-to-Point. That was the arrangement." He paused, and then concluded with a cliché: "But the best-laid schemes of mice and men gang aft agley."

"Well," said Anthony, "you have my sympathy. It's bad enough to feel ill when there are helping hands close by, but to be alone—and really alone—as you seem to have been, well, that's nobody's cup of tea."

"What will you drink?" said Fothergill, "if we get a move on, we shall just have time to catch the speaker's eye. According to my time, there are only about a couple of minutes to go. Beer? Right! It's my shout."

He gathered up the tankards with the adroitness of an old hand and moved quickly to the bar. When he returned to the table, there was just enough time to drink up and for Anthony to say good night.

He decided to walk back to Verne. Walking he always found a highly conducive exercise to intensive thought and mental concentration.

So far, he had seen Catchpole, Willmott, Doctor Harradine, Maurice Fothergill, Harcourt, Bentley and Paula Secretan. And although Keegan had been propelled towards him by more than one agency, he had, strangely enough, not been able to extract any information from the man himself. This omission did not greatly concern him, for the reason that Anthony was already beginning to have very definite opinions with regard to the two murders. No doubt, too, MacMorran would bring further news of the Madrigal end, on the following morning, when he returned from town.

4

Anthony went along to the station at Verne, on the next morning, to meet MacMorran. He had a certain amount of time on his hands and an inspection of the time-table had told him that the 'Yard' inspector would be almost bound to catch the particular train he had gone to meet. He bought a platform ticket and made his way to the farther side of the station where the London trains invariably run in. Loitering near an automatic weighing-machine he was somewhat surprised to see the journalist, Bentley. Anthony fell to wondering whether he, also, had come to meet somebody from town. A second or so afterwards, this wonderment expired and gave place to a fairly sharp and certain suspicion that Bentley was watching him.

These newspaper wallahs let nothing thwart them in their pursuit of news. Individual privacies went by the board. The last thing he wanted, though, was an intervention from Bentley when MacMorran arrived, so that when Bentley's gaze appeared to be averted for a fleeting second, Anthony dodged into a convenient waiting-room. Here he stayed and waited for the next few minutes and until MacMorran's train came in. As the luck ran, the inspector slipped out of a compartment almost exactly opposite the waiting-room door behind which Anthony was sheltering. Anthony caught MacMorran's eye almost immediately and beckoned to him.

"What's afoot?" inquired MacMorran with a quick glance round.

"Nothing of much importance. All I'm doing is trying to dodge an ultra-enthusiastic news-hound who's been on my track, I'm afraid, since last evening. It's the *Fanfare* reporter and he's knocking around the platform. I've already had one dose of him. He collared me in the 'Wheatsheaf' last night. He's been in on the Flagon business since the trouble started and naturally he's all out for 'scoops.' Catchpole seems to have taken advantage of the fact that he was on the spot and used him. At the present moment, it seems to me that this room is far preferable to his company."

"If we wait in here for a few minutes, he may think he's missed you and clear off."

"Good for you, Andrew. That's exactly the idea that I had."

"I'll tell you what. There's a buffet next door. Let's slip in there. I can do with a drink. May be able to get a coffee or something."

"The chances are certainly in favour of the latter," murmured Anthony.

It was the work of a moment for the two of them to slip out of the waiting-room and into the refreshment-room. As Anthony had feared, this last description was very definitely a euphemism. MacMorran brought two cups of dark, muddy liquid which masqueraded as coffee, to a side table and for some seconds did persistently aggressive work with a spoon. Anthony let him alone for some minutes and then came to the point.

"Well, Andrew, did you get it?"

"I did. I saw Lady Madrigal yesterday evening. While you were wasting your time drinking that disgusting alcoholic poison in the 'Wheatsheaf' and yarning to avid reporters, I was workin', my boy! The hours of overtime I'm called upon to do are nothing more or less than a public scandal. Still, where am I?"

"Drinking Lady Madrigal's best Scotch, if I'm any judge."

"You misjudge me. Sorely. If I did join her in a wee spot, it was merely out of courtesy to her, and just to keep her company. You ought to know by now that I rarely drink when I'm on duty."

"I do. There's not a lot offered to you these days. Opportunity would be a fine thing. But go on, you old scoundrel."

"I wasn't with her overlong. She's a ladylike old girl and badly cut up at her husband's loss, as you may well guess. And what makes it a bit worse for her, there are no bairns. Neither chick nor child. The only boy was killed in the spring of 1918 when Jerry broke through the Fifth Army round Amiens. I asked her about the anonymous letter and she produced it for me. Here you are. Here it is."

MacMorran took an envelope from his pocket and handed it over to Anthony. "Before you examine it and read it, I'll tell you something. I'll make you a present of the information. It's almost exactly the same in every particular, bearing in mind the different conditions, as the one Flagon had. That Salt handed to Inspector Catchpole. With one exception."

"That's a bit Irish. Where's the difference?"

"Postmark," replied MacMorran laconically. "Flagon's was posted in Verne, Madrigal's was posted at Hammersmith."

Anthony looked at the postmark on the envelope. "H'm. Yes, so I see."

He opened the envelope and took out a single sheet of poor quality writing-paper. Anthony read it. "The printing is the same as that of Flagon's letter," prompted MacMorran.

Anthony saw that it was illiterate and the letters generally ill-formed. It ran thus: 'Just a line to inform you that you'll come to Quiddington to-morrow for the last time, you bastard! Why? Because you'll give up the ghost and go to Hell in the same way as your pal has done. From One who Knows.'

Anthony went back to the envelope and looked at the address.

'Mr. Justice Maddrigal, 19 Amersham Mansions, W.1.' He looked across at MacMorran.

"There's something phoney about all this, Andrew. To me that fact sticks out a mile. Say what you like about it. You can't pair up this sort of thing with the 'sharp quillet.' They're as far apart as the poles. It just doesn't make sense." He tossed the envelope back a little impatiently.

"You mean these anonymous letters are all boloney?"

"Of course I do, Andrew. Whatever angle I take, I can't think otherwise. Don't you agree with me?"

MacMorran picked up the envelope again and looked at it. "I'm not so sure," he said after a moment's consideration. "Listen to me for a moment. I look at it like this. It may not be the work of one man only. There may be *two* people at work on this job. One on the letters, and the other on the darts. Doesn't that strike you as a distinct possibility?"

"It's possible, of course," admitted Anthony, "but I don't think so myself. By the way, how did Madrigal take that letter? Was Lady Madrigal able to help you there?"

"Yes. I asked her that same question. The judge received the letter on the actual morning of the funeral. First post."

"Just a minute, Andrew, and forgive me the interruption. But a point's just occurred to me and I don't want it to slip by. How was the writer of the letter certain that Madrigal would attend Flagon's funeral? Doesn't it argue something to you?"

"You mean a certain amount of inside knowledge?"

"Of course. I think the point's a good one."

"Well, leave it where it is for the time being, we'll come back to it."

"O.K., Andrew."

"As I said, Madrigal received the anonymous letter by the first post on the morning of the day Flagon was buried. And, quite naturally, he told Lady Madrigal about it. She says she was frightened. 'Scared to death,' was her expression. She couldn't forget, she says, what had happened to Justice Flagon. On the other hand, Madrigal himself made light of the whole matter. Laughed the whole thing to scorn. Said that a practical joker was at work, banking on the Flagon affair."

Anthony rubbed the side of his nose. "Funny line, don't you think, for a trained and logical mind to take seeing the fate that had befallen Flagon in similar circumstances a few days previously? Wouldn't have appealed to me in the light that it apparently did to Madrigal. Oh, no, far from it. Still, go on, Andrew."

"Well—there isn't a lot more for me to tell you. Madrigal pooh-poohed the whole thing. Lady Madrigal argued. Wanted him to ask for police protection. But she cut no ice with the old boy at all. Madrigal refused and still muttering 'stuff and nonsense,' or words to that effect, went out to the funeral—and paid the penalty."

"I still say that none of it makes sense, Andrew. There's no consecutive or symmetrical shape in the pattern anywhere. And whichever way you look at things, you're always brought up with a jerk when you come to examine the question of motive. Take Flagon to start with. If we're inclined to stretch a point for the sake of discussion, we can collect two people with motives—or perhaps 'half-motives' would be the better term—for killing Flagon. Number one—this bucolic gentleman by the name of Mike Keegan. We are told that Keegan has been heard to breathe fire and slaughter against the deceased judge. Why exactly, we don't know. That's the part we're *not* told. Number two. Paula Secretan."

Anthony paused. To see how MacMorran would take the statement. The pause did not go entirely unrewarded.

"What?" exclaimed MacMorran almost incredulously, "how do you arrive at that?"

Anthony grinned at the way MacMorran had risen to the bait. "In this way. Although I'm perfectly willing to admit that it's something like a hundred to one chance. But if Flagon *had* managed to find time to execute his will in her favour—I'm accepting the lady's story as true—then she stood to gain pretty considerably by Flagon's death. I should say from the financial angle. That's so, isn't it, Andrew?"

"Hold on a minute," interposed MacMorran. "You're running on a trifle too fast. I can answer that. I can answer it in more ways than one. That is to say both directly and indirectly. First of all, Paula Secretan would hardly have murdered the man she was about to marry, on the mere *chance* that she *might* inherit his money. Because that's all there was in it. Will you give me that one?"

"No, Andrew. She may have *said* she wasn't sure. She may have had the knowledge all the time that Flagon *had* altered his will in her favour. Which, I think, would effectively dispose of your condition of mere chance. We must find out the truth from Flagon's solicitors. Will you give me that one?"

"No," returned MacMorran in a flash.

"Why not?"

MacMorran smiled a slow smile of triumphant satisfaction "Because I have found out. I called on Flagon's solicitors this morning. I went there before I caught my train down here. You weren't expecting that, were you?"

5

"You cunning old twister," said Anthony, "and you've been sitting there all this time with Sugden, Ward and Blake of Basinghall Street, all nice and cosy up your sleeve—eh?" He grinned. "You wait. I'll have my own back, Andrew, and you'll moan like hell when I do. Still—what's the dope?"

"Flagon had *not* altered his will. Miss Secretan's story rings true in every respect. What had happened was this. Flagon had written to Messrs. Sugden, Ward and Blake quite recently, hinting at his intentions *re* the will and saying that he would fix an early appointment with them to round the job off. That appointment never took place and will never take place. You know why."

Anthony sat silent. "Well," said MacMorran after a decently respectable interval, "haven't you got it yet? If you haven't, you're much below your usual form."

Anthony looked up—a little startled at the inspector's remark. It was evident that his thoughts had strayed elsewhere. "Why—how do you mean, Andrew? Oh—I get you. The bequest to Miss Secretan entailed altering Flagon's will. There was a will already in existence. By jove—now we are getting somewhere. Motive—eh, Andrew? Motive. Well—come on, man, tell me the worst."

"Flagon," said MacMorran, "was, as you are aware, a man with few or no living relations. Certainly no close ones. And his will, save for a few special pecuniary bequests, is in favour of a great friend of his. No doubt you will be able to put a name to him."

Again MacMorran waited. Anthony's thoughts harked back. He remembered the interview they had had at the outset with Inspector Catchpole.

"I know whom you mean," he said slowly, "you mean Salt! Keith Salt, K.C. Good Lord—this breaks the case wide open. Salt! A few days later and Flagon would have altered his will and Salt would have been the loser of—what's the size of the estate, Andrew—any idea? Did you find out?"

"Over six figures," was MacMorran's laconic reply, "so you see Mr. Salt had something more to play for than a box of kippers. His visit to Catchpole with the first anonymous letter was a blind, of course. Looks as though he wrote the anonymous letter himself and then followed it up with a similar one to Justice Madrigal. Cunning piece of work and quite likely to throw the local police off the scent."

"To say nothing of their expert brethren from Scotland Yard." After delivering himself of this, Anthony was silent again. Some seconds elapsed before he spoke. "No, Andrew," he said at length, "I'm sorry—but I still don't get it. We're all wrong."

"Why? What's the trouble now?"

"Madrigal! Still Madrigal. Madrigal was and Madrigal is. I can stomach the idea of Salt or somebody else even sending him an anonymous letter as a highly-seasoned red herring—but to kill him as well, Andrew—" Anthony broke off. But he continued. "Well—that's a bit too steep for me to swallow. It's just murder for murder's sake."

"Not if it seals up the case and saves the killer's neck. That was your own idea a couple of days ago. You've got to look at it from that point of view. *You* gave that to me. Now I give it back to *you*."

Anthony shook his head. "I'll tell you what, Andrew—find out whether Salt plays darts. With any degree of skill."

"That is already listed on my personal programme. And if I was informed that he didn't, it mightn't make a lot of difference to me."

"Why not?"

"He might be a dark horse. He might have boxed clever and kept his dart-playing skill under a bushel. It's difficult to *prove* that you *can't* do a thing. Whereas to prove that you *can* may be a comparatively simple matter."

"Yes. I see your point. It's a good one. All the same, I don't know that I'm altogether satisfied."

Anthony fell to meditation. "We haven't traced those darts yet, you know, Andrew. The substituted ones. Where they came from."

"That's in course of being done. I left them with Chatterton last night. With full instructions as to what I wanted. When the midnight news was coming through. If he strikes lucky, we may get a line on that by this time to-morrow morning."

"Good. We may find something highly interesting."

"Perhaps. Mustn't bank on it. We're up against a cunning criminal. I haven't the slightest doubt about that. One who I don't think will make many mistakes."

"I should say you're right, Andrew, with regard to that. And I'll tell you something else that I think. I'll have an interview with Keith Salt. This afternoon if I can manage it. You don't mind my taking that on, do you? After all, neither you nor I have ever seen the man and all we have with regard to him is Catchpole's account and subsequent reaction. Which from our point of view may be anything or nothing. If he's left this district, I'll run up to town this afternoon and try to see him. O.K. with you, Andrew?"

"Yes. Quite O.K. And in the meantime, we'll be strolling back to the 'Saracen's Head' for a spot of lunch. I didn't have a lot of breakfast this morning, so I'm a bit peckish."

"Right-o, Andrew. Suits me." Anthony got up and walked to the door of the refreshment-room and looked out. "The coast seems clear. I see no sign of Comrade Bentley. He's probably got browned-off and gone home."

"Right," said MacMorran, "I'm with you. Looks to me as though his patience has been definitely exhausted."

CHAPTER IV

1

KEITH Salt, K.C., was undoubtedly a man of distinction. This, mentally as well as physically. He was of Irish stock, and after a brilliant career at the Royal University, Ireland, had taken degrees of B.A., LL.B. and LL.D. with first honours. In many ways he was the favourite of fortune. He had an imposing presence, a fine resonant D voice, a really remarkable gift of memory and an extraordinarily valuable sense of humour. He would, in all probability, have never claimed to be a profound lawyer. Or even scientist. The human aspect of his work made, to him, by far the strongest appeal. As a graduate of a University he had eaten his thirty-six dinners under the supervision of the Benchers of his Inn and had there made the acquaintance of Nicholas Flagon, then, like him, commencing on his career as a barrister.

In this same capacity, Salt had been successful. Two reasons had materially contributed to this. For one thing, he made it an invariable rule right from the beginning of his career never to be engaged on more than one case at a time. He was thus enabled to give his entire attention to it and he never lost grip of its salient points until the verdict had been given and the curtain rung down. At first, this policy entailed a certain loss of income, but against that Salt gained in legal prestige and moral stature. Secondly, he never allowed himself to make the grave error of quarrelling with any of the judges. Even though it might be glaringly obvious to everybody in court that Salt was right and the judge wrong, he never lost that most admirable self-control of his in an effort to adjust an inequitable position. He also had the enviable reputation of extreme courtesy and consideration towards his juniors.

Almost from the first day they had met, he and Flagon had become fast friends. They had been briefed together once during their early days, and although Flagon had outdistanced Salt in the end this fact had not been permitted by either of them to disturb the even tenor of their friendship. Neither man had married and neither had been attracted by the prospects of a Parliamentary career, that graveyard of reputations of so many brilliant members of the Bar.

As he looked at Anthony Bathurst's card that had just been presented to him, Salt pushed back his chair, stroked his chin reflectively and thought over one or two matters very carefully.

"All right," he said eventually to his clerk. "I'll see him. Show the gentleman in."

Anthony was amazed at Salt's extraordinarily fine physique when he was shown into his room. He had expected to see somebody entirely different, and this sun-tanned giant with the sailor's eyes was so different from the many eminent members of the legal profession whom he had been previously privileged to meet.

"Sit down, Mr. . . . er . . . Bathurst," said Salt in his impressive voice, and Anthony murmured a conventional 'thanks,' as he accepted the invitation.

"What is your business, Mr. Bathurst—may I ask?" said the giant.

"In the matter of the death of the late Justice Flagon. And subsequently, the death of Mr. Justice Madrigal. The local police authorities have enlisted the help of Scotland Yard and I have been asked—unofficially, of course, by the Commissioner of Police, Sir Austin Kemble, to have a look at the affair generally."

"I see." Salt's brows contracted into an unmistakable frown. Anthony formed the instant impression that he had not expected this. "And where exactly do I come in?" inquired the K.C.

But Anthony was ready for this. "You called on Inspector Catchpole with regard to a certain anonymous letter which was received by the late Nicholas Flagon just prior to his death. That is so, isn't it?"

"That's quite true. What about it? Did Madrigal get one too? Because in the light of what's happened since, I'm quite prepared to hear that he did."

For this question, Anthony was not quite so ready. He decided, therefore, seeing the calibre of his questioner, to tell the bare truth. "Yes, Mr. Salt. You are right in your surmise. The police have been informed that he did."

"From an unimpeachable source, I take it?"

"From the widow, Lady Madrigal."

"Is the letter in their possession?"

"Yes."

"What's it like? Similar to that which Flagon received?"

"Almost identical. Allowing, of course, for the somewhat different conditions."

The K.C. knitted his brows. "How do you mean? I don't quite understand."

"Well—Flagon was riding in a race. Madrigal was merely attending Flagon's funeral. That's the main 'difference' to which I referred." At the receipt of this information, Salt caressed his chin with strong, supple fingers. "And Madrigal went the same way as Nick Flagon did. I knew them both. Flagon was my friend. But I also knew Justice Madrigal well—if not intimately. Amazing business—all of it. More like fiction than fact. Are the police on the point of making an arrest?"

Anthony realized that the boot was gradually and decidedly cleverly being fitted on to the wrong foot. Instead of him questioning Keith Salt, Salt was putting questions to him.

"I am not in charge of the case, Mr. Salt. I think that you should clearly understand that. It's in the hands of Chief Detective-Inspector MacMorran. But I'm afraid that at the moment we're—"

Salt cut in brusquely: "Running round in circles—eh? Well—I'm afraid I can't help you. You've come to the wrong man, my friend." Anthony grasped his chance at once and took full advantage of the opening. "I disagree. I think perhaps you may be able to. That's the reason I came here." Anthony paused. He wanted a full dividend from his next remark, because it was his key question. "You were aware, I presume, bearing in mind your close friendship with the late Mr. Justice Flagon, that he was being married at Whitsun?"

Salt looked at him as though Anthony were a chameleon which had just exercised its particular power in supremely brilliant fashion.

"What?" he ejaculated. "Who's stuffed you up with that piece of arrant nonsense?"

Anthony replied according to plan. "I'm sorry," he said, "but I imagined that you would have been in Flagon's confidence to that extent."

Salt gave another impatient exclamation. "It's rubbish. Utter rubbish. Take it from me. Nick Flagon was a dyed-in-the-wool bachelor. Helen of Troy herself wouldn't have tempted him."

"Nevertheless, Mr. Salt, I have every reason to believe that he would have married at the coming Whitsun."

Salt shook his head. "If you told me that a thousand times, I still would refuse to believe you. Anyhow, putting that on one side in a genuine thirst for information—who's the lady, may I ask?"

"Miss Paula Secretan."

"What?" Salt roared again. "Paula Secretan! What utter rubbish! Why, she's been running around with Sir Claude de Monterey for some time now. You can take it from me that Nick Flagon wouldn't have looked at her twice. Pardon me, Bathurst—but who passed this preposterous nonsense on to you? Am I permitted to enquire?"

Anthony replied quietly. "I can assure you that it's not nonsense. Not only have I Miss Secretan's word but also—"

Salt intervened again impulsively. "Miss Secretan! Why—the woman's pulling a fast one on you for some absurd reason known only to herself. I wouldn't trust any woman—"

Anthony held up his hand to check the torrent. "But also the lady's story is confirmed in every detail by the late Justice Flagon's solicitors, Messrs. Sugden, Ward and Blake of Basinghall Street."

Salt's open mouth closed. This last statement of Anthony's was calculated to clinch the matter. Anthony went on to establish the position he had gained.

"There is a further point I will elaborate. The late Justice Flagon was about to execute a will in favour of Miss Secretan—that is to say—his fiancée."

Anthony watched Salt closely as he made this statement, and he had the satisfaction of seeing that Salt was considerably taken aback. But the barrister said nothing for some little time.

"You mean, Bathurst, that Flagon died before he . . . er . . ."

He stopped abruptly. Anthony filled in the gaps.

"Exactly! Before he could carry out his intentions with regard to Miss Secretan. That is so."

"I'll be perfectly frank with you, Bathurst. Within the last few days, Messrs. Sugden, Ward and Blake have been in communication with me in relation to my dead friend's will. They tell me that, to all practical purposes, I am the sole beneficiary." Salt's voice was dry and harsh. "I'm glad now," he continued, "in view of what you have just told me, that Nick Flagon did not confide in me with regard to his intended marriage. Where ignorance is bliss, etc." He looked up at Anthony and added, "although I fully realize that you have only my word for that."

Anthony made no immediate reply to this. He felt that in this mood, Salt might go on and say something further of interest. But the policy met with no reward. Salt knew all his vegetables and remained silent. Anthony resolved, therefore, to ask him another question.

"Did you attend the funeral?"

"Of course. I told you. He was my closest friend."

"How far were you from the late Justice Madrigal when he fell?" Salt bit his lip at the question. "I didn't go to the graveside for the interment. I suppose I ought to explain that and the sooner the better. I left immediately after the service in the church. From no wish of my own, I can assure. I had no option in the matter. It was a case of leaving Quiddington St. Philip for important business here in town. A long-standing engagement which I couldn't possibly put off. So I can't assist you at all in connection with the death of Madrigal. I only wish I could. I see your difficulties."

'Check again,' thought Anthony to himself. But he did his best to follow up without delay. "You know of no common enemy, I suppose, to both the dead men? You can't help me in that direction?"

Salt pursed his lips and thought over the question. "You'll forgive me," came his rather curt reply, "but I can't help thinking that that question borders on absurdity. It's . . . er . . . sensational. It smacks of the penny dreadful to me. It suggests that your mind rejects the penny plain and simply must have the twopence coloured. And, to my mind, has little or no relation to life. Certainly not to the life lived by Nicholas Flagon. *And*, I should say, by Mr. Justice Madrigal as well. Because, until I find convincing evidence to the contrary, I shall presume the late judge lived a normal life in the same way that Flagon did."

Anthony bore the criticism with imperturbability. "Very likely. And you may be entirely justified. But forgive me, too, if I point out that neither of them died normal deaths. Which fact alone is surely *my* justification for asking the question that I did. Somebody liked them so little that he murdered them. Sensational? Perhaps—but unfortunately true. And decidedly uncomfortable for the two people principally concerned. You have no other answer, then, to my question?"

"I'm afraid I haven't, Bathurst—but now that you've asked me, I should say that Nicholas Flagon, whom I *can* speak with certainty about—hadn't an enemy in the world. If he had, I am equally certain that there was no real reason for that enmity."

"Jealousy is also a vice," said Anthony.

"Yes. I've been thinking that myself. But jealousy, more often than not, refuses to unmask itself. It lies hidden in the heart and mind of the offender."

Salt closed his lips as though he had spoken the last words. Anthony began to feel that the interview had brought him comparatively little, and he wondered whether any good purpose would be served by his prolonging the conversation. Salt, if he knew anything, wasn't giving it away—that was becoming increasingly evident. The matter was crystallized, however, by the K.C. himself. He rose with the obvious intention of giving Anthony his quietus.

"Well, Bathurst, I'm sorry, but my time's not exactly my own, and I'm particularly busy to-day. I shall have to ask you to excuse me."

Anthony rose too. "Thank you. I understand perfectly." Salt came and faced him. "But there's one thing I'd like to say to you. And I don't intend to let you go without saying it. And that's this! I don't think you quite understand how I felt towards Nicholas Flagon or even what we were to each other. I'm not a sentimentalist. Nor am I an emotional man. And you may or may not be familiar with those beautiful words of William Johnson Cory."

"I think," said Anthony quietly, "that I know what you are about to say."

"Good. Nevertheless, I'll say it." Salt's resonant voice rang through the room. "'They told me, Heraclitus, they told me you were dead. They brought me bitter news to hear, and bitter tears to shed.'" Salt paused. There was a long silence. Salt turned away and as he did so Anthony heard him say very quietly and scarcely above a whisper "How often you and I, had tired the sun with talking and sent him down the sky."

Anthony closed the door gently behind him and made his way out. He felt that no other course was open to him.

2

"H'm," commented MacMorran, when Anthony reported to him the gist of his interview with Keith Salt. "Pretty negative, on the whole. Certainly not a lot to hang your hat on. But, apart from all that, what was your own reaction to the interview? I always think that one's own personal impressions are best from contacts of that kind. Especially when you come to look back on them afterwards. In effect—how did Salt strike you? Favourably or otherwise?" Anthony thought over the question before he answered it. "Well, Andrew," he said eventually, "I'll begin by confessing that I find that question decidedly difficult to answer. Much more difficult than ordinarily. You'll agree that I'm not usually in that position. As a rule I come away from interviews of that kind with fairly clear-cut ideas. I found myself, when I was with Salt, continually alternating between acceptance, doubt, and acute disbelief. I shouldn't have said 'alternating'—I should have said 'vacillating.'"

MacMorran grinned. "I'll hand it to friend Salt, then. If he can put you on a spot like that. Must be a chap in a thousand."

Anthony grinned back. "All right, Andrew. I can take it. But seriously, now, and going back to your question, that's exactly how Salt had me feeling. You see he stalled first of all over the will. When we got down to serious business, he was forced to admit that Flagon's solicitors had already been in touch with him and had acquainted him with the fact that he had been left a considerable sum of money. But there had been no frankness at all with regard to that, at the commencement of our interview. That was the point when my doubt condition made way to definite disbelief. Afterwards, though, he impressed me much more favourably. He seemed to exhibit genuine grief at Flagon's death. I'm ready to admit, though, that the man may be a damned good actor. One must be prepared for that sort of thing on jobs that come our way."

MacMorran nodded his head. "He denied all knowledge of Flagon's intended marriage, you say. Well—I wouldn't judge him too harshly on that account. I'm inclined to be fifty-fifty on that. When I analyse it thoroughly. On the one side, you have the fact that he was Flagon's close friend. On the other, you have the 'secrecy' condition agreed upon by Flagon and Miss Secretan. Seems to me it's quite a probable assumption that Flagon would place the lady's interest before that of the friend. It's eminently reasonable and history tells us it's been done before."

Anthony listened. He heard MacMorran out. When the inspector had finished Anthony said: "Yes, Andrew. I think that's quite fair. Like you, I'm not one to judge friend Salt on that one showing."

MacMorran took out his tobacco-pouch and carefully filled his pipe. "I've been thinking," he said contemplatively, "while you were up in town. On certain lines. Certain very definite lines. Have you ever thought that there's one person who appears on the fringe of this business—and when I say 'on the fringe,' I *mean* on the fringe. I chose the phrase deliberately. Can you guess the fellow I've in mind?"

Anthony nodded. "Yes—I'll bet you a level half-dollar I click in one. Are you taking me on?"

"Not on your life. There's no prize for the correct answer. It's not as difficult as all that. I quite expect you to get it. Still—have a go. Who is it?"

Anthony smiled. "Sir Claude de Monterey. Your words 'on the fringe' gave it away to me."

"Yes," reiterated MacMorran. "That's the man. And 'on the fringe' is right in more directions than one. According to Catchpole's version of the death of Flagon, de Monterey turned up almost at once to assist in the removal of the body. Acting, of course, in his capacity as steward. Note that to begin with. Point number one. Then—we also find him on the fringe of the Secretan and Flagon business. There's the pretty general story that he was well in the lady's favour prior to Flagon taking over from him. It may be that we're facing one of the oldest of old stories and that there's one of those inevitable triangles in front of us. That de Monterey was a rejected suitor who vents his spite on the man who's supplanted him in a lady's affections. That's point number two."

MacMorran had his pipe well going now and puffed away with serene satisfaction. "Well?" he concluded, "what about it? Going to pick the bones out of it?"

"Still the same old answer, Andrew. The same answer that I have to apply to myself when I start to theorize as you're doing."

"Which is?" asked MacMorran with complete composure.

"One word, Andrew—and one word only. And the same word as before. Madrigal!"

"H'm! I thought you'd say that. But let that rip for a minute. The answer to that, when we do find it, may be a very simple one. I'm putting it clumsily, perhaps, but this is what I mean. We shouldn't refuse to explore certain roads just because the signpost to them doesn't obviously display 'Madrigal.' That it *appears* to have only Flagon on it. Do you get me?"

"Yes, Andrew—and I think you've made a good point *there*. Congratulations."

"Well, then," went on MacMorran, delighted at Anthony's reception of his argument, "apart from the Madrigal angle—ignoring that entirely for the moment—how do you like my remarks *re* de Monterey?"

Anthony demurred a little. "He's oldish, Andrew. I should say, from what I've heard of him, he isn't far short of sixty. On the other hand, he's an all-round sportsman, with an almost international reputation, and I believe a remarkably well-preserved man for his age. If it's any use to you, I should say he plays a good game of darts." Anthony laughed and went on. "I don't know, of course, how hard hit he is over la Secretan. A man at that age, sometimes, takes his medicine very badly. And then—oh and then, I always come back to Madrigal! Just can't help it, Andrew."

"If you ask me, you're inclined to exaggerate the importance of the Madrigal murder. I keep on hammering that point home. I firmly believe it was wantonly conceived and executed, for the express purpose of throwing us fellows off the scent. Your own first idea."

Anthony shook his head. "Comfortable words, my Andrew, but as I've said so many times, 'I hae ma doots.' I'm very much afraid that you're producing a thought very much fathered by my own original wish. I may be wrong now—my first impressions may have been correct—but until I feel differently about things, I must maintain my present position. If, of course—"

He was interrupted by the approach of one of the hotel maids.

"If you please, sir, you're wanted on the telephone. The one by the receptionist's." She addressed the remark to MacMorran.

"Thank you, Miss."

The Yard inspector jumped up to answer the call. "I'll wait here for you, Andrew. Come back when you're finished. Hope it's news that will lead us somewhere."

"You never know," MacMorran called over his shoulder, as he disappeared down the corridor.

Anthony Bathurst waited patiently for the return of the inspector. MacMorran was away at the telephone for some time. When he returned, he was shaking his head.

"That was Chatterton on the line," he said, "I'd put him on to that darts investigation as I told you. It's not been plain sailing for him, by any means, according to what he's just told me."

"Didn't think it would be. Darts aren't exactly old masters. Has he got anything?"

"No. Nothing to speak of. All he's picked up is that they were purchased, in all probability, in Sussex somewhere. The makers of that particular variety sell wholesale to a sports agency which supplies the South Coast towns—Brighton, Hastings, Bexhill, Lewes, Worthing, Shoreham, Eastbourne, Bognor, etcetera. As well as the villages and towns inland and near the Downs. I'm afraid that as far as that goes, we're stymied. It isn't as though we had the box they were sold in. All we have is the darts themselves. Little hope there, I'm afraid. Might mean weeks before we clicked on anything—and then no certainty attached to what you might be lucky enough to discover. We shall have to call it off, I fear. Anyhow, I told Chatterton to pack it up until I gave him further instructions."

Anthony signified his assent. "Just as I feared, Andrew. From the beginning of the clue. We shall be forced to work on other lines. What do you say to my making a call on Sir Claude de Monterey? I might fare better with him than I did with Salt. He's of a vastly different type, I should say. You said yourself how valuable personal impressions were. You never know—he might open his mouth and something jump out. What do you say?"

"Where does he live? Far away from here?"

"No. Reasonably close, I believe. His place is just on the outskirts of Sword. I looked him up in *Who's Who*, yesterday. He's a man of parts. Son of Sir Montague de Monterey, the well-known banker. Clubs—the Junior Carlton, the Belsize B.C., Leander—he's also played for the M.C.C. on their Channel Island tours and turned out more than once years ago for the Corinthians."

"Soccer—eh?" remarked MacMorran. "I should have thought he'd have been a Rugger man with that record behind him."

"Winchester, my dear Andrew, is a Soccer school. William of Wykeham probably played it himself. At any rate, I'll assume that he did."

"Well—if you want a word with de Monterey, by all means go and have it. Although personally—" MacMorran paused.

"Although personally—what?"

"I think you're barking up the wrong tree. I've changed my mind somewhat. I'm pretty certain in my own mind that you won't find the murderer in Flagon's own class."

"No. Where then?"

"In the Keegan class. The 'old lag' class. I've been looking into that particular gentleman's movements on the day of the murder. He attended the Point-to-Point meeting and backed the horse that beat Flagon. I'm interested."

"Did he also attend the Flagon funeral? One of the chief mourners perhaps?"

"I don't know—yet! But he had a day off from work, let me tell you. Supposed to have had 'one-day' flu! Yes—I'm rather more than interested."

"If you feel like that, Andrew, why don't you explore the *reason* of his dislike for Nicholas Flagon? You might then be able to clinch the matter."

MacMorran's eyes twinkled. "I'm at work on that, don't you worry. I'm not standing still and letting the grass grow under my feet. And I'll bet you a level bob that Comrade Michael Keegan has been a guest of His Majesty at some previous stage of his career— and that Nick Flagon was the judge that sent him down. There you are, there's a sporting offer for you."

Anthony let go a low whistle. "Oh-ho! So that's the lay, is it? 'The Old Lag's Revenge,' or 'The Prison Walls have Left a Shadow.' So that's what you're after? Well—it's an idea, Andrew—and who am I to pour scorn on any idea? Michael Keegan—eh? Well—well—the future will prove which one of us is right. And likewise which one wrong. And in the meantime, if you agree, I'll stroll over and have a pow-wow with de Monterey. And I'll do the thing properly. I'll 'phone him first and let him know I'm coming."

"Wouldn't be a bad idea," supplemented MacMorran, "then he can get the silver dusted and the red carpet put down."

"Naturally," replied Anthony smiling, "after all, 'Manners Makyth Man.'"

3

It was a glorious spring morning when Anthony strolled along the road from Verne, through Quiddington St. Philip towards Sword, and he rejoiced to be alive. He quoted Belloc to himself as he saw violet and cowslip, breaking in prodigal profusion along the budding countryside. "The faith in their happy eyes, Comes surely from our Sister, the Spring, When over the sea she flies; The Violets suddenly bloom at her feet, She blesses us with surprise."

As he walked, a host of song-birds piped anthems of sweet music. The sun was moving to its zenith and the ripples of the little river Quidder which he could see every now and then were on fire at their eager edges. The air was wondrously mild for the time of the year and away in the distance, towards the coast, he could see many patches of marsh cotton, looking like exquisite clouds of burnt silver and stretches of samphire—like wet emerald.

"Samphire," he said whimsically, "the samphire of East Anglia, which, pickled, tastes as fine as it looks unpickled."

De Monterey's house was about a quarter of a mile the Quiddington side of Sword. It lay well back from the road. Directly Anthony saw it, he knew it to be Elizabethan, but it lacked the common compliment to Gloriana, of the three gables. Foursquare it stood, strong and unyielding, upon a slight slope, with a sweeping descent of wavy red-brown roof towards the mouth of the valley, well-sheltered from the winds that swirled up to it from the sea. A plethora of chimney stood out against a dullish background of wood. As Anthony walked towards it, there rose from one of them a straight column of blue smoke, unwavering in the clear spring air. Anthony turned up the drive and saw, for the first time, the house's name 'Brightworthy.' He saw but little garden. Most was orchard with thick plantings of many-coloured flowers under each window of the house. Gaunt poplars lined the drive like a rank of stark sentinels.

He had almost reached the house when he heard the rattle of a car in the drive behind him. Stepping to one side, he let a car pass him and swing round outside the front of the house. A tall, spare man, of obvious middle-age, alighted and waited for him to come up. It was clearly de Monterey himself.

Anthony saw a big, broad, sun-burned man with a thick crop of brown hair on his head that was beginning to turn grey. He was alert and loose-limbed, however, for his undoubted age, and looked a man skilful at most ball games, and when he stood up he extracted the full value of every inch of his height—which Anthony, with quick assessment, placed at six feet two. As Anthony drew abreast of him, he closed the door of the car and drew a handkerchief across his forehead. The veins were swelling in that forehead.

'Here is a man,' commented Anthony inwardly, 'who is moved quickly to temper and passion. But as soon as that passion is expended, he readily reverts to mental doubt and hesitation. Blows hot and cold—and after a time, inevitably cold.'

De Monterey advanced towards Anthony and held out his hand. "Good morning, Bathurst. Although you may not be aware of it, we've met before. I didn't tell you so on the 'phone just now." Anthony shook his hands. "First blood to you, sir. I am not aware of it. Time and place?"

De Monterey laughed. "Guessed you wouldn't remember the incident. But I'll recall it to you. It was at Canterbury. During the week. 'Old Stagers.' You were with Gerry Crookley, Angus McKinnel and Gervaise Renton. Play: *Lady Windermere's Fan*. Am I right? You were introduced to me during the evening of Ladies' Day by Lady Crookley after the show. In the dressing-room. I rather fancy, from memory of what you told me, that you had been staying near Bramber in Sussex. Well? How many out of a hundred?"

"Full marks, Sir Claude. You're right in every particular. You've raked me fore and aft. We were both younger in those days."

"Naturally. But come along in and we'll have that talk you say you want with me."

Anthony followed him into a room with heavy dignity of line in old walls and oak-ribbed ceiling. There was an abundance of silver almost everywhere. Much in cabinets and some on a massive sideboard. It was ponderous stuff—most of it, probably, Anthony thought, eighteenth-century date. His eyes also caught sight of fine Georgian and Queen Anne glass and an absolutely magnificent Spode dinner-service.

"Sit down and make yourself at home," said de Monterey.

Anthony took a chair. De Monterey sat opposite him. The morning sunlight poured into the room—golden and clear. One of the larger windows was open. The garden was noisy with birds, but Anthony shut his mind to all outside sounds and external influences.

"Now," said Sir Claude, "what can I do for you? Or I suppose I had better say, what can I tell you? That's probably nearer the mark, isn't it?"

Anthony decided to be as frank as possible. "I told you why I was coming. Tell me everything," he answered, "that you imagine may be likely to help me. That is, if there is anything."

De Monterey shrugged his shoulders. "Believe me, Bathurst—there's—precious little. Across my heart! I scarcely knew Flagon. His life lay far apart from mine. I've spoken to him, I think, on not more than three occasions. The last time was on the afternoon of his death. I was a steward at the Point-to-Point meeting and I had a conventional word with him just prior to his weighing-out."

"How did he seem?"

"So far as I could judge—in the very best of spirits. Yes—I can assert that without the slightest hesitation. Certainly normal." De Monterey hitched himself a little closer to Anthony and fixed his eyes upon him. "Flagon was a man of outstanding ability in many directions. Have you considered the matter from that particular angle?"

"What exactly is your point in emphasizing that, Sir Claude?"

De Monterey pursed up his lips and tapped his right knee with his fingers. Anthony waited for his answer. De Monterey stopped tapping his knee, joined the tips of his fingers and looked up to the ceiling. His attitude seemed to have undergone a complete change. Anthony still waited patiently. He was wondering what lay behind this change.

"Well—let me put it like this. Hasn't it occurred to you, Bathurst, that having that unusual ability, and being very largely something like the darling of the gods ever since he left his cradle, he may well have made a number of . . . er . . . violent antipathies during the course of his career. And probably, more than one serious enemy?"

"It's a point certainly. And, of course, one that we've been bound to consider. Beyond its mere consideration, though, we haven't got very far. I mean by that, that we haven't yet succeeded in running against one of these enemies. No one has as yet popped out. Or even shown a hair."

Anthony purposely left Keegan out of this issue.

"Very likely," returned de Monterey, with a twist of his powerful shoulders, and with almost an air of triumph, "but that doesn't mean there's no wood-pile and no nigger."

"Agreed. But let me ask you a more practical question, Sir Claude. How far away were you when Flagon fell?"

"Quite a mile."

"You didn't see the incident?"

"Oh no. Nowhere near it. Word came to me that there had been an accident and I went down to the place where Flagon was, as hastily as I possibly could. I thought that he'd just taken a toss. Thought perhaps his mount had pecked at the last jump." De Monterey paused. As Anthony made no intervention he continued almost immediately. "There's nothing more to tell. You know all the rest. Or if you don't—you ought to. No doubt you've seen Harradine and you've seen Catchpole."

"Yes. I've heard all they have to say. I take it you saw or heard nothing to make *you* in any way suspicious?"

"No. Nothing whatever."

"What do *you* think happened to Flagon?"

De Monterey raised his eyebrows. "I'm sorry," said Anthony, "if I were vague. My apology. What I meant was how do you think the murderer worked?"

De Monterey shook his head. "Now it's my turn to be sorry. I can't answer that. Actually, I haven't the slightest idea."

"Were there many people, in your opinion, near where Flagon fell?"

"From what I saw when I got to the body, I should say not a lot."

"There were trees and hedgerows near the course."

"Oh, yes. In many places. A Point-to-Point isn't like an ordinary race meeting."

"I appreciate that. So you can't help me much."

"I was afraid I couldn't from the outset. I tried to make that clear to you."

Anthony had timed his thrust. Leaning forward to stub out his cigarette in a convenient ash-tray, he said quietly: "Were you aware of the late Judge Flagon's approaching marriage?"

De Monterey gave no sign that the thrust had gone home. "No. Can't say I was. But . . . er . . . that's a question at a tangent, isn't it? Should I have been?"

"I wondered." Anthony cut short his reply, thereby forcing de Monterey to come again.

"What was the point, Bathurst, underlying your question? I think that there must have been one. I may be a trifle dense, but I can't quite see how Flagon's . . . er . . . intended marriage affects me?"

"Merely from the standpoint of personal interest. I understand he was about to marry a lady, both well-known and resident in this district. That's why I asked you the question."

De Monterey still exhibited no obvious sign of vulnerability. But Anthony, watching him closely, thought that his jaw was hard set.

"Oh, and who may this lady be? Do I know her?"

"Miss Secretan," said Anthony cheerfully.

There was no doubt about it now. The umpire's finger had gone up. De Monterey was having a hard struggle to control the tell-tale features.

"Miss Secretan? Really? I won't say I'm not surprised. Because I am. I happen to know the lady fairly well. Very charming girl, in every respect. I should say they would have made an ideal couple. Dear me. What frightfully hard luck for her. Damned shame! But if I may ask you, how do you know all this? I've neither seen nor heard any . . . er . . . announcement of the engagement. Surely, if it were . . . ?"

"My informant is the lady herself. The late judge's solicitors were also aware of the understanding. There can be no doubt with regard to its truth."

De Monterey rose. "And yet," he said almost to himself, "I might have guessed."

There was a certain wistfulness in the tone of voice which appealed to Anthony hearing it, and in a way weakened him to a condition against which both his better judgment and inclinations contended. De Monterey was standing to his full height and gazing out of the window. The look of sadness which his face had held had now passed from it. It had become a strange mixture of curiosity, perplexity and dismay. He half-turned and looked anxiously down to where Anthony was sitting.

"Is there anything more you desire to ask me, Bathurst? Because if not . . . I'd be rather glad if . . . in the circumstances. . . ."

Anthony rose and stood with him. "Certainly. I'll clear. You're a busy man, no doubt. I'm sorry our interview hasn't been more profitable. More profitable mutually, I mean. But one can't arrange these things, unfortunately, try how we will. Will you forgive me if I ask you one last question?"

De Monterey appeared to have recovered himself. He came away from the window and faced Anthony.

"Of course."

"Did you attend Flagon's funeral?"

"Yes. I felt that I should. Out of courtesy. I had been closely connected with the Point-to-Point arrangements. I felt that out of courtesy—"

Anthony nodded. "Quite so. I understand. Were you close to Justice Madrigal when he was struck down?"

"No-o. Not to say close. He had been an intimate colleague of Flagon's, you know, whereas I wasn't. I might have been a dozen to twenty yards in his rear. But not more than that, I should say."

"You saw nothing in any way suspicious?"

"No. I didn't even see him actually fall. I just heard the, er . . . hum of excitement from the people in my vicinity. You can guess what it was like."

"I see. So I've drawn another blank. Well, thank you very much, Sir Claude. I'm indebted to you."

De Monterey shook hands. "Don't mention it, Bathurst." Anthony walked back along the drive. 'He's shaken,' he said to himself. 'Distinctly shaken. Now I wonder why, exactly. Is it only because of the lady, or is there something else giving him the headache? A nice sharp quillet, eh?'

Anthony shook his head. A quillet! He repeated the word to himself more than once as he walked home. For MacMorran or no MacMorran, he felt that therein lay the kernel of the mystery.

4

When Anthony arrived back to the 'Saracen's Head,' he learned upon inquiry that MacMorran had gone out. According to the message the inspector had left for Anthony, MacMorran was having a further conference with Catchpole at the Verne H.Q. If MacMorran had not returned to the hotel by lunch-time, so the message ran, Anthony was not to wait.

When that time arrived, therefore, Anthony obeyed the instructions he had received and went into the luncheon-room. MacMorran made no appearance, so Anthony made a good lunch on his own and decided to devote the afternoon to his own pursuits. He therefore walked as far as Lode Park which lies about a mile out of Verne. Anthony had come here with definite and deliberate intention. He desired conditions of complete tranquillity and solitude, because there was a problem within a problem which he knew he must solve quickly, if he were to solve, eventually, the major riddle.

Anthony found a secluded seat which the sun served, by a stretch of reeded water, and sat down. To the best of his vision there wasn't a soul in sight. Which was the condition of his desire. The afternoon was comparatively young yet. The people and the children would come later. By his own reckoning, he thought he could look forward to a couple of hours in reasonable comfort and seclusion. Anthony packed the bowl of his pipe with tobacco, lit up, arranged his back muscles as best he could against the hard unyielding wood of the seat, put his feet towards one end and took his etymological dictionary from his jacket pocket.

'Quillet!' Anthony knew, of course, what the word meant. Had he been asked, he would have answered 'a legal quibble.' Catchpole's acceptance of the word as a 'small dart,' and MacMorran's apparent acquiescence in the position, had both interested and amused him. But he had resolved to lie low with regard to the matter, until he had made a closer acquaintance with the word and its absolute, etymological meaning. What he must do now was to make himself more sure of his ground.

"Ah, here we are!" The dictionary told him this. "Quillet. An evasion. The word may be an abbreviation of the old world 'quillity' (formed on analogy with quiddity) meaning a quibble, or it may possibly be from the Latin 'quidlibet,' meaning 'anything you like.' A more fanciful suggestion of some scholars is that it came to England from the French law courts, where each separate allegation in the plaintiff's charge, and every distinct plea in the defendant's answer to that charge, began with the words 'qu'il est,' whence 'quillet,' to signify, therefore, 'a false charge' or 'an evasive answer.'"

Anthony replaced the book in his pocket, having read the meaning through again. He had satisfied himself, now, without any doubt. That is to say, more precisely, he had no doubt left now in his own mind.

'A false charge!' Exactly! Just as he had thought! And yet, he must admit that the phrase was elastic and capable of a variety of meaning. And there was still something eluding him! Some stray reference against which his imperfect memory was fretting and fuming, as it were, in an abortive attempt to run it to earth. 'A sharp quillet.' Where had he met that particular combination of adjective and substantive? As his brain struggled, another memory came to him. A memory of association, this time. It brought a phrase to him, as a retriever will bring the quarry to the hunter, and laid it on the threshold of his mind. 'The quirks and quillets of the law.' A quillet, then, was 'false,' 'evasive,' 'a piece of smug trickery' and very definitely 'a shady piece of business.' Yes, that fitted the pattern all right. The pattern which he himself was in the process of forming.

But a *sharp* quillet! He was still groping for the main discovery that he desired. Now where the heck had he heard that particular phrase before? 'A sharp quillet.' And as he groped and grasped with his mind questing and darting hither and thither, like a terrier seeking a lost ball or a hidden slipper, a phrase swam into his ken and slipped unobtrusively, almost, from the shadowy darkness into the smooth niches of his mind. The phrase was 'the sharp quillets *of the law*.' Yes, the *law* again. There it was, too plain to be overlooked. The law! And both Flagon and Madrigal had been judges. But *where* had he heard it?

Anthony shut his eyes and let his mind float off again, unfettered and unbound, to fend for itself. When it returned to him it *might* bring back the desired object. And then—gradually—as was invariably the case when his memory went a-seeking—clearness began to come to him. An auditorium! A knot of Americans seated in the row of stalls behind him. In the summer of the year. A river near. Swans and cygnets. Swans! The Swan of Avon! Shakespeare! Stratford-on-Avon! The Memorial Theatre. A matinée. Of course— of course! What was the play? *King Henry the Sixth*. Yes! He was there! The words came rolling back to him. Smoothly and easily! No hitch. No feeling for them now with either mind or tongue. They came in clear and clean completion. "But in these nice sharp quillets of the law, Good faith, I am no wiser than a daw."

And then, as the effort of reminiscence had come to the success of fruition, as so often happens, a second kindred memory came flooding into his brain in the wake of the other, as one wave ripples to the beach and creams there, behind its predecessor. "Oh, some authority how to proceed; Some tacks, some quillets how to cheat the devil." 'Shakespeare again,' thought Anthony, but for some time he was uncertain as to which play was its source. Eventually, he came to the decision that the second quotation he had remembered came from *Love's Labour's Lost* and that he had met it in reading, and had not heard it spoken in any performance.

Anthony bent down to the path at his feet, found six small pebbles and threw them singly and with *élan* into the water. So far so good! Flagon and Madrigal had been murdered, and at last, he thought, he was beginning to see why! Yes—as he thought things over more and more—he felt pretty certain that he now knew 'why.' But 'who?' There still remained that more important half of the problem. And then, as he sat there and scrabbled for more small stones to throw, it came to him that he thought he also knew 'who.' He reviewed with meticulous care the various persons who had figured in the drama and the different stories they had told him. He sifted the details of those stories with due deliberation and scrupulous exactitude. It had always been his contention—he had instanced it at the very opening of his career as an investigator and he still maintained it—that the detective's major task in the solution of his problem was to work carefully through all the clues which the problem presented, and his major difficulty to separate the true from the false, the wheat from the chaff. In the case of Madrigal and Flagon this task presented, he thought, even more difficulties than was usual.

He examined, as he sat by the reed-pond, as a whole, and also in detail, Willmott's story of the 'Wheatsheaf' darts, Paula Secretan's account of Flagon's funeral (most important, this), the various Keegan entanglements, Fothergill's account of his afternoon at the Point-to-Point meeting, his friend Harcourt's story of the sudden illness which overtook him, the little newspaper-man's narrative, the official reports of Inspector Catchpole and Doctor Harradine, Keith Salt's more intimate 'fillings-in' of Flagon's life and career, and the particulars of that last interview he himself had so recently had with Sir Claude de Monterey, boxer, Corinthian footballer, cricketer and Leander oar. "Yes," he murmured, as he tossed another pebble into the reed-pond, "I know 'why' and I'm confident that I also know 'who.'" He would see MacMorran at once. Then he brought himself up with a jerk. Argue as cleverly as he might, his proofs, as yet, were of the flimsiest. Before he could close in for the kill, there remained much for him to do.

It would be necessary to explore the more detailed reasons which governed the 'why' and to establish, beyond any measure of doubt, that the trail, which he was convinced *did* exist, led unerringly back to the guilty person. All this meant time and, in all probability, a considerable degree of trouble. Nevertheless it had to be done, and done it should be.

Anthony rose from his seat, tossed his remaining pebbles into the water and stretched out his long arms. A most unusual case, certainly, and much as he might endeavour to persuade himself to the contrary, he had to admit that the rest of the journey before him would be difficult and up-hill going. He walked back to the 'Saracen's Head' to find MacMorran, and exhilaration walked with him.

5

Anthony ran into MacMorran in the vestibule of the 'Saracen's Head.' To all appearances, the inspector had just come in.

"Can't altogether make out this fellow Catchpole," he declared, "seems completely out of his depth."

Anthony was particularly interested to hear this. "Why exactly, Andrew, may I ask? What's the latest?"

"Well, he doesn't seem certain in his mind as to *anything*! Seems to grow more bewildered every day. Runs from one set of tracks, as it were, to another, before he's satisfied as to where the first set leads. No progress is ever made on those lines. It's like the hunter who switches from one spoor to another which may happen to cross his path and comes to the end of the day with an empty cooking-pot."

Anthony said: "The case may be too big for him. Don't suppose he's used to murder. Must make allowances for him, Andrew."

The inspector grunted. "For two pins I'd say his heart wasn't in the chase. To me it looks very much like that."

"It's rather funny you should say that. I've just been in Lode Park and spent two hours on the case."

MacMorran said: "Two? I've spent a hundred and two." Anthony said: "That's different. I meant two hours of intensive thought. You know my methods, my dear Watson."

MacMorran snorted at the reminder. "Must I always—"

Anthony said: "Listen, Andrew, seriously now. I've made considerable progress. Via *Love's Labour's Lost* and the sixth Harry of England."

MacMorran ejected indignation. "I know. *A Midsummer Night's Dream* which I suppose will end in *Much Ado About Nothing*. I can guess what you were going to say. Now it's your turn again."

Anthony grinned. "Andrew—desist! I say 'I have made progress,' and when I say 'I have made progress' I mean 'I have made progress.' Are you going to listen to me, you old ruffian?"

"Carry on," said MacMorran, a trifle sulkily. "I'll listen."

"In the first place," said Anthony, "cast your mind back to the amazingly important point of the 'nice sharp quillet.' Got there?"

"O.K."

"Good. Then immediately disabuse your mind that a quillet is anything like a dart such as our murderer uses. Well—that's stage one of your mental excursion."

"It's not—eh? And we've been barking up the wrong tree—eh? Well—what is it then? Something the missus uses to skewer up the Sunday joint?"

"It does sound something like that—doesn't it? No—I'll explain what it is. You listen to me."

The inspector paid attention to Anthony's expounding. When the explanation was finished Anthony said: "Well—and what do you deduce from all that?"

MacMorran scratched his cheek as he pondered the question. "You mean that the murderer must be an educated man? Or at least, one that knows his Shakespeare?"

"Not exactly, Andrew. I didn't mean it in that way. Although the point's taken. No—what I meant was that the genesis of these crimes goes back to the legal side of Flagon and Madrigal. That they died—primarily—because they were justices of the high court. Don't you agree?"

MacMorran, however, was still not wholly convinced. "Maybe. Maybe not. It occurs to me that the murderer may know the law and has—how shall I put it—translated his revenge or even his motive for revenge into legal terms. Which may mean in turn that *those* are the terms with which *he* is most familiar. Get the idea?"

Anthony thought over carefully what MacMorran had just said. He knew that Andrew was pretty sound as a general rule.

"You mean," he said at length, "that the legal side of the *murderer* is featured and not necessarily, as I was insisting, the legal side of Flagon and Madrigal? Is that your position?"

MacMorran was smiling all over his face. "Exactly. That's just what I do mean. You've put it just right."

"It's a possibility," said Anthony slowly and turning it over in his mind. "I'll admit that, but I don't agree with you. I think mine's the right angle. In fact the more I consider all the details, the more certain I am about it. If I can only pick up the one remaining link necessary for my complete chain, I'll prove it to you."

MacMorran's eyes twinkled. "Ah! If! It's those 'one remaining links' that are the very devil. And well I know it."

"I shall go up to town in the morning, Andrew. I've made up my mind on that. The link will be there—not here."

The inspector's eyes still held their twinkle. "Town's a big place. Hope it won't be a case of the needle and the haystack. If it is, it'll try your patience. You have my sympathy."

"Not for the first time. I'm used to it. Yes—I'll be in town to-morrow morning and—this is for your private ear alone, my dear Andrew—I am not entirely destitute of ideas. Far from it. So you can reserve your sympathy, you old scoundrel, until I come back empty-handed and ask you for it."

But although Anthony spoke so confidently, all unbeknown to him the Fates had already taken a further hand in the game, and his visit to town on the morning of the morrow took place in very different circumstances from those which he had visualized in his conversation with MacMorran. Actually, had he but known it, the curtain was slowly rising on the third act of this dreadful drama. Perhaps it would be more correct to describe the act as the fourth. But whether or not it was in truth the third or the fourth it most certainly was the final. Because, to the names of Flagon and Madrigal, there was to be added another.

Part Three
THE LORD CHIEF JUSTICE

CHAPTER I

1

THE Right Honourable Gervaise Dewar Melbourne, Viscount Fifoot, came down to breakfast on the morning of the anniversary of his seventy-first birthday in good health, better humour and the very best of spirits. He looked through the window of the morning-room at the glorious spring sunshine and remarked to his wife, who had already wished him "many happy returns of the day"—"My dear, what a wonderful morning—the champagne of all weather—the Merry May's begun."

It will be seen that the Lord Chief Justice of England was nothing if not original.

"Yes," returned the lady. "A perfect morning. Now come and sit down to breakfast, my dear, otherwise it will begin to get cold."

Fifoot obeyed. The Lord Chief Justice took his seat, a copy of *The Times*, and the respective items of his morning's post, which according to the routine of years had been scrupulously and studiously arranged for him at the side of his plate. He put them on one side for the moment, in order that he might be free to attend to the somewhat more important duty of skinning a pair of peaches. For some minutes there was silence. Fifoot was busy disposing of the kindly fruits of the earth. At which exercise, it may be remarked, he was no mean exponent.

"Not quite up to standard, my dear Sybil," remarked the Lord Chief Justice as he finished the last fragment. "Just a little lacking in flavour. I shall have to have a word with Saville. He should be getting better results. He gets plenty of assistance from the under-gardener. He'd have to travel a long way to get a better man than Wontner. Can't complain that he's over-worked and under-staffed. You simply have to keep these fellows up to scratch. If they think you aren't troubling—well, then, they don't."

"Yes, dear," said the dutiful Sybil, "they're nearly all the same these days. It's the same everywhere. The old type of servant is dying out and will soon be as extinct as the dodo. I've just had a letter from Edith. You know—Tunbridge Wells. She makes a point of saying very much the same thing."

"All—that reminds me. Haven't opened my post yet."

The Lord Chief Justice surrendered *The Times* to the table-cloth and pulled his pile of letters towards him. His wife heard him muttering as he examined them one by one.

"H'm, Shepherd and Murless. Bill, I suppose! Usually is. Yes—thought so. H'm—details of to-morrow evening's dinner. H'm—h'm—confounded cheek! Who does he think he is—mayor of some tin-pot borough! They amuse me. these people. Ah—yes. Legal Society. Yes—yes—that's all right. H'm—h'm—three invitations for three extremely undistinguished platforms. Can't be done. I'm not exactly on tap as it were. Dodge those in some way—hallo—what on earth's this? Looks as though it might have come from the 'moor' itself. Envelope's filthy enough."

The Lord Chief Justice took the paper knife which was always laid near his plate and slit with fastidious care the top of the envelope which had so excited his criticism. He frowned as he read it. Before he came to the end, the frown had reached prodigious proportions. Sybil, his wife, looking up from her finger of toast, noticed her husband's alarmed and alarming expression and put her curiosity into words. "Gervaise! What on earth's the matter?"

The Lord Chief Justice took a little time to answer his wife's question. As she looked more carefully at him she noticed, to her great surprise, that his hand which held the letter was shaking. A most unusual physical feature on the part of the Lord Chief Justice. But he put the letter in front of her and said quietly: "Read that, my dear . . . to say the least of it . . . it's . . . er . . . disturbing." The lady adjusted her glasses and read the letter. "The handwriting—or printing shall we call it," she said, "is most disgustingly illiterate."

"Read the contents," he insisted testily, "never mind the quality of the script."

"Just a line to inform you that when you recieve this, you'll have less than forty-eight hours to live, you old bastard. Why? Remember your two pals, Flaggon and Maddrigal and what has happened to them and you'll know the reason why. From one who knows even better than you do."

"Disgusting," said the lady again—"an utterly abominable and ill-spelt letter to be sent through the channels of the post."

"Yes, I know," replied the Lord Chief Justice even more testily than before. "I know all about that side of the question. But what about me? Nick Flagon and Theo Madrigal have both been killed. They've both been murdered. Am I to . . . er . . . disregard the implications because of its execrable penmanship? Am I to sit down quietly and be murdered in the same way as my two colleagues? I tell you, my dear, I don't think that I'm a coward, but this thing frightens me." There is little doubt that herein Fifoot was speaking no more and no less than the truth. Great beads of sweat stood in profusion on his florid brow. He found his handkerchief, put it on his lap and in his perturbation wiped his forehead with his table-napkin. Sybil Fifoot saw that he was, indeed, badly shaken.

"What will you do then?" she asked.

"I shall waste no time, for one thing," came his reply. "I don't intend to so like a lamb to the slaughter as Flagon and Madrigal did.

No, my dear—I certainly do not. I shall grasp the nettle. I'll ring the Commissioner of Police *now*! What's the precise time, my dear?"

His wife glanced at the big clock on the mantelpiece. "Nearly twenty minutes past nine," she answered.

"It's a bit early," he muttered, "but if Kemble's not there, I'll leave word for him to ring me the moment he comes in."

"If he *does* come in," corrected the lady, "they don't always, you know. People in his position."

"We'll see about that. I'll 'phone now."

The Right Honourable Gervaise tottered out to his library and to the telephone. Sybil Fifoot waited anxiously for her lord and master's return. He was absent for over ten minutes. When he came back, it hurt her to see that he was still white and trembling.

"As you said, Kemble's not arrived yet. I spoke to an A.D.C. Farrell-Knox, I think his name was. Kemble's expected at ten o'clock and they've promised me he'll 'phone through to me the moment he arrives."

"Well, then," said his wife gently, "that's all right. Now sit down and finish your breakfast. You won't feel any better having nothing in your inside."

"Breakfast," snorted the Lord Chief Justice, "breakfast! My dear Sybil—please show a little sense of proportion. I feel bound to point out to you that my position is very different from yours. Very different. It has a resemblance—compared with yours—to at least one of Aesop's better known fables."

"My dear," protested Sybil Fifoot, "I understand *exactly* how you feel and I think you're doing absolutely the right thing in getting to grips with it at once. It's a pity those other two poor people didn't act similarly."

"As I said just now—grasp the nettle," murmured the Lord Chief Justice, "grasp it fearlessly. It's the only way. With all life's problems. It's always been my rule and I'm not departing from it now."

"So you're determined not to have any more breakfast?"

"Please don't refer to breakfast again, my dear. Food has become an excessively minor consideration. A drowning man isn't tempted by a lobster mayonnaise. I'm going back to the library to wait for my telephone call."

His wife bowed her head in submission and his lordship rolled out of the breakfast-room. Perhaps it was as well, from the point of view of Sir Austin Kemble himself, of the Lord Chief Justice and ultimately of Anthony Lotherington Bathurst, that the Commissioner reached his office at the 'Yard' on that particular morning, comparatively punctually. The first thing he did was to read the scribbled message lying on the front of his desk and, realizing the social altitude of its origin, he at once put a 'phone call through to Downland 22.

The Lord Chief Justice, waiting for it in an agony of suspense, answered it a trifle quicker than immediately.

"Is that Sir Austin Kemble?"

Sir Austin Kemble listened to Fifoot's story and realized without hesitation that the matter confronting him was serious in the extreme.

"I'm very glad you rang me at once, my lord. Very sound on your part. Delays in matters of this kind are invariably most dangerous. Now do you mind reading this letter to me over the 'phone—slowly—if you please. I'd very much like to hear it. Thank you very much."

The Lord Chief Justice read the letter slowly and deliberately.

"H'm," said the Commissioner of Police, "yes . . . I think I've got the gist of it. Let me see now. With regard to time. Less than forty-eight hours after you received it—that's the threat. And you received it—you say—about an hour ago. Yes—I see—first post, this morning. That—er—to my mind indicates that the attempt will be made to-morrow evening. Or possibly a little later than that. Now first of all, sir, what are your arrangements from now onwards?"

"Nothing on at all to-day, Sir Austin. I'm quite free as it happens. An absolutely blank day. I'm in the chair at the dinner being given by the Middle Temple to the Dean of Faculty, Sir Wardlaw Henderson, to-morrow evening. The American Ambassador will also be present. To say nothing of the Minister of Justice for Canada. Shall I cancel it? In these terrible circumstances? It's being held at the Diadem Rooms." Sir Austin Kemble considered the question the Lord Chief Justice had put to him and knew that he was in a quandary. Consultation on his part with certain of his officers with regard to this particular point was clearly demanded and necessary.

"Look here, my lord," he replied. "First of all, I shall have to take certain precautionary steps. And before I decide anything definite, I must have a conference up here with some of my principal officers. Look here, sir—" Sir Austin thought quickly, "I'll be at your place as soon after lunch this afternoon as I can make it. Say between three and four o'clock. Stay indoors all the time. Don't let any stranger come near you under any pretext whatever. Get Lady Fifoot to stay with you all the time until I come down."

"Very good, Sir Austin. I'll expect you then after lunch. Will you come by road?"

"Yes. Through East Smilstead. I know the road well."

"Good. I'll tell my wife. And I'll do exactly as you say." The Lord Chief Justice rang off, and judging by the tone of his voice, the Commissioner of Police saw no reason to doubt his last statement.

Sir Austin Kemble put down the post-office telephone, thought for a moment and picked up the internal one. He asked for Superintendent Hemingway.

2

"Oh—Super," said the Commissioner, somewhat severely, when Hemingway put in an appearance, "I want you to get into touch with Chief Detective-Inspector MacMorran. At once! And when I say at once, mean at once. Tell him from me to leave Verne directly he gets my message and to come straight here. Tell him you can't answer any questions. Just that he's to come here at once and report direct to me. Also—and this is most important—he's to bring Mr. Anthony Bathurst with him. Is that clear?"

"Yes, sir. Inspector MacMorran and Mr. Bathurst to leave Verne and to come here to you immediately."

"That's right, Hemingway." Sir Austin Kemble looked at his watch. "A quarter past ten. They should be here soon after one o'clock. Oh—and make arrangements for a fast car to leave here for Hart's Heath at two o'clock prompt. Get the Daimler."

"Very good, sir." Hemingway made his exit.

Precisely at eleven o'clock, the superintendent had a further audience with the Commissioner.

"Everything in order, sir," he reported. "Inspector MacMorran and Mr. Bathurst left Verne by the eleven-eleven train, sir. Scheduled to reach Liverpool Street at seven minutes to one. And the car you ordered, sir, will be ready to leave at two pip emma. All arrangements are made. Miss Repton will be driving, sir."

"Thank you, Super. That's all right then."

When MacMorran and Anthony walked in, the Commissioner was waiting for them.

"Leave the questions for the moment. I'll satisfy your curiosity later," said Sir Austin, "get away for a quick snack and be back here at two sharp. According to my watch, you've got exactly thirty-three minutes. So step on it."

"I suggest, Andrew—seeing that it's got to be a quick one," said Anthony as they made themselves scarce, "a hunk of bread and cheese at a pub washed down with copious draughts of the wine of the country. What do you say? Are you on?"

"Suits me. Can't do better. What in the name of Hades has happened, do you think?"

"Something pretty tempestuous, I should say, judging by the old man's manner. Can't remember ever having seen him so hot and bothered. Still—sufficient for the day, etc. We shall know all about things in half an hour's time. Till then, Andrew—patience and snaffle the Cheddar. Perhaps."

"What concerns me," said MacMorran, "is what's coming on the menu at two o'clock? Where are we bound for, do you think?"

"Well," said Anthony, "there's not the slightest point in guessing. So why worry? But it's fairly obvious that the focal point of interest has been transferred from Verne. Otherwise we shouldn't have been yanked away from there as we have been. Question is, which balloon has gone up, where has it gone up, and—equally important—who sent it up? Here we are, Andrew. This place looks O.K." Anthony pushed open the saloon-bar doors of the 'Silvery Moon.' "There you are, Andrew. The 'Silvery Moon.' People used to sigh for it. At least, so I've heard it said. What will you have? Guinness with the bread and cheese or plain wallop? Which is it?"

"Guinness," said the Chief. "I'm partial to the Celtic brew." Anthony gave the necessary order, collected the essentials and they repaired to a side-table.

"You know, Andrew," went on Anthony, "I find this sudden translation a trifle disturbing. I had all my plans mapped out for to-day, as I had already outlined to you."

MacMorran disposed of a goodly portion of his Guinness with obvious enjoyment. "Yes. I know. You told me. But there you are—man proposes—you know the rest."

"Very true. I'll tell you what I was after, Andrew."

"I know—you needn't trouble."

"What?"

"A murderer!" The Chief grinned at his witticism.

Anthony shook his head. "Agreed. Ultimately! But I was on the track of something which was antecedent to that. Not a bad piece of cheese this. Trust a pub to get hold of decent stuff. No, Andrew—I was after a birth-certificate."

MacMorran looked at him with newly-awakened interest. "Whose?" he asked.

Anthony grinned. "That's my main difficulty. I don't know the name."

MacMorran stared at him. "Do you mean the birth-certificate of the murderer?"

"No—Andrew. To say that wouldn't be *strictly* correct."

"Moving in the dark a bit—aren't you?"

"That's the devil of it. Cimmerian darkness. Need a supply of carrots and cat's eyes. Still—I live in hopes, Andrew. Unless of course—"

MacMorran interposed. "Unless what?"

"Unless," Anthony spoke slowly and deliberately, "unless, Andrew, what we hear at two o'clock clears the air for me. For us. It's on the cards it may. Come on, finish up those crumbs, and we'll get cracking. Fit?"

MacMorran drained his glass and the two men walked quickly back to the Yard. When they arrived there, the clock showed the time at two minutes to two.

"He can't grumble at that," said Anthony.

"You don't know him," replied MacMorran.

3

"The car's ready and waiting," announced Sir Austin. "Sorry to cut your lunch so fine, but I had no option. Get in."

Anthony waved to Helen Repton at the wheel and was rewarded by a charming smile in return. What Miss Repton thought of Mr.

Bathurst was equalled by what Mr. Bathurst thought of Miss Repton. Each admired to the full the other's extreme efficiency. Sir Austin gave the signal and the car got under way.

"Hart's Heath, Miss Repton," he said to the chauffeuse, "via East Smilstead."

Then he turned to Anthony and MacMorran. "I haven't forgotten that I owe you fellows some sort of an explanation. You'll have the full story from me on the way down. Justice Flagon had an anonymous letter, a threatening letter. He ignored it. He died. Justice Madrigal received an anonymous letter of the same kidney. He ignored it. He died."

Anthony was listening avidly. He told himself he knew what was coming. Not particularly—nothing like that—but generally. Not with any details as to person or persons but in principle. Sir Austin, however, was continuing.

"Yet a third . . . er . . . threatening and . . . er . . . anonymous letter has been received. On this occasion by no less a personage than the Lord Chief Justice himself, Viscount Fifoot. He, however, has *not* ignored it. Very properly, he has placed the matter in my hands. Moreover he acted with exemplary promptitude. He received the letter this morning and 'phoned me at once. Of course he couldn't possibly have done better. I told him so. We are going straight to his house at Hart's Heath. That's why I sent for you, MacMorran, and you, Bathurst, and that's why you're here now."

Anthony took in the details of the Commissioner's statement. As far as he was concerned this latest development was not disturbing to him but, on the other hand, fitted the pattern of the crimes as he saw it. And it might well be, he argued to himself as the car wheels skimmed over the road, that the Lord Chief Justice's action, prompt as it had been, would give them a much greater chance of coming to close quarters with the criminal. Forewarned is forearmed all the world over. He turned to the Commissioner and sought for greater detail.

"When's the threat due to be effective, sir?" he asked.

"In less than forty-eight hours after the receipt of the letter. Do you regard that as of any importance?"

"Yes, Sir Austin. Let us look back. In each of the previous murders, the original threat referred to the next day for its fruition. And the writer, on each occasion, kept faith with the promise. Less than forty-eight hours—eh? That brings us in all probability to to-morrow. With the balance towards to-morrow evening."

"What instructions did you give his lordship, Sir Austin?" inquired MacMorran.

"Told him to stay put until we came. After that, it will have to become a question for our joint conference and decision. I suggest we keep an open mind on the matter until we've discussed all the details fully with Viscount Fifoot. Does either of you disagree with that suggestion?"

"No, sir," returned MacMorran, "I can't see any better course. Yet."

"What about you, Bathurst?" demanded the Commissioner.

"No, Sir Austin. In the absence of the entire data, I don't see that you could have recommended anything better. All the same, my thoughts are running on rather. I'm wondering what will be the best course for us to adopt afterwards."

"How do you mean, Bathurst—afterwards?"

"To-morrow, sir. The day after to-day. We shall have to walk very warily. The criminals have brought it off twice, you know. Whatever we do—we mustn't treat the threat cavalierly—and forget that. Frankly, sir, I'm worried. It's a matter of time. That's where I'm so awkwardly placed. If only I had more time. Another day might have made all the difference."

The Commissioner looked at him sharply. "How? What difference could a day have made? I'm afraid I don't follow you, Bathurst."

Anthony shook his head. "I think, sir, that I know who's responsible for these murders. I'm fairly certain that I've narrowed it to one of two people. But I am woefully short of proof. I had intended to use to-day in an endeavour to make sure. Before your summons came. Now—to save the life of our worthy Lord Chief Justice—I'm compelled to take a chance. And I hate a risk when another man's life's at stake. At the same time—"

Anthony paused somewhat abruptly. Sir Austin Kemble cut in. "At the same time—what?"

"This new move, sir, is not all to our disadvantage. I can see that. It brings one vital advantage with it. If my instinct's right— and God grant it may be—the next twenty-four-hours will bring us all the proof we want. But—and it's a big but—I'm compelled to call, as it were, to the toss of a coin which has two sides. *And I may call wrong.*"

Sir Austin caressed his chin. "H'm. Yes—I see the difficulty."

Suddenly, Anthony brightened. "Don't worry, sir, I've just thought of something. I think I can see my way out."

"Good. I'm relieved. You'll confer with MacMorran, of course."

"I shall, sir. We shall work together—as in the past."

"Good again. Where are we? Can you see?"

Anthony looked out of the window. "Lottingham, sir."

The Commissioner looked at his watch. "I promised—or half-promised—Viscount Fifoot that we'd be at his place some-where between three and four o'clock. We shall do that easily, that girl's going well."

"There's one thing I'd like to know, sir," said MacMorran, "and that's this. Have you any idea of his lordship's arrangements in respect of to-morrow? We shall have to watch them very carefully. It seems to me that a great deal depends on that."

"He has a dinner in the evening. So he told me on the telephone. Pretty big affair. Fifoot's in the chair. He asked me if he should cancel it in the circumstances. I thought we'd better discuss it first. You know—leave it until we'd had a word with him. Far better."

"Where's the dinner taking place, sir?"

Sir Austin furrowed his brows. "Now where was it he told me? For the life of me I can't remember. Anyhow, he'll tell us when we chat it over with him."

"Is it in town?"

"Oh—yes. It's in town somewhere."

MacMorran heaved a sigh of relief. "Well, that's one good thing anyway. I was worried that it might not have been. The murderer will have less chance to operate in London than in one of these country districts. Similar, for instance, to Quiddington St. Philip."

Anthony looked at him. "Don't you agree, Mr. Bathurst?" asked MacMorran with a smile.

"Not altogether sure, Andrew. I know what you're thinking of, though. But don't forget we're dealing with the throwing of a poisoned dart. The victim might, for example, be on the point of entering an hotel and the dart be thrown at him from the top of a London Passenger Transport Board omnibus. Still—on the whole, I'm inclined to agree with you."

The car flashed over a level-crossing. "Where are we, Bathurst?" the Commissioner asked again.

"Mercer's Common, sir."

"Good. We must be just on East Smilstead, then."

The car took a bend in the road and Helen Repton hugged the left-hand hedgerow. Then the road twisted on and up the hill and came out on to the straight stretch which runs along the whole length of the 'Rector's Elbow.' Helen Repton let the car have its head and smoothly pushed up the speedometer needle to a steady fifty. They came to the four cross-roads which mark the end of 'Rector's Elbow.' Helen Repton swung right here and they went down a narrow winding road with high hedges. About two miles from East Smilstead.

"First turning left," said Anthony, "and we're in East Smilstead."

As he spoke, a turning to the left showed just ahead of them. The car took it and sped along a road which was pocked by holes. The sandy surface had been undermined by heavy rain. Five minutes later, they flashed through the pretty little town of East Smilstead and to their right they could see the beginnings of Goodacre Forest. Anthony glanced at his watch. The time was ten minutes past three.

"Goodacre Forest, sir," he said to the Commissioner of Police. "You'll make the time all right."

Sir Austin grunted unintelligibly and stirred uneasily in his corner seat. The road now began to twist and turn again until Helen

Repton took the car up a sharp rise and to a cross-roads signpost with a triple-fingered sign. Anthony read it as they purred by—the road to the right went to Cherry Vintner, that to the left to Silken Courtway and the road straight ahead to Hart's Heath and Dennis Crossing. Helen Repton took the car straight across.

"Last lap," said Anthony—"and a mere nine miles to go."

Sir Austin nodded and the remainder of the journey was encompassed in silence. Helen Repton took the next turning to the left which showed 'Hart's Heath—2 miles.' The car slid past two farmhouses and, close by, a number of grandly-timbered old-time barns. And almost before he could properly realize it, Anthony felt Helen Repton slowly easing the speed down.

"I rather fancy," he heard Sir Austin say, "that this is Journey's End."

He saw a square house of red brick with a lodge-keeper's cottage at the beginning of a well-tended gravel drive which sloped rather steeply up to the house. There was a trim hedge which bordered it, and as he turned back and looked at the country through which they had just come, Anthony saw that Viscount Fifoot, Lord Chief Justice, certainly knew all his gherkins and had done himself gratifyingly well in his selection of his country residence.

A manservant answered the bell which Sir Austin had pressed. He was erect of figure and austere in manner. A fitting servant, thought Anthony, for such a master.

"Sir Austin Kemble?" he inquired of the Commissioner.

The latter nodded corroboration.

"Come in, sir. His lordship is expecting you."

The Commissioner stepped smartly over the threshold, followed by Anthony and MacMorran.

"His lordship is in the library. I will inform him you are here. If you gentlemen would kindly step this way. . . ."

The manservant went and came back. Within a few minutes they were conducted down a wide passage and to a door which was partly open. As they waited on the threshold, the sunlight could be seen shimmering through. The manservant ushered them into the room. Viscount Fifoot rose to greet them. As he did so, Anthony saw a lady rise and stand just behind him.

4

Anthony noticed that the Lord Chief Justice of England was surprisingly tall. Almost as tall, in fact, as Keith Salt. But he lacked the latter's magnificent physique. The Lord Chief Justice was thin and spare and a mane of grey hair swept back untidily from his high, intellectual forehead. The clean-shaven face had the brow of the scholar and the mouth was long and thin-lipped.

"Good afternoon, Sir Austin," said Fifoot, "this is my wife. I don't think you've met her. You see how explicitly I'm obeying your instructions. She hasn't left my side since we spoke to each other on the telephone."

Anthony saw with surprise that Lady Fifoot was nearly as tall as her husband. For a woman, she was amazingly tall, slim and with a rather small head covered with wavy white hair and set on a long, slender neck. Her hands were long and aristocratic. Her wrists and ankles were fine and shapely and her feet narrow and delicate.

She had been a beauty in her day, Anthony thought, but now she was drawn by the mesh of circumstance which had caught her up, and a trifle haggard. Her eyes were dark and rather magnificent and the gaze which came from them was keen and intelligent. She was plainly dressed in black—and wore no ornaments, Anthony noticed, with the exception of her wedding-ring and two drop emeralds in her ears. These stones were tiny and beautiful.

"My wife," said Fifoot again.

Sir Austin bowed gallantly over the lady's hand. Then he turned and introduced Anthony and MacMorran. When Lady Fifoot spoke, her voice was caressingly low and husky.

"Sit down, gentlemen," she said; "and if you don't mind and can put up with me, I'd like to stop and hear what you're going to say. Such a procedure may not be strictly in order, but I'd like you to allow it." She flashed a quick smile at her husband as she spoke.

"Certainly," said the Commissioner, "and I'm sure you'll forgive me, if I at any time appear a little curt. That's not my fault. The main point that we have to remember is that we have so little time. You do understand, don't you, Lady Fifoot?"

"I understand perfectly," she replied, "now you men talk and I'll listen. My husband will tell you that I *do* know when to keep my mouth shut."

The Commissioner took on himself the self-contained and rather detached manner of the experienced courtier, mingled with the aplomb of the old soldier suddenly called upon by a mischievous fate to deal with a critical situation.

"Certainly, Lady Fifoot."

She gave him a deliciously kind, yet impersonal smile. He turned to the Lord Chief Justice.

"First of all, may I see the threatening letter?"

It was handed to him immediately. Sir Austin adjusted his heavy horn-rimmed glasses and read it without comment. He passed it to Anthony who read it and handed it to MacMorran. Nobody spoke. Eventually Sir Austin broke the silence and put a question.

"Well?"

MacMorran shook his head and gestured to Anthony to answer.

"Same as! Same as before! Same handwriting or 'printing' if you prefer to call it that. Similar sheet of letter-paper. Same person undoubtedly. Posted, you will have observed, in Whitechapel of all places."

Fifoot nodded. "Yes. I noticed that."

"Now, my lord," went on Sir Austin, "can you yourself throw any light on it? Amy glimmer of light? No matter how small. Is there anybody you suspect may have sent it—even though the suspicion may appear to have the flimsiest foundation?"

"Nobody at all. I can't think of anybody. There's no doubt that there may be thousands of criminals who've crossed my path of duty and who possibly . . . er . . . harbour a certain resentment . . . against me—but certainly not any particular one whom I could separate from the rest and . . . er . . . class as a definite suspect."

"That leaves us still in the dark then. And it means, too, that we can't waste time casting round and angling for the murderer. That must wait for future action. In the meantime, we must devote our entire energies to saving you."

Lady Fifoot nodded. Anthony saw her. Sir Austin continued.

"Now, I've brought Bathurst and Inspector MacMorran along with me, primarily, to decide on your programme for to-morrow. They've been working on the Flagon and Madrigal end of the affair. Up to now we've come to no decision with regard to *you*. We thought we'd see you first and talk things over. Please tell us about your engagement. With details. You mentioned it to me on the telephone."

"To-morrow evening," said the Lord Chief Justice, in precise tones, "I have an engagement of long standing. I'm due to take the chair at the Diadem Rooms. At a dinner to be given by the members of the Middle Temple to the Dean of Faculty, Sir Wardlaw Henderson. Just prior to his retirement from office. I shall be supported by the American Ambassador, Mr. Hillman Horniman, and the Minister of Justice for Canada, Mr. Louis something or other, in particular, and by many learned members of the legal profession in general. As you know, the Diadem Rooms are in Salopia Circus. I had proposed to go up by car. The dinner is at half-past seven. Reception at seven-fifteen. That constitutes my sole engagement for the day."

"Thank you," returned Sir Austin.

He turned to Anthony and Inspector MacMorran. "Well, gentlemen, you heard what his lordship said. Point number one—shall he keep the appointment or ... er ... call it off? I have my views—but I'd like to hear yours before I express them."

MacMorran had first say. "Seems to me, sir, it comes to this. Does Viscount Fifoot put himself in our hands—unreservedly? I mean—does he leave the decision to us as to whether he keeps his engagement or not?"

The Commissioner looked toward the Lord Chief Justice for the answer to MacMorran's question. Fifoot glanced across at his wife and then cleared his throat nervously.

"Yes. If you feel you can offer me adequate protection, I'll put myself entirely in your hands. I'm quite prepared to do that."

"Well then, sir," said MacMorran, "I counsel that Viscount Fifoot fulfils his engagement. If he does, then it seems to me that we shall have a gr-r-eat chance of putting our hands on the murderer. Yes!"

He turned and invited Anthony's opinion. "Do you agree, Mr. Bathurst?" he said.

"I agree entirely."

"In that case," contributed Sir Austin, "seeing that you two are of one mind, I'm prepared to accept the position. You take the chair to-morrow evening at seven-thirty, in the Diadem Rooms, my lord. You'll travel from here in a closed car. We shall supply escort all the way to the restaurant. If the attempt is made during the dinner, adequate measures will be arranged to defeat it. I can assure you of that. They will have to be considered and developed, but I give you my word now, my lord, that you shall be made fully cognisant of them."

"When?"

"You will not leave this house until you leave it for the dinner to-morrow evening. That will be in the region—say—of five o'clock. Your chauffeur, I take it, will drive you up to town. In addition to the escort cars, one of my men will be with your chauffeur in the front of your car. But I will see that you have full instructions with regard to every possible point, not later than midday to-morrow."

"I'll put all that in Hemingway's hands," Sir Austin added to MacMorran as an afterthought.

Fifoot nodded. "Have you any objection to Lady Fifoot accompanying me in the car to the restaurant?"

"None at all," replied the Commissioner with warm approval—"actually I should welcome it."

"Good. She'll come then. It was not her intention to come originally—but we'll remedy that."

"If I may be allowed to butt in, sir," said Anthony, "I'd like to suggest that the Lord Chief Justice acts to-morrow evening, as far as he himself is concerned, just as though there had been no menacing letter. It will help our plans if he will do that." He turned to Viscount Fifoot. "I realize that perhaps I'm asking a little too much of you, but I've no doubt you'll play up all you can."

Anthony smiled and Lady Fifoot half-fell in love with him at that moment.

"I'll do my best, Mr. Bathurst," answered the Lord Chief Justice, "but I'm not as young as I was, you know. I've passed the allotted span. Well, then. That's more or less settled. I place myself unreservedly in your hands, gentlemen, and you complete all your instructions to me not later than midday to-morrow. I go up to town by car—under your escort—and I do my best to forget all the abnormalities that the evening may possess for me. Is that my programme?"

"That's it, my lord," said the Commissioner, "and if we have any luck, we'll have the murderer of Flagon and Madrigal in safe custody, before the evening's through."

Viscount Fifoot turned to his wife. "On that note, then, my dear Sybil, I *think* we'll have tea. At the same time, though, I feel just a little like the kid that's the bait for the tiger."

CHAPTER II

1

HELEN Repton turned the car down the gravelled drive at six o'clock exactly. The radio pips were actually sounding as the wheels began to revolve.

"We have just about twenty-four hours," said Anthony. "No more. That's the part which is worrying me. Now, have I your permission to monopolize the conversation for the next half-hour?"

"Go ahead, boy," said Sir Austin, in high good-humour—because the case suited his social pretensions very thoroughly and would benefit him considerably if he could round it off successfully.

"Right, sir. Now first of all, there's little doubt, in my mind, that the dinner will be the venue of the attempt. The old boy in the chair's a sitting bird—agreed on that?"

Sir Austin and MacMorran each signified acquiescence.

"O.K., then. Now granted that—which is it (a) guests, (b) waiters, (c) Press or (d) alien influence?"

MacMorran knitted his brows. "Interpret the last, please."

"Well, Andrew, what I meant was this. Between his leaving the car and reaching the chairman's table in the Diadem Rooms, there will be people making certain contacts with him. Contacts that can't very well be avoided. People, for instance, attending other functions. Ordinary diners, moving in the restaurant. Attendants—cloakroom and lavatory, for example. He *must* be exposed to certain risks. You appreciate the difference. That's what I meant by alien influence. So I come back to my first question—in which category do we look for the murderer? Please be as quick as you can because I've a hell of a lot to do in these coming twenty-four hours."

"Guests," said MacMorran emphatically.

"The last lot. Alien influence," said the Commissioner.

"Guests—without a doubt," reiterated the inspector. "With all respect, sir."

"Well, we don't know," said Anthony reflectively, "but I'm *inclined*, just at the moment, to agree with you, Sir Austin. But it means this. Hemingway must cover the cloakroom, the lavatory, the staircases and, I think, the waiter's staff. MacMorran and I will see to the rest. And by the way, Andrew, I'd like Helen as an extra waitress. I want her to have the L.C.J. under her nose all the time he's in the chair. And by 'under her nose' I mean 'under her nose.' I don't want her to let him out of her sight. She must be in close attendance all the time. Will you see to that?"

"I will."

"Thank you, Andrew. Now Hemingway's fixed and Miss Repton will be all right. Number Two. I want, as early as possible, a plan of the dinner-seating in detail. Names of guests and all that. Also any other johnnies expected to be present. Press reporters, newspaper wallahs, etcetera. You get the idea. O.K., Andrew?"

"O.K., Mr. Bathurst."

"Right. Number Three. I want—and this is going to give you something like a headache—the birthplaces and birthdates of Maurice Fothergill and Ronald Harcourt. They're still staying at the 'Wheatsheaf'—as far as I know. You must extract the information from them somehow. *You yourself!* Number Four—John Bentley—Reporter. Attached to staff of *Daily Fanfare*. I want similar information *re* him. Perhaps Hemingway can put a really good man on to that. Screw it out of *him* somehow. That will mean, in each case, a second string to my bow in the event of my own failure. Now—the time! That's the snag, Sir Austin! Worries me! We shall be in town by—say—eight-thirty this evening. I want that information, Andrew—all of it—by nine o'clock to-morrow morning—not a second later. That's vital. Everything hinges on it. And listen, Andrew—I'll 'phone *you* for it."

"Where?"

"Don't be a goat, Andrew. Verne, of course. Where else? Not forgetting Fothergill and Harcourt—are we? You won't let me down, will you?"

"I'll do my best," said MacMorran, "but you're asking a lot, you know—all these points. I may not be able to get to grips with all of them."

"I know. You must forgive me. I'm trusting to luck and hoping for the best. But I *must* eliminate. It's the only course open to me. If not all, then as many as possible."

"You think you know the murderer, Bathurst?" said the Commissioner.

"I'm *almost* certain, sir. Say about five per cent of doubt still sticking at the bottom of the glass—not more. But sufficient to cause me to hold my hand for a little while. I hope to make absolutely certain this evening and to clinch it by what MacMorran tells me at nine o'clock in the morning. If I do, you shall know the name tomorrow And you, Andrew." Anthony chuckled. "And when you hear it, I fancy you'll whistle your surprise. A clever criminal, gentlemen. With *one* extremely clever touch."

He looked at his watch. Helen Repton was already through Lottingham.

"Shall we recapitulate, Andrew? To see that we've neither omitted nor neglected anything?"

MacMorran agreed and proceeded to tick off the items on his finger-tips as Anthony ran through them. Anthony took the list methodically and Sir Austin commented on it here and there. The inspector ticked off the last item on the list.

"That's all right," confirmed Anthony, "and I think it covers everything." He turned from MacMorran to address Sir Austin again. "One more thing, sir. And another request, I'm afraid. I want you to put this car and also Miss Repton at my disposal. Until, say, to-morrow evening. It will ease matters considerably for me. MacMorran can get back to Verne to-night, from Liverpool Street. There's a train at ten-twenty. Which will give him time to attend to those matters for me. I'm sorry to rush you all so—but there's no option. We've so little margin. Is that all O.K., sir?"

The Commissioner nodded. "Yes, that can be arranged. I'll see to it for you. You take the car. MacMorran can go back by train. And I'll put Hemingway to work directly we arrive."

Helen Repton brought the car to a standstill outside the 'Yard' and the Commissioner and MacMorran alighted. Anthony spoke to her down the communication-tube. The time was now twenty-two minutes past eight.

2

Helen Repton swung herself from the seat at the driving-wheel and came round to the window.

"If you like, Mr. Bathurst," she said, "I'm ready to start at once. I don't mind a scrap going straight on."

Anthony smiled at her. "Good for you, Helen. Still, it'll be better for you to have a snack now while you can get it. I'd take you out to dinner—but there simply isn't time. As a matter of fact, Helen, we're up against it."

Helen Repton knew what that meant. When Anthony Bathurst spoke in that strain, she understood that he had good reason.

"All right," she smiled, "I'll be back in twenty minutes. So that we'll be away sharp at a quarter to nine. And mind you have a bite of something, yourself. You need it just as much as I do."

Anthony grinned at this expression of solicitude. "Don't worry. I've nine wolves in my genealogical table and they've never had reason to be ashamed of me yet. See you at eight-forty-five, then."

They were each as good as their respective words and Helen Repton turned her wheel punctually at a quarter to nine on the journey Anthony had described to her down the speaking-tube. The streets were clearing now and there weren't too many vehicles on the road. Helen made good time with steady continuity and had astoundingly good fortune with the traffic-lights. After a time, Anthony noticed that she was endeavouring to attract his attention. He spoke to her.

"What's the headache, Helen?"

She brought the car to a standstill by the side of the road and came round to him.

"Mere feminine curiosity, Mr. Bathurst. You know how we women love to interfere, don't you?"

"What is it you're so curious about?"

"Why are you doing this? Why didn't you pass it over to the regulars?"

"My dear girl—how could I? My conscience would have tormented me till I turned my face to the wall. Have a heart, Helen!"

"Well, if that's how it is, I think you're no end of a sport."

"Besides," Anthony went on, "I've given Andrew MacMorran something like a shipping order to see to before the clock strikes nine to-morrow morning. Believe me, his hands are as full as they possibly can be. Fuller than mine, by a long chalk."

Helen Repton hoisted herself back into the driving-seat. "All right," she said. "I'll believe you, Mr. Bathurst, where thousands wouldn't. We're O.K. for time. I've a fairly straight road now, and I'm going to step on it."

"Nothing," returned Anthony, "would suit me better."

Helen lived up to her declaration and the car purred on, fairly eating up the road. Suddenly, Anthony leant forward in his seat and spoke through the tube again.

"First left—then first right. After that you can't miss it. But do as I told you."

He found himself wondering, now, whether MacMorran had run into any awkward obstacles and also whether he had reached Quiddington St. Philip yet. Also, as to how Hemingway was faring on his particular job. A glance at his wrist-watch told him that the inspector must still be in the train.

The car swung to the right and the road rapidly deteriorated in quality. Then he realized that Helen Repton was pulling up. She came round to the window again.

"Am I far enough away—do you think? I should say it's a good quarter of a mile."

Anthony approved. "Just about the right distance, Helen." He got out and stood at the side. "Wait for me here, will you. Unfortunately, I can't promise you how long I shall be. But I assure you I won't make it a minute longer than necessary."

The time was now seventeen minutes past eleven.

3

When Anthony came to the house he saw, to his satisfaction, that there was no glimmer of light anywhere. Not a window showed the normal sign of room-occupation. He worked round to the back, and then carefully took off his shoes. He put these underneath a largish bush. There was a kind of loggia behind the french doors at the back of the house and it struck him that his luck *might* be in and the doors of it not too securely fastened. After all, he wasn't standing on the corner of Piccadilly Circus. At any rate, he would try those loggia doors before he decided on any other method of entry. But fortune, this time, was *not* on his side. The doors were locked, so Anthony turned his attention to the conservatory which, from what he could see of it, probably opened on to the lounge.

The door of the conservatory was also locked. Anthony deftly removed a pane of glass, flashed his torch through the aperture and turned the key on the inside. As far as he himself could tell, he had done his work noiselessly. A second later, he had closed the door behind him and felt the thick warm air of the greenhouse meet him and the heady fragrance of the plants within it. His torch then showed him the outline of a door. He opened it and entered a large room. It was empty. No sound came to him and he saw from the appointments that he was in the dining-room. He crossed it silently, opened another door and closed this behind him. This brought him into a wide passage along which he passed. He then came to another door on the left-hand side which he opened carefully and soundlessly.

After a few seconds' wait on the threshold, Anthony used his torch again. This room was also empty and, from the quick glance he was able to take at it, looked very much like a library and in all probability, he considered, the room he wanted. There were the remains of a fire on the hearth and his nose caught the tang of stale tobacco-smoke. Anthony went in on tip-toe and shut the door silently behind him. He stood and listened carefully for any sound from either above or below, but all was as quiet as the grave.

'A desk,' he whispered to himself, 'a desk! Much more likely a desk, I think, than a safe, in a house of this kind. Now where is it likely to be?'

A large book-case was prominent in the far corner of the room and at one side of the fire-place, which faced him, was a curtain, heavy in texture, which covered, doubtless, the window. But there was no sign in the room of either desk or safe. Anthony moved over to the curtain and pulled it to one side. To his surprise, it masked the entrance to a bedroom—which like the other rooms he had seen, was empty.

'Not in bed,' he thought, 'but out. I was wrong in my first impressions. Good job I was. I shall have to work quickly.'

He crossed the threshold of this bedroom and then, to his intense satisfaction, saw the desk for which he had been seeking. It was small, with brass bands, and a lock on the front of it. His hope was emptied in delight when he tried the lid and lifted it. As he had anticipated, the desk held documents and letters of importance. One by one, he examined the envelopes or outer coverings by the light of his torch and tossed them aside. There were a bundle of receipted bills, two insurance policies, several newspaper-cuttings, five stacks of letters neatly tied and, for one moment, as he looked at the heap on the floor, Anthony felt that he was destined for acute disappointment. But he continued to search methodically and rapidly through the contents of the desk. Eventually, he found a leather wallet. He emptied out the various compartments. But there were only visiting cards and a number of small photographs—of nobody whom he knew, as far as he could tell, from the cursory glance he gave them. Anthony replaced them in the wallet and bent again to his task. As a precaution, he held his torch as close to the floor as possible. Time was passing all too quickly for his peace of mind and he could see that he was now not a long way from the bottom of the pile.

But he still cherished hope within his bosom, because right at the lowest level he could see a number of large, legal-looking envelopes of extra-quality paper. Save an old programme of Henley regatta, there was nothing of any interest until he came to them. And then his heart gave a leap, for the third of these envelopes held what he had come for! Anthony examined it with the greatest curiosity and made a quick mental calculation. Yes—the date fitted—this should give him the vital clue necessary to forge the final link in the chain which he had constructed. With a concentrated effort of visual memory, he mastered the required details and put the papers back into the envelope. Then he swept the heap of papers from the floor beside him back into the desk, shut the lid and placed the desk itself in its original position. Now for his shoes, the car, and Helen Repton!

He made his way back to the conservatory, went out through the door, put his arm through the empty space of his own making, replaced the key in the lock and turned it. He then went into the garden, found a large stone, held the pane of glass in its place for a moment and smashed it with the stone so that the fragments fell inside the conservatory. Grinning to himself, he hied to the bush which concealed his shoes, found them there, and put them on. Just as he was tying the lace of the left shoe, he heard the sound of a car pulling up at the house, or at any rate, close to it. Luckily he was at the rear, so he stood in the shadow of the bush where he had hidden his shoes and awaited developments. At the same time, he was not absolutely certain as to where the garage was situated. Anthony stood by the bush for about half a minute before he heard the clearer sound of approaching car wheels. Judging by the route the car was taking, the garage must be somewhere near where he was standing. He immediately dropped down, therefore, and lay prone on the grass.

As he lay there, face to turf, he heard the sound of a man's footsteps, too close to him to be pleasant, and then the sound of the car door shutting. Then came another sound of a heavier door closing and more sounds of car wheels moving away again. To be followed by complete silence. Anthony raised himself on his elbows and listened carefully. All was quiet. The countryside was caressed by the Goddess of Night.

Anthony resolved to stay where he was for another couple of minutes before he moved. The time he had allotted himself brought him no further moments of apprehension. All remained quiet. He picked himself up from the grass, skirted the house and walked sharply back to where the 'Yard' car was waiting for him. Helen Repton was standing quietly at the side of it smoking a cigarette. Her eyes lit up with pleasure and relief when she saw Anthony.

"Thank heaven," she said; "I was just beginning to get a wee bit anxious about you."

He grinned. "Everything O.K.?" she asked.

"Helen," he replied. "Couldn't be better—I think I've got everything."

"I've thought that for a long time," she replied roguishly.

"I didn't mean that—flatterer! I meant all that I went for."

"Good," she said, "I'm so glad—*and* thrilled."

"Tell me, Helen," he went on, "did a car pass you a little while ago? Going in my direction?"

"No. Nothing. Nothing's been on the road at all. I've stayed here all the time in splendid isolation."

"My judgment was right, then. Good business. That's why I parked this side of the house."

"Where to now, Mr. Bathurst?" asked Helen Repton.

"The 'Yard,' Helen—and as soon as you can make it."

The time was now twenty-two minutes past midnight.

4

Anthony slept soundly in a large chair at the 'Yard' and breakfasted, feeling reasonably fresh in the circumstances, at eight o'clock sharp. Two messages had been left for him. Each seemed satisfactory. The first, that Superintendent Walter Hemingway would see him at nine a.m., and the second that Sir Austin Kemble, the Commissioner, would be along for the same purpose at ten o'clock precisely.

Anthony returned from breakfast at ten minutes to nine and asked the telephone operator to get him Chief Detective-Inspector MacMorran at the 'Saracen's Head,' Verne. He smiled to himself as he issued the instruction.

"I'll jolt him out of bed if necessary, the old scoundrel."

He waited patiently at the telephone for MacMorran to come on at the other end. At length the effort was rewarded. He heard the Inspector's familiar voice.

"Good morning, Mr. Bathurst. How's tricks?"

"Good morning, Andrew. Hope I haven't disturbed your porcine slumber. And the answer to your question—is—'mother and child both doing well, thank you.' My end's all gone according to plan. I'll let you have all the details when you come up here. Now—what about your end?"

"Well—I'll tell you what I've got. Don't know whether you'll be satisfied or not. Better get a pencil and paper and put this down."

"Shucks," returned Anthony—"sounds good—now, Andrew, I'm waiting for it. What have you got?"

"Well, as soon as I got back to Verne last night, I picked up a taxi outside the station and drove out to Quiddington St. Philip. To the 'Wheatsheaf,' as you may guess. The place was closed, of course—it was well after hours, but I told my taxi chap to wait and I walked up to the window of the bar-parlour which opens on to the road and knocked. . . ."

5

MacMorran tapped again with his knuckles on the window of the bar-parlour of the 'Wheatsheaf.' For the second time, he received no answer. But a third, and much louder, attempt brought him the required answer. Old man Willmott came shuffling to the door and MacMorran heard him unfasten the bolts.

"Who is it?" he called out and then spotted the inspector.

Without further ado, MacMorran slipped into the house and spoke quietly to the landlord.

"I didn't recognize you, sir, for the moment," apologized Willmott, "and o' course I wasn't expectin' you—no more trouble, I hope? To bring you 'ere as late in the day as this?"

MacMorran shook his head and told the landlord quietly what it was he wanted. Willmott nodded confirmation.

"They're both 'ere," he replied, "both o' the young gentlemen you mention. And I don't fancy as 'ow they've gone to bed yet. Still in the saloon, I believe. They're stayin' in the 'ouse, you know."

"Yes. So I believe. That's why I came along now."

"Come this way, sir," went on Willmott—"you can speak to 'em private like—they've got the saloon to themselves."

He opened the door of the saloon to usher the inspector in. Willmott had been right. Fothergill and Harcourt were in there playing darts.

'Most appropriate,' thought MacMorran, as he signed to Willmott to refrain from announcing him. He stood in the doorway and watched Fothergill, who had his back to him, go 'round the clock' with ease, certainty and deadly accuracy. Harcourt then took a turn, performing with an almost equal measure of skill. MacMorran stood where he was until Fothergill, turning slightly to pick up a glass, saw him and waved a cordial salutation.

"Come in, Inspector. Harcourt and I were just spoiling a quarter of an hour before hitting the hay."

MacMorran walked towards them. "If it's not too inconvenient, I wanted a word with you two gentlemen," he said with a benignant smile, "it may be that you'll be asked to come up to the 'Yard' in a day or so. With regard to certain information affecting Keegan. The chap was heard to threaten the late Justice Flagon in this pub. The Commissioner is considering the possibility of interviewing several people, and you two gentlemen are amongst the number. Shall I find you here, say, at the beginning of next week?"

"You'll find me," said Fothergill, "at Seven, Little Fanthorpe Street. I'm returning to town to-morrow. Harcourt can speak for himself." MacMorran jotted down the address. "Should never have taken you for a Londoner, Mr. Fothergill. Shows how mistaken one can be. I'll bet you weren't born there."

"You'd win," replied Maurice Fothergill shortly.

"Kent?" queried MacMorran with a knowing look.

"No. Sussex, Hayward's Heath."

"Go on. That's rather interesting. I had an uncle lived there. Used to play for the local cricket team. Went there in 1919."

"Two years before I entered this vale of tears, Inspector. And I didn't stay there long—so I probably had to forgo the pleasure of meeting him."

MacMorran nodded casually. "Reckon you're right." He turned to Ronald Harcourt. "And what would your address be, Mr. Harcourt? For the next few days? In the event of your story being wanted in support of Mr. Fothergill's?"

"Number eleven, Lancaster Mansions, S.W." Harcourt appeared to be on the point of adding something to the bare statement, but pulled himself up rather abruptly. MacMorran didn't miss the opportunity. He cut in like a shot.

"Yes? You were about to say?"

"Merely that I can't tell you much. Really nothing at all. So I don't feel that I—"

"That's all right, Mr. Harcourt. Don't worry about it. Very likely you'll not be called upon at all. I shouldn't be a bit surprised."

He assessed Harcourt's features with an amused look on his face. "Lancaster Mansions—eh? Now I should say you *were* a Londoner. Bow bells and all that."

"Then you'd be wrong again," replied Harcourt curtly. "I was born in Simla." He turned away with more than a hint of discourtesy and started to replace the darts in their respective boxes.

"Well, gentlemen," said MacMorran, "that's how it is. I happened to be passing on my way back to Verne and I thought I'd fix that up while I had the chance. Wasn't sure, you see, how much longer you'd be staying here. And now, I'll wish you both a very good night."

MacMorran found Willmott and the latter showed him out of the front door. The inspector signalled to his taxi that he was ready. As he was about to enter the cab, a car passed him before pulling up by the kerb a few yards away and a man got out. To MacMorran's intense surprise, he saw that it was Michael Keegan—almost the very last person he would have expected to alight from a car of that description. The car then made off again at a good pace.

"'Saracen's Head,'" said MacMorran, pondering deeply over the incident.

The time was then ten minutes past twelve.

"So there you are, Mr. Bathurst. That's the lot," concluded Mac-Morran over the telephone. "That's precisely what happened."

"So that's up to the fall of the last wicket—eh, Andrew? Good man—you've done well."

"What about Harcourt—though? That's a nasty one. Can't see that Simla's much good to us from any point of view."

Anthony chuckled over the telephone. "So he pulled an Indian trick, did he? Master Harcourt! Don't worry over that, Andrew. There are others. I can approach that in another way. Now—Fothergill. Hayward's Heath 1921, I think you said. I'll deal with that one, too. So your part's over. What time will you be up here?"

"By midday, Mr. Bathurst. I'd better not make it any later, considering what's in front of us for the rest of the day."

"No. Perhaps you hadn't. And I've got a special commission in front of me this morning. Thank heaven it'll be the last one, I fancy. As far as this particular case is concerned. Now there was one other thing I wanted to ask you about. What the blazes was it? Oh—I know—the seating plan of this evening's dinner. Were you able to manage that for me?"

"I think that'll be all right, you'll find. Superintendent Heming-way'll see you with regard to that when he contacts you this morning. The old man gave him special instructions himself. You won't have long to wait. That all O.K.?"

"O.K., Andrew, and thanks for the 'gen.' See you later then—and I'll make your old flappers waggle when we do meet. Cheerio—and many thanks."

Anthony replaced the receiver. So much for Part One.

6

Superintendent Walter Hemingway arrived punctually at nine o'clock. His face was wreathed in smiles and generally exuded satisfaction when he came in to Anthony.

"Good morning, Mr. Bathurst. Pleased to see you looking so fit. Now which would you like first?"

Anthony grinned. "Good morning, Super. The compliment is returned. This is very nice of you. Now—let me see." Anthony caressed the ridge of his jaw. "Bentley—I fancy, first of all. Yes— that'll be best friend Bentley. In whom I have a certain interest. What can you tell me about him?"

Hemingway hooked a chair towards him with his toe and sat on it. "I handled that myself, Mr. Bathurst. In the circs I fancy it was just as well I did. Well—first of all I rubbed along to the offices of the *Daily Fanfare* in Fleet Street. I got in there about half-past eleven, I should think. A chap came to meet me, quite the la-di-da, don't you know—and sang out what did I want. . . ."

7

"Good evening," said Superintendent Hemingway.

"What can I do for you?"

"I'm Superintendent Hemingway of the C.I.D. Can you put me in touch with one of your chaps by the name of John Bentley? If you could I'd be very much obliged—I'd like a word with him."

The man whom he addressed looked at him a little doubtfully. "I'm afraid," he said, "that Bentley's not on the premises, just at this moment. So you're unlucky. But I'll inquire for you to make certain. You won't mind waiting a minute?"

Hemingway kicked his heels in the general inquiry room of the *Daily Fanfare* offices for a matter of nearly five minutes before the well-groomed gentleman returned. There was any amount of bustle and activity in the office, and he began to wonder if he would be destined to spend the remainder of that night and the early hours of the following morning in a fruitless hunt for this reporter, Bentley. Which would be definitely not so good! Especially bearing in mind the vital importance with which the old man had invested this particular piece of business. Still—it was no good meeting trouble half-way, thought Hemingway—and perhaps when this *Fanfare* fellow came back, he would bring him more reassuring news, or at any rate, something a little more tangible for him to work on.

But Superintendent Hemingway, alas, was doomed to disappointment. The man returned and shook his head.

"I'm frightfully sorry but, as I thought, Bentley's not on the premises. I've spoken to his particular 'buddy' and as far as the chap knows, Bentley's not covering anything special this evening. So that it's just on the cards you may find him at home. More than that, even, he *might* be between the sheets. At the same time—you know—reporters are notoriously late birds—so you can't bank on that. Is it terribly important that you see him to-night? Because to-morrow—"

"Yes. It is, rather. I think you'd better give me his address and I'll pop along there."

"Right-o. That won't be any trouble. Hope it won't be too far afield."

Hemingway waited a second time for the newspaper man to come back to him. But on this latter occasion, the delay was of considerably shorter duration. The man for whom he waited entered with a slip of paper in his hand.

"Here you are, Superintendent. Nineteen, Ringwood Avenue, Hammersmith."

"Might have been worse," commented Hemingway, "might have been a great deal worse. Might have been Isle of Wight." He turned to his companion. "Many thanks for the information. Sorry to have given you so much trouble."

"No trouble," came the reply. "Pleased to fix you up. Good night and good hunting."

Hemingway turned on his heel and walked up Fleet Street until he spotted a taxi that was disengaged. He beckoned the driver over to him and the cab pulled up at his side with a grinding of brakes. The 'Yard' superintendent indicated the address he wanted and said in addition: "And I don't mind how quickly you make it."

The driver obliged to the utmost, did good time, had more than average luck with the traffic-lights, and deposited Hemingway outside Bentley's place of residence as Big Ben struck twelve times.

"Wait for me," said the superintendent curtly, "the man I want may be out. But wait, in any case."

Hemingway walked quickly up to the door of a small villa-type house and rang the bell. It jangled noisily through the quietness of the night. But that was all which did happen. No answer of any kind from the interior of the house came to the questing Hemingway. He took the natural course and rang again. With the same negative result. Hemingway thereupon rang for a third time, but once again the effort was unproductive. He stood there on the step for a moment weighing many 'pros' and various 'cons.' Then he ran quickly down to the waiting taxi-cab.

"Fleet Street again, driver. *Daily Fanfare* offices."

The cab slewed round and started the return journey. Hemingway dashed into the offices and had the good fortune to find the same man there who had attended to him before.

"Sorry to trouble you again, but our friend Bentley's not at home. So I'm still where I was. I've tried three times at his house and got no answer."

"H'm. That's strange—that. He's certainly not out on anything for us." The man thought for a moment and then his face cleared a little. "I know," he volunteered, "I've had a brain-wave. Not too soon, you probably think. I can tell you where he is probably. Down in the country. He's got a country cottage out in the wilds, somewhere. You know—the sort of place he uses for week-ends and holidays. No water, no light, no indoor sanitation! A home from home. I believe he occasionally spends a night there when he feels in the mood. That's it. That's where he is in all probability. I only wish I'd thought of it before."

Hemingway realized that, if possible, he must force the issue. "That's a pity," he said, "as I told you, I wanted to see him on a matter of some importance and I'm up against the time factor. I've never actually met him in person. 'John Bentley,' isn't it? I knew a family of that name near my home town when I was a boy."

"Bolton—would it be?" inquired the *Fanfare* man.

"No. Miles from there. East coast. Near Ipswich. Pin Mill locality."

"Wrong man, then. I can tell you that for a certainty. Our Bentley's a Lancastrian—born and bred."

"My man would be about forty-five," said Hemingway meditatively, "between, say, forty-five and fifty. How old's your Bentley?"

"I can tell you. I can easily turn it up for you. I've all the staff records in the next room. Wait half a jiffy, and I'll let you know." The man disappeared into the adjoining room. He was soon back with a card in his hand.

"Bentley was born in 1882. At Bolton—Lancashire. You know— 'The Trotters'—Pike's Lane and Burnden Park. Expect you've heard of 'em. You remember the white horse at Wembley, don't you?"

"I get you," returned Hemingway—"and he's certainly not the man I was thinking of. Can't be. Well—many thanks again for all your trouble. I must try to contact him somewhere sometime early to-morrow."

"Good. If I were you, I'd 'phone him here, somewhere about lunchtime, to-morrow. You'd stand a good chance of picking him up. This place is stiff with reporters about that time. He usually pops in before going out for his snack."

"Many thanks for the tip. I will."

Hemingway went back to his taxi. "Scotland Yard," he said, "and that'll be the bundle."

"So I don't know whether you'll be satisfied with that, Mr. Bathurst, or not. In the circumstances, it was the best I could do." Hemingway concluded his recital on a note of apology.

Anthony chuckled. "Out at his country residence, was he? Out in the wilds somewhere—eh? I'll say he was, Walter. Anyhow, don't you worry. I'm not going to, I assure you. Now—listen—instructions passed to you. Put this down for me, will you, please?"

Hemingway produced pencil and pad. Anthony dictated. "Fothergill—Maurice. Born Hayward's Heath, Sussex, 1921. Got that? Good. Bentley—John. Born Bolton, Lancashire, 1882."

"Yes, Mr. Bathurst."

"I want those verified if possible through Somerset House before twelve o'clock noon. If anything's wrong with either of them, let MacMorran have the dope at once. Is that clear, Super?"

"Yes, Mr. Bathurst. I'll see to that for you."

"Good. That's nice of you."

Anthony looked down at his watch. "A quarter past nine, Walter. If only I had another twenty-four precious hours. All the same, we haven't done too badly." A smile twisted his mouth. "We're up against it, Walter me lad." Anthony looked at the superintendent, but in a second his mind was off again. "Kick me, Walter. Kick me hard in the tenderest part. 'Twould be well merited. I was on the point of forgetting something. Plan of the dinner-seating! Got it?"

"Yes, Mr. Bathurst. All ready for you. I was waiting for you to ask for it. Here we are."

Hemingway went to a side-table. "Wrap it up for me, there's a winsome Walter."

"Wrap it up for you? Don't you want to look at it?"

"No time now, Walter. Later on. In the car, I will. Sorry, old man, and all that—and bags of thanks for all you've done. But it's this ruddy time-factor that's the nigger in the wood-pile. Oh—I know—be an angel and tell Miss Repton to have the car ready in two minutes. And give this note to Sir Austin Kemble for me. Thank you, Walter."

"Yes, Mr. Bathurst."

Hemingway took the letter, shrugged his shoulders and went to find Helen Repton. He'd never before seen Anthony quite so worried as this.

The time was now seventeen minutes past nine.

CHAPTER III

1

THE car was waiting for him when Anthony went down. Helen Repton was walking up and down by the side of it. She turned and saw Anthony with a parcel under each arm, and brightened perceptibly.

"Good morning, Helen," said Anthony. "How on earth do you manage to do it? I confess I wish I knew the secret."

In the precincts of the 'Yard' Helen was regimental.

"Do what, sir?" she asked demurely.

"Look so fresh after being up half the night."

She coloured, much to her own annoyance, and gave him a smile for an answer. Then she walked to the door and opened it for him. "And where to, this morning, sir?"

"The same journey, Helen, as you took me yesterday afternoon. Hart's Heath. The Lord Chief Justice, Viscount Fifoot. Oh—and Helen!"

"Yes, sir."

"I shall probably want you all day. You know that?"

"Yes, sir. I was told."

"You got my message—in full?"

"Yes, sir."

"Where's the . . . er . . . thingummybob?"

She blushed again. "In the front, sir. Both lots are there. You'll tell me, I suppose, when I'm to—"

"I will, Helen. The very moment."

"Very good, sir. And I hope I shan't let you down, sir."

"I'm sure you won't. You never have yet. And if you can knock a few minutes off the time you took yesterday to get to Hart's Heath, the other half of my kingdom's yours, Helen Repton."

"I'll do my best, sir."

She closed the door on Anthony and went round to the driving-seat. The time was now nine-thirty.

2

At Lottingham, Anthony told her to pull up. She brought the car to a standstill outside an hotel which showed the sign of the 'White Bear.' Anthony got out and walked round to her.

"You've done well so far, Helen. So well that we'll stop and have one. We can afford to. Country hours out here, you know."

He turned away to enter the hotel and then realized that Helen Repton was still sitting at the wheel. He went back to her.

"Come in, Helen. That was an invitation. With me."

She shook her head. "I'm quite O.K. here, sir."

"Don't be ridiculous. I want to buy you a drink."

She laughed attractively and got out. Anthony shepherded her into the bar. "What shall it be?" he asked.

"One half-pint of bitter, sir—in a tankard, please. If you wouldn't mind asking."

Anthony grinned. "Cut the parade stuff, Helen. We're well away from the 'Yard' now."

She laughed. Anthony ordered the beer. "May I drink you a toast, Mr. Bathurst?"

He shook his head. "That's the wrong way round. I should drink to you and your bright eyes."

"No. Not this time. This is a special occasion." She raised her tankard. "Here's to your success—*to-night*."

Anthony cocked his head at her quizzically.

"I'm 'in' on it, you know," she explained, "just a little."

"Thank you. I appreciate the interest. Now drink up and back to the road again."

The remainder of the journey was executed at a pace which suited Anthony down to the ground, and when Helen Repton drew up outside the residence of the Lord Chief Justice, she walked round to Anthony with an eager question.

"Well, Mr. Bathurst. Have I done well—or have I?"

Anthony looked at his watch. "I'll say you have. What do you reckon you've knocked off, Helen?"

"I know," she said with a laugh, "I just looked at the clock in the dash-board. I've cut yesterday's time by eight minutes. Not so bad, considering we stopped on the way at the 'White Bear,' Lottingham."

"I make it nine, but we won't argue about it. What's an unforgiving minute?"

"What do I do now, Mr. Bathurst?"

"Wait here, I think. For the time being. I'm afraid you'll have to. But I'll come out and see you again before very long. I shall know most of what there is to be known within the next half-hour. Cheer-o for now."

He waved to her and walked up to the house. Anthony knew that if the edifice he had erected were soundly foundationed he was on the verge of revelation.

The time was now sixteen minutes past eleven.

3

The Lord Chief Justice and Sybil Fifoot came to him in the morning-room. Anthony could see at once that each was living perilously. Each was the victim of the erosion of anxiety.

"Good morning, Mr. Bathurst. We won't pretend we aren't pleased to see you. Because we are." They each shook hands with him cordially. "Sit down, do. And—please—have you any news for us?"

Anthony took a comfortable arm-chair. "Yes, my lord. I can say that I do bring you news. And to my mind, very vital news."

A flicker of apprehension passed over Viscount Fifoot's face.

"Do you mean . . . er . . . that you are the bearer of bad news?"

Anthony shook his head. "Not at all, my lord. Far from that. In fact I think we might almost embrace optimism and call it definitely good news. At least, that's my own opinion."—

"I am most relieved."

"I cannot thank you enough," added Lady Fifoot. "I haven't had a very good night and I had hardly dared hope that you were a harbinger of good tidings. Now I'm beginning to feel better already."

"Yes. I think it's good news," went on Anthony, "because it gives us, or I think it's *going* to give us, a certain degree of knowledge, which we were previously without. And knowledge *must* mean, not only that we possess a more adequate equipment in defence, but also a more potent striking force in attack. You agree with me, sir?"

"Most certainly do I agree, Mr. Bathurst. It's almost a case of 'ça va sans dire.' You will tell me, of course, what exactly this knowledge consists of? Because, I take it, you were referring to something— shall we say—entirely new? Something which previously you hadn't been able to consider?"

"Oh—yes—that is my intention. But first of all—in order that I may make sure of the position—I'm bound to ask you certain questions."

Lady Sybil intervened with a smile and an outstretched hand. "Before the inquisition starts—may a mere woman interfere? With a purely mundane, but nevertheless very necessary question! And that's this—you'll stay to lunch, Mr. Bathurst, of course?"

"Thank you, Lady Fifoot—I'd love to—but no. Please excuse me. I'll tell you the reason. I can't afford to lose a minute, there's so much for me to do. But if you could do a few sandwiches for me in, say, ten minutes from now and also send some out to my chauffeuse, I'd bear you eternal gratitude. And perhaps the lunch you spoke of may belong to the future."

"I shall be only too pleased—although I'm an acutely disappointed woman. I'll see to it at once for you." Lady Fifoot rang the bell.

"Can I start now?" inquired Anthony.

"Certainly," replied the Lord Chief Justice. "I shall be all attention."

Anthony chose his words carefully. "A threat which was offered against Mr. Justice Flagon and Mr. Justice Madrigal, unhappily, has proved only too real and has meant death to each of them. That threat is now overhanging your head, my lord, as you yourself are aware. I have been forced to look, therefore, for the common factor as it affects Flagon, Madrigal and you, my lord. Call it, if you like, the natural L.C.M. of the whole ghastly business."

Fifoot nodded and smiled. "I'm not in any ... er ... way attracted by what I've always regarded as the low cunning of mathematics, Mr. Bathurst, but I think I know what you mean."

Lady Fifoot leant across the arm of her chair and said: "Even I can understand that."

"Good," remarked Anthony, "that disposes of Stage Number One. Now, my lord, if I asked you to supply an immediate answer to the question—'can you furnish me with that L.C.M.,' realizing the number of years you have devoted to your most distinguished career—I should feel that I was taxing your memory far too heavily and imposing a far greater strain on you than would be fair. In other words, I should feel that you had acquitted yourself creditably if you supplied me with that answer within a week."

"Again, I think I see what you mean, Bathurst, and again I think that I agree with you. But a week's a long time, isn't it?"

"Excellent. You get my point entirely. We'll call that Stage Two." This time Anthony leant forward in the direction of his two hearers. "But suppose, my lord, and Lady Fifoot, *I* give *you* the name of that L.C.M.—as I feel confident I can—can you then give me the foundation-stone of the little edifice that I've been able to build up?"

"Go ahead, Bathurst," said the Lord Chief Justice quietly, "and then it'll be my turn to see what I can do for you."

Anthony rose from the arm-chair and stood in front of the fireplace. The Lord Chief Justice and Lady Fifoot looked up at him expectantly.

"The key-word to the puzzle, my lord, as I see it, is the name of 'Pemberton.' Does that convey anything to you? Does it in any way strike a chord of memory?"

He waited with a mixed emotion of eagerness and anxiety for the response. He was overjoyed to see Lady Fifoot nod understandingly. Viscount Fifoot also accepted the reference.

"Yes," he said in measured tones, "I can tell you what the name of Pemberton means to me."

Anthony heaved a sigh of relief. He knew now, with a completely satisfying certainty, that he had not laboured in vain. But he asked yet a further question to make assurance doubly sure.

"*And* to Justice Flagon and Justice Madrigal? It must be relevant to all three?"

"Yes, Bathurst. To all three. To Flagon, to Madrigal and to me. Come and sit down in the arm-chair again, and I'll explain in greater detail the terms of the reference. You'll be interested."

Anthony obeyed and sat down again.

"Arthur Pemberton," went on the Lord Chief Justice, "was a young fellow sentenced to death for the murder of a prostitute at East Dulwich just over a year ago. He was quite young as things go, somewhere round twenty-five, I should think. He was a member of a Lancashire family—the father had come to London some years previously in connection with his business. I fancy he was a printer or something of that kind. Mr. Justice Wilbraham tried the case with Sir Graham Preston appearing for the Crown. Pemberton was defended, and defended most ably, by Keith Salt. The defence which he presented pivoted on an alibi. But the witnesses for the defence were not exactly noteworthy for their integrity. And the jury decided against him and rightly so, in my opinion. Well—as you may guess—Pemberton appealed against the verdict. I presided at the Court of Appeal and sat with Flagon J. and Madrigal J. in support. The grounds of appeal were misdirection by Wilbraham. The appeal was lost—my learned brethren and I were unanimous—and Arthur Pemberton paid the penalty for his crime a few weeks later. There you are, Bathurst—there you have the Pemberton case as I can remember it."

Anthony thought for a moment. "Was there any demonstration, can you remember, when you pronounced judgment?"

Viscount Fifoot's brows furrowed in thought. "Let me see now—was there?"

Anthony waited patiently for the answer. Lady Fifoot was leaning forward anxiously, hanging on her husband's words. Eventually,

Anthony saw the Lord Chief Justice nod to himself and seemingly emerge from his reverie.

"Yes. Yes. I can remember now. It's come back to me. There *was* some sort of demonstration when I gave judgment and dismissed the appeal. I'd better describe it, perhaps, as an incipient demonstration. It never developed into anything at all serious. A man stood up and shouted something. A protest of some kind, of course. I fancy it was Pemberton's father. But he was soon pulled down by the people who were with him and the incident closed."

His mood and manner suddenly changed and he faced practical issues. "What does it all mean, Bathurst? Is it revenge?"

"I fear so, my lord, if I read the signs aright."

"I see. Yes—yes! Well, we know now where we are. It's better like that. One feels that the ambush, as it were, is no longer there." Anthony was considering something. "Tell me, sir," he said, "going back to that day when Pemberton's appeal was heard, how did Keith Salt take the decision?"

Fifoot smiled and shook his head. "Rather badly, I'm afraid. He'd put up a really brilliant defence—you know—worthy of Marshall Hall at his best—and it was a bitter blow to him to be beaten at both the trial and the appeal. But I'm rather afraid that Keith Salt has always been that way inclined. A bad loser, I fear! He has an extremely brilliant mind—and like many other men—finds it frightfully galling when an inferior one gets the better of him—as occasionally, of course, in life, must happen."

"I see. I'd wondered about that. You've heard, no doubt, what was attached to the two darts which killed Flagon and Madrigal?"

"Some sort of slip of paper, wasn't it?"

Anthony nodded. "Yes. With these words. 'A nice sharp quillet'! Ay!"

He paused deliberately to see what reaction came from the Lord Chief Justice. Viscount Fifoot frowned and Lady Fifoot looked puzzled. There came a fairly lengthy silence.

"Yes," said his lordship eventually with a nod of the head. "I think that again I see. I had to cast my mind back several years to capture the allusion. And then it eluded me for some considerable time. I'm afraid I'm getting old. It's Shakespeare, isn't it? 'These nice sharp quillets of the law?'" He paused as Anthony had before him. "Yes," he said again, "I'm beginning to see even more clearly than I did. The quillet—eh?"

He turned to Anthony and now there was fire in the old man's eyes. "Bathurst—my most sincere congratulations! An amazingly able piece of work on your part and one that any man living might well be proud of."

"This is all very well," burst in Lady Fifoot, "but—*pour moi*—I'm completely in the dark. And I simply hate that to happen. It would be very sweet of somebody to lighten an old woman's darkness."

Anthony seized the opportunity thus afforded him. It gave him the chance to ask the Lord Chief Justice the question that had been on his lips for the last few moments.

"Explain to Lady Fifoot, sir, what you understand by a quillet."

"I'm sorry, my dear," said Fifoot, "I forgot. If I interpret a quillet as a 'false charge,' or an unjust accusation, you will see where our friend Bathurst is getting to."

"I see," said Lady Fifoot. "Now I, too, begin to understand."

There came a tap on the door. "Here are your sandwiches, Mr. Bathurst. And I thought you'd probably like a bottle of beer with them. You look that kind of man. Oh—it's all right, don't be alarmed—I mean that as a compliment, I assure you."

"And Miss Repton?" Anthony answered.

"She has hers, too," replied Lady Fifoot.

"Thank you very much. And I rather fancy she's that kind of woman."

"How delightful," answered Lady Fifoot.

The time was now nineteen minutes to twelve.

4

Ten minutes later, Anthony rose to take his departure. "You'll receive full and detailed instructions, sir, from Sir Austin Kemble within the next half an hour. Don't worry with regard to anything. We have everything well in hand. Adhere rigidly to all the plans that are made, try to forget the abnormal side and take the entire evening in your stride. Right from the moment you leave here until the peril has been averted. And if you obey implicitly, I'll give you my word, sir, that we won't let you down."

The Lord Chief Justice and Lady Fifoot each shook hands with him.

"Mr. Bathurst," said the latter, "I for one cannot thank you enough. When I think of all you have done for my husband and in so short a time, too, and of all you are going to do—"

"That's all right," smiled Anthony—"wait until it's all over and then ask me to lunch. An invitation I've been forced to refuse to-day. But I'm sure you understand."

"Where are you going now—back to Scotland Yard?"

"Not yet, Lady Fifoot. I'm going now to make my preliminary contact with an extremely skilful dart-thrower who is also a close student of Shakespeare. That contact, which I hope to make before very long, will then remain unbroken until the arrest is made.'; Wish me luck."

Viscount Fifoot sat down. His face was heavy and troubled. Part of the dreadful truth had now been revealed to him.

Anthony ran down the drive to the car and Helen Repton. She had finished her sandwiches and beer and was ready and waiting.

The time now was exactly twelve o'clock.

CHAPTER IV

1

"I WANT to 'phone, Helen," said Anthony, "at the first available place we come to. Keep a look-out for me, will you? And you know where to make for now, don't you?"

"Yes, Mr. Bathurst. And I'll keep an eye open for a 'phone. Oh—and thank you for the sandwiches. They were really delicious." Anthony shook his head. "Not me, Helen. Thank rather (a) Lady Fifoot or (b) Lady Fifoot's cook." His eyes twinkled.

"Do I drive fast?" enquired Miss Repton.

"You do. As though you were the devil herself."

"Herself?" she queried.

"'Twill do," answered Anthony, "for this particular occasion. Seems more appropriate somehow."

He got in and she shut the door. "O.K., Helen. Push her along." The car ran for a matter of four minutes and then stopped. Anthony saw the telephone-kiosk on the left-hand side of the road. Helen came round and opened the door for him.

"Shan't be overlong," he said as he alighted—*"we hope!"*

The box, fortunately, was unoccupied and he was quickly through to Inspector Catchpole.

"Your message received, Mr. Bathurst," said the Verne inspector, "and everything arranged as you wanted it. An officer named Chatterton has been sent down from the 'Yard' and he's already been on the job for over an hour. He seems to be right on top of what's required and he's reporting back to me every half-hour. His last report—about twenty minutes ago, to be precise—was 'everything O.K. and well in hand.'"

"That's splendid, Inspector," replied Anthony. "That's a load oft' my mind, I can tell you." He thought for a moment or so and then put another question. Again Catchpole's ready reply reassured him.

"He's actually *in* the hotel at the moment, Mr. Bathurst. I believe he returned yesterday. Inspector MacMorran made sure of that before he left for town and he hasn't moved since. What's that? Oh—I see—all right—very well—I'm pleased to hear that's satisfactory. Good-bye, Mr. Bathurst."

Anthony hung up and walked back to the car. "O.K., Helen. No more interruptions. Buzz along."

She lingered for a second. "When do I—?" She paused.

He grinned at her cheerfully. "Not yet. I'll tell you when. Possess your soul in patience and don't be in such a flaming hurry. You girls are all the same."

"Very good, Mr. Bathurst. I'm in your hands."

She returned grin for grin, skipped back to the wheel and slid into speed almost immediately. Anthony took up the parcel which Superintendent Hemingway had wrapped up for him, untied the tape and opened it. He took out the plan of the seating for the dinner that evening which the Middle Temple was giving at the Diadem Rooms. He placed it across his knees and studied it carefully. Keith

Salt was not at the top table. Anthony had thought that he probably would be. Actually, Anthony saw, Salt was at a side-table on the chairman's left hand. Anthony examined the plan with scrupulous and painstaking exactitude. He went through the various names one by one, sifting each one, as it were, through a sieve of his own mental consciousness.

The occupants of the Press table were shrouded, as he had anticipated, with anonymity. This fact, naturally, afforded him no help. It was when he reached the close analysis of the special seats at the chairman's table, that he received a jolt of surprise. For at Viscount Fifoot's immediate left he read this. 'The Minister of Justice for the Dominion of Canada, Mr. Louis de Monterey.'

Anthony sat back in his seat and whistled softly under his breath. This was an absolute eye-opener for him. "So that's how it is, is it?" he murmured.

The complementary position he discovered five seats away—'Sir Claude de Monterey.' "Must be either his brother or his cousin." commented Anthony.

He looked at his watch. The time was half-past twelve.

2

Anthony picked up the speaking-tube and called through again to Helen Repton.

"Miss Repton—I'm sorry—Helen—stop at the next hotel on the right. The name should be familiar to you when you see it. Run the car into the garage and then I'll come in with you. I'm first of all going to telephone again. You go to the receptionist and ask for the number of your room. When she tells you—'then' will be the time for which you've been so anxiously awaiting. When you're ready after that, make for the vestibule by the receptionist's and wait for me. I shan't keep you waiting too long, I hope. Everything O.K.?"

Helen Repton turned and nodded to him. "Yes, Mr. Bathurst." She ran the car into the hotel garage as Anthony had instructed her, grabbed her case, waved her hand to him and proceeded on the lines he had indicated. Anthony, fully prepared, returned the wave, followed her in, and straightway found the hotel telephone. Again he called Inspector Catchpole at Verne and repeated the terms of the previous enquiry. And again the Verne inspector was able to reassure him.

"Don't worry. Everything's still all right, Mr. Bathurst. No need to be anxious at all. I'm still getting regular messages from Chatterton on the 'phone as you arranged and he reports 'everything still O.K.'"

"Good. When's he due on next?"

"In about three minutes from now, Mr. Bathurst. Would you like a word with him yourself when he comes through?"

"I think I should, Inspector Catchpole. If it's no trouble to you, I'll 'phone through again then in exactly four minutes' time. He's pretty punctual as a rule, isn't he?"

"So far, he's been on time on every occasion. So you should be all serene at the time you mention."

"Excellent. Expect my call, then, when I said."

Anthony rang off and then waited by the telephone until the due time had elapsed. When he got through to the police station at Verne for the second time, his luck still held. Chatterton was on the line to Inspector Catchpole.

"Good afternoon, Mr. Bathurst," said the plain-clothes man, "the inspector here just whispered you wanted a word with me. Well, you can rest easy, sir—everything's O.K. this end and going according to plan. Our friend's in the house and the car's still in the garage. Not a smell of any sort of move yet awhile."

"That's good, Chatterton. I'm more than satisfied. My opinion is the move'll take place somewhere round four o'clock. That's how I read it. And that's when I shall turn up."

"Suppose it's before that?"

"You must telephone Inspector Catchpole at once in that case and he'll tell you how to act. He has full instructions for all emergencies. But I fancy I'm on pretty safe ground. Four o'clock, you'll find, won't be very far out. It's on the cards I'll speak to you again before I make my next move."

"Right-o, then, Mr. Bathurst. I'll ring off now and get back on the job. There's one thing, I can actually cover the place from inside this box. But I expect you know all about that."

"Cheer-o, Chatterton, until about four p.m., then. Thanks for the 'gen' and good hunting."

Anthony replaced the receiver and walked slowly back to the receptionist. He smiled at her. She smiled at him.

"What number?" he asked simply.

"Twenty-seven, sir," she answered.

"And you fixed Miss Repton up all right?"

"Yes, sir."

"Good. Thanks very much."

As he made his way upstairs, carrying one of the burdens he had brought with him, he looked at his wrist-watch. The time was now twenty-five minutes past three.

3

When he met Helen Repton again, it was just outside the office of the receptionist.

"My dear Helen," he said, "to compliment you on your appearance would be the equivalent of gilding the lily. You almost take my breath away. You look a really lovely lovely. *You've got it all!*"

Helen Repton made a mock curtsey. "I am delighted that Mr. Bathurst is satisfied with Miss Repton's appearance."

Anthony continued: "Your evening coat is exactly right, and your make-up a work of art. Also, the long cigarette-holder couldn't be improved upon. It gives just the right touch. All I wish is that this joint effort on our part had been dedicated to a better cause."

"Such as?" asked Helen with a spice of mischief.

"Well now—what can I say? I know. Dinner with me—*a deux*."

A spot of colour, born of a blush, showed momentarily on Miss Repton's cheeks. "How are things—otherwise?" she inquired, changing the subject.

"O.K. Everything's going splendidly. I've just had my last word with Chatterton, and we're all right. Drive straight along the main road and turn down by the avenue of poplars. You can't miss it. It's about five minutes' run—not more. I'll tell you when to pull up." Anthony adjusted his monocle and draped the white evening-dress scarf round his neck and across the front of his collar.

"We are, Helen," he murmured, "very definitely—the berries."

They walked to the car. The clock in the receptionist's office showed the time at five minutes to four.

4

Helen Repton, assured, poised and débonnaire, drove the car along the main road as Anthony had directed her. She came to the avenue of poplars on her left and turned down it. About three hundred yards down the turning Anthony, now at her side, turned in his seat and tapped her on the arm. Helen pulled up. The car waited. Anthony made no move. Within a matter of seconds, a man came running towards them. It was Chatterton.

"You were right, sir," he said, rather breathlessly, and flinging one arm up. "The car's out of the garage and in the front runway. It was moved about three minutes ago. Will you be guided by me and take a chance? I don't think, in the circumstances, you can possibly do better."

"Tell me, Chatterton," said Anthony quietly—"what you advise I should do."

"Don't wait here any longer. Run your car round to the main road again and cruise fairly slowly towards town. The other car'll pass you, I should say, within ten minutes at the outside. It's a dark blue limousine, and I fancy—though I won't be absolutely sure—that the number's 2153. If you aren't passed in ten minutes, slow down for a while—and then I'm pretty certain you soon will be. O.K.?"

"O.K., Chatterton, and thanks a lot for all you've done. Tell Miss Repton, will you?"

Chatterton's head bent towards Helen Repton. Anthony saw her listen to him and then nod. Chatterton stood away to the kerb and the car slid smoothly forward again.

The time was four-four.

5

Helen and Anthony made the main road again as Chatterton had suggested they should and the car headed west. They cruised along for about a quarter of an hour without being passed on the road. Anthony thought of Chatterton's words and gave Helen the signal to decrease speed a bit. The last thing he wanted at this stage of the proceedings was to get too far ahead. A few minutes later, however, his period of suspense ended. Suddenly he saw Helen make a quick movement with one of her hands. He guessed the intention behind the movement and waited for what was coming. He hadn't to wait long. A dark blue limousine came up behind them. Helen casually gave it the road and it swept by them. Anthony was just conscious of a man's face above a huddled coat-collar and saw the wispy smoke of a cigarette. He tried hard to catch a glimpse of the car's registration index mark and number, but its pace was too quick for him and the effort was unsuccessful.

As the car tore by, Anthony saw and entirely approved Helen's nonchalant pose at, and handling of, her driving-wheel. She looked exactly as he had wished and arranged for her to look. That she was with him and that the two of them were as two people going to a dinner and a show. Helen permitted the blue limousine to get well ahead, but not too far. The road was comparatively clear, so her job of tailing it was simplified. It was an excellent thing, too, Anthony thought, that the blue limousine had overtaken them, instead of the reverse process. The driver of the car in front would be scarcely likely to think that he was being tailed by a car which he had, in the original instance, passed on the road.

Thus they proceeded west. Helen alternated between being well behind and merely moderately so. She had no difficulty whatever in keeping the blue limousine taped, and on one occasion they were able to draw sufficiently close for Anthony to read the number in a fleeting moment. Chatterton's version had been correct. But just as he attempted to obtain a view of the occupant, the car was away again. On the outskirts of London Helen's task began to get more difficult. Streams of traffic in all directions had to be negotiated and the work of keeping the blue limousine in sight all the time taxed the girl's judgment and resource to the utmost. More than once, when the luck of the lights went against them, Helen momentarily lost track of the quarry, but by quick recovery and well-timed acceleration she was able always to establish touch again. In this way and by this method of approach, they came to Kingsway where the traffic congestion was worse than ever.

Anthony knew that the 'Diadem' was down a turning on the left-hand side, and as luck would have it, it was here that Helen ran into one of the worst traffic-blocks of the whole journey. Held up by the lights, she lost the blue limousine altogether and Anthony realized that it had taken the turning necessary for the restaurant whilst his car was still held stationary. When they did eventually get going again, and turned down on the left-hand side, Anthony saw to his surprise that the blue limousine was a good three hundred yards in front of them and, moreover, had passed the front entrance of the 'Diadem' restaurant. He had not expected this eventuality, and the sudden realization of it momentarily unbalanced him. He immediately knew that he would be compelled now to make a snap decision. He at once communicated this to Helen.

"Keep going, Helen. We can't afford to stop as I had anticipated. Get on its tail as close as you dare. I'm not at all sure now what's doing, but the safest plan is to follow the car. It can't be moving minus a driver, can it?"

Helen nodded that she understood. After a time the blue limousine turned west and Helen kept the car tucked well in behind it at an average distance of about a hundred yards. On and on went the blue limousine until Anthony began to realize that they were running straight for Hammersmith Broadway. The blue limousine passed the Metropolitan railway-station and then turned off as if it were making for the Lyric Theatre or its vicinity. At this, Anthony, for the first time, began to feel a certain anxiety. Whereas previously he had been a little puzzled, now his mild bewilderment was joined with definite apprehension. Here was a contingency with which he had definitely not reckoned.

But the blue limousine passed the Lyric Theatre and then turned down a road of houses and villas. Anthony, unable to see the name of it, was more perturbed than ever, for the traffic was thin here and it seemed a dead certainty that the driver of the limousine must, before long, wake up to the fact that Helen Repton had been on the trail for all those miles.

Just as Anthony's mind was registering this disturbing thought, however, the blue limousine halted suddenly outside a small house. Luckily, Helen was well behind it when this occurred and she immediately brought the car to a crawl.

"Take the first turning you come to," Anthony gave her, "and I'll get out. I *must*—there's no option. Then cruise up and down as best you can till I rejoin you."

The time was now half-past six. It was beginning to approach dusk.

6

When Anthony emerged again into the street of the house before which the blue limousine had stopped, he was relieved to see the car still there. More than that, he was just in time to see a dark figure emerge from it, run quickly across the pavement and knock on the door of the house. He strolled slowly, therefore, in that direction. When he arrived the door was shut, so it was evident that admittance had been gained by the person who had sought it. He was now in something of a quandary as to his best policy. For one thing, he was in full evening dress plus monocle, and although he was now wearing an overcoat, he must be, he felt, in this particular neighbourhood, a rather conspicuous figure at this time of the evening.

He walked slowly past the house, crossed the road and then up on the other side. When he passed the turning down which Helen had taken the car on his instructions, he could see the car coming slowly up it and towards him. Good girl, he thought—thinks quickly—all set for another sharp getaway when the moment comes. He decided then to keep, if practicable, on the Helen Repton side of the house which at the moment contained his quarry, in order that he would be able to establish the quicker contact with Helen directly it should become necessary. How could he best achieve this condition without the running of any serious risk? He turned again and looked up and down the street in which he was standing and noticed that in the middle of the row of villas, there were tucked three shops. They were a café, a florist's and a 'newspapers and tobacco,' and as luck had it, they were almost opposite to the house of his particular interest. On a wire frame in the doorway of the newspaper shop were a number of assorted domestic advertisements. He could stand here, he decided, for a few moments at least and read some of them without exciting much comment, and at the same time, he would be able to keep his eye on the doorway of the house of his attention and the waiting limousine outside. After all, he persuaded himself— his period of waiting couldn't be too protracted—the dinner at the 'Diadem' was timed for half-past seven.

Anthony read through the advertisement cards with laborious interest. 'Piano for Sale,' 'two rooms required for respectable elderly couple,' 'Alsatian puppy (pedigree) for sale,' 'sitting-room to let—would suit refined lady out all day preferably,' 'twelve Buff Orpington chicks for sale,' 'copies of the *Children's Encyclopedia* (unsoiled) etc., etc.,' without apparently satisfying his wants, and then began to read them all through again. One intrigued him immensely. 'Mr. and Mrs. Cohen, 43, Ringwood Crescent, Hammersmith, wardrobe experts, have cast-off clothing of all descriptions—inspection invited.' There was an undeniable savour about this one which tickled his mental palate immensely. He was still chuckling over this when he heard a door slam near at hand. Glancing quickly in the direction of the house under his surveillance, he saw a man's figure in evening-dress come running quickly down the step of the house and jump into the waiting blue limousine.

Anthony snatched a paper from a near-by rack, threw a penny on the counter and walked quickly away. The car had not yet started. As he hurried along, he made a pretext of opening the newspaper he had bought and reading it. This action, he thought, might well serve two purposes. It might destroy suspicion (were there any), and it might also assist to conceal his face. The blue limousine passed him, travelling along the road by which he had come. No sooner had this happened, than Anthony began to run. He ran hard towards the side-turning in which he knew that Helen Repton was somewhere waiting. When he made it, he knew that he had the break. For the car was travelling in his direction and was but twenty yards away when he saw it. Helen accelerated and he jumped in. He called to her what he had seen happen. Helen swept away in pursuit and picked up the blue limousine again in under a couple of minutes.

They began to retrace the journey which they had just previously covered. Traffic was thick again now, and before they came back to Kingsway, Helen passed through many anxious moments. But she made no mistakes and had the satisfaction of seeing the blue limousine pull up outside the parking-place for the Diadem Restaurant and a man get out. She took her own car in and parked there likewise. Anthony jumped out like a flash.

"Good work, Helen! Thank you. You know where to go and what I want you to do. Ask for Mr. Casson. There's the ticket to let you in. 'Anthony L. Bathurst and Lady.' See you later and jolly good luck."

He entered the restaurant in advance of her and saw the figure of the quarry he had tracked for miles just in front of him. He noticed certain sartorial details. "Good Lord," he said to himself, "so that's how it is—is it? Well, well, lucky I batted right through as I did and took no risks."

A man in some sort of uniform came to meet him. "I want the *maître d'hôtel*," said Anthony, "and Chief Detective-Inspector MacMorran. They're expecting me."

"That's O.K., Mr. Bathurst," came the reply. "And I have been, too. Come this way—will you please."

The time was now five minutes past seven.

CHAPTER V

1

MacMorran and Monsieur Regnault were awaiting Anthony in the latter's private office. MacMorran sat in his overcoat.

"Good evening, gentlemen," said Anthony, "and thanks for all the arrangements that you've put in hand for me. Now please pardon me if I'm a little on the rapid side with regard to one or two questions. I have so little time. First of all—Miss Repton?"

MacMorran let Regnault answer this. "That is all fixed, Mr. Bathurst—just as you asked. Casson has all the particulars and everything's ready. You told the young lady, of course, to make direct contact with him at once?"

"Yes. That end of it's all right. I saw to that coming along. That's good. Now for question number two. Which one of your waiters lives at Hammersmith—just behind the Lyric Theatre? Any idea?"

"Although I can't answer that off-hand, I will ascertain that for you at once, Mr. Bathurst."

Regnault turned and lifted the telephone-receiver. They heard him ask several questions appropriate to Anthony's request.

Regnault waited for the reply. It was not long in coming. Regnault nodded, replaced the receiver and spoke to them quietly.

"It is a Charles Smith by name, Mr. Bathurst. But I'm afraid that I do not know a great deal about him. He has not been on the staff here for very long."

"Well—that's the man I'm interested in, Monsieur Regnault. I'd like the head-waiter to have a look at him and then report back to you immediately. Will you see to that for me?"

Again Monsieur Regnault had recourse to the telephone. MacMorran and Anthony listened while the necessary instructions were given over the line. Again Monsieur Regnault put down the receiver. He sat there quietly with his hands folded over his lap.

"That information will come through in due course. And now, what next, gentlemen?" he inquired.

MacMorran looked across at Anthony for the appropriate answer. But Anthony shook his head.

"Nothing more from me, Monsieur Regnault, until we have that report from your head-waiter that you just 'phoned for. That's the king-pin of my case. Can't move further until I know where I am on that."

"You won't have to wait very long," said Regnault, "Casson is both thorough and quick in everything he does. I have never known him to waste time. Give him, say, two or three minutes and I am confident you'll have all you want."

The three men sat there in silence. MacMorran fidgeted with one of his thumb-nails. Anthony and Regnault kept perfectly still.

The time was now seventeen minutes past seven.

2

At nineteen minutes past seven, Regnault's 'phone rang. MacMorran was so nervous that he jumped a little in his chair at the sound of the bell. Regnault picked up the receiver and spoke—just as quietly and unemotionally as he had spoken previously. Anthony listened, acutely sensitive.

"Yes," said Regnault, "you have? And the result? It's not? You're quite certain of that? Positive—eh! Well, well, that's pretty conclusive from all points of view. No-o—I don't think so in the circumstances.

I've an idea that it was, from what I've been told, more or less expected. Hang on for a moment, Casson."

Regnault put his hand over the mouthpiece and spoke to Anthony. "It's not the Charles Smith that Casson knows. That's his report. And he's positive of it, he says. How does that suit you, Mr. Bathurst?"

"Beautifully, Monsieur Regnault. You speak honeyed words. Nothing you might have said could have pleased me better. Tell Casson that Chief Detective-Inspector MacMorran will be with him in a couple of minutes with full instructions as to what he must do."

Anthony turned to MacMorran. "Casson, Andrew, at once, please. You heard what I told him. He'll show you the person you've to arrange about. And you'll see to all the rest for me, won't you? Thanks so much."

MacMorran rose. It was characteristic of the man to make no demur.

"Oh—and by the way," added Anthony, "put Miss Repton wise, do you mind, Andrew? You know where she'll be. Then you'll have another string to your bow. And on your way to Casson, take a dekko at this."

Anthony slipped a small piece of paper into his hand. MacMorran took it and went. As he departed, Sir Austin Kemble entered in the company of the Lord Chief Justice. The Commissioner looked pale and excited. Regnault was on his feet in the twinkling of an eye. He bowed to the incomers.

The time was twenty-five minutes past seven.

3

Viscount Fifoot, Anthony Bathurst thought, was looking a little fine-drawn, but taking things by and large, the old man was standing up well to the strain that had been imposed upon him. If he were highly nervous, he certainly wasn't showing it to the extent that the Commissioner of Police was. The latter came to the point immediately after the conventional greetings had passed between them.

"Well, Bathurst, how are things going? Is everything all right?"

Anthony smiled at him reassuringly. "Everything is well in hand, Sir Austin. MacMorran has his men placed and they're all fully primed as to their individual courses of action. It will be difficult, believe me, for a guilty elbow to be even raised for the purpose of the gentle exercise of dart-throwing let alone for the dart itself to be thrown." He turned to the Lord Chief Justice after he had spoken. "I hope that hearing that has reassured you too, my lord."

Fifoot smiled at him and jerked back his head courageously. "I put implicit trust in all of you, Bathurst. Otherwise I shouldn't have come here this evening. If you tell me that you and your colleagues are ready and prepared to deal with any and every possible emergency, that's good enough for me. I'm perfectly satisfied—and that's that."

Sir Austin burst in fussily. "I've been thinking, Bathurst. All the way here this evening. Why not make the arrest at once? I feel that we should. Why risk such a valuable life as that of the Lord Chief Justice in the way that you propose doing?" Sir Austin almost purred the words of the title. "If anything went wrong, you know," he continued, before Anthony could reply, "it would place me in a deucedly awkward position. It might well be the finish of my career."

Anthony thought hard before he answered. He had been expecting this question from the Commissioner and had been surprised that it hadn't come before.

"I don't mind, sir," he said, "if you'd rather have it that way. The only thing is that my way will give us overwhelming proof of guilt. It will be a case of *in flagrante delicto*. And I give you my word of honour that if I thought there were the slightest risk, I wouldn't take it. There isn't. The moment the guilty hand is raised, the game will be up. You can't throw a dart, you know, without giving some indication of the intention. There will be ten terriers at least to deal with the one rat—and all of them within an absurdly short distance."

"I'm satisfied, Sir Austin," said Fifoot, "if it will help you to know and to feel that. All the plans for my safety seem to have been well and truly laid. You know, Sir Austin, I like to think I'm a gentleman. Well—what is gentility worth, if it can't stand fire."

As he spoke, he shook hands with both Anthony and the Commissioner of Police. Then he turned and with rare courtesy extended the same compliment to Monsieur Regnault.

"And now," said the Lord Chief Justice, "we mustn't delay any longer. I must go and meet my guests. I see the time is just half-past seven."

4

Anthony took his seat quietly and unobtrusively at an obscure end of one of the more obscure tables. He could see from where he sat, in addition to the chairman, Sir Austin Kemble, Keith Salt, Sir Claude de Monterey, Lady Fifoot, MacMorran looking rather uncomfortable in evening dress, and also, moving smoothly among the waitresses, Helen Repton. He knew that MacMorran's men were well-scattered amongst the guests and waiting-staff and that each, by now, had received implicit and definite orders as to the necessary action if contingency arose. He watched Helen Repton closely and he saw that she had now placed herself between two waiters. The guest of honour, Sir Wardlaw Henderson, the Dean of Faculty, was on the immediate right of the Lord Chief Justice, with Lady Fifoot next to Sir Wardlaw on the other side. On Fifoot's immediate left was the American ambassador, Mr. Hillman Horni-man, and next to him, obviously, to Anthony's eye, was seated Louis de Monterey, the Minister of Justice for the Dominion of Canada. Directly he saw him, Anthony had detected a pronounced family likeness to Sir Claude. They were of similar physique, with hair and eyes strongly alike.

Keith Salt was at a table on Fifoot's left and Sir Claude de Monterey was seated but a few seats away from his distinguished relative. There was the customary buzz of conversation during the preliminaries and, when Anthony sat down, there were still half a dozen or so vacant seats at different tables. But these, however, gradually filled up and, within a period of about ten minutes, the first course was in process of being served. Waiters moved quickly and efficiently from place to place.

When Anthony saw this continuous movement of the waiters and the general bustle from the service-room to the various tables, he felt supremely thankful that he had covered that position and placed Helen Repton where she was and also that Helen was who she was and nobody else. He continued to watch her from the corner of his eye and he saw with intense satisfaction how close she kept to the waiter who had signed the staff-book that evening in the name of Charles Smith.

For Viscount Fifoot, the Lord Chief Justice of England and the chairman for the evening, Anthony felt nothing but the most sincere admiration. He thought of almost the last words he had heard him speak, concerning gentility and standing fire. The old man was acquitting himself splendidly and not a soul in the room would have guessed or even suspected that the dinner held anything in the nature of an ordeal for him. He was conversing with each of his immediate neighbours in turn and generally holding with poise, facility and distinction the delicate balance of the various discussions which were taking place not only within his own personal area but even, also, a little beyond it. He betrayed in no way by his manner or bearing that Anthony could see, that the dinner at which he was presiding was in any degree unusual or abnormal.

As Anthony withdrew his glance from Helen Repton for a mere second, to watch the Lord Chief Justice, he saw Viscount Fifoot wave gracefully to a person sitting some little distance away from him.

The salutation was returned at once and Anthony observed that the acknowledgment had come from the tall figure of Keith Salt who raised himself in his chair a little, in order to give it. Salt looked flushed. Anthony thought that he had been drinking rather heavily.

It was at that moment that Anthony had something in the nature of a brain-wave, and as it came to him he could have kicked himself that the idea had not occurred to him previously. Because it undoubtedly should have. He glanced across at the Press table to see if, by any chance, the man who had called himself John Bentley was present. As far as he could see from where he was sitting, there were four Pressmen in attendance, but Bentley was not one of them. As he thought this, Anthony found himself pondering on the strange tricks which Life plays—both on us and for us, as its caprice has it. The thought, however, suffered disturbance by reason of the waiter removing his soup-plate and placing in front of him an attractive-looking portion of *sole à bonne femme*. Anthony bent over and regarded it with appreciation.

The time was now ten minutes to eight.

5

The service of the succeeding courses slowly passed to the sweet. This consisted of *Pêches flambées*. But these, Anthony considered, to be at their best, needed Perrier Jouet. Thus the dinner proceeded, normally and entirely uneventfully, until the toasts.

The Lord Chief Justice rose to a storm of applause. The movements of the waiting-staff gradually subsided, and the buzz of noise and snatched conversation died down, until quiet reigned in the room. As Viscount Fifoot stood up to propose the toast of the guest of honour, the Dean of Faculty, Sir Wardlaw Henderson, Anthony felt a condition of aggravated tension. He felt certain that the psychological moment of peril must be very near. For now, he knew, the Lord Chief Justice was presenting himself as a target. The target of the aggressor's desire. Every eye in the room would be turned on to him. And more than that—he—Anthony—had deliberately allowed this position to come about. If he made a mistake and anything went wrong—

Fifoot began to speak in the well-modulated, carefully measured tones that most of the members of the company had heard before and meant to signify that all was in order and that there was no need for him to be unduly anxious. Anthony returned the signal, but only MacMorran himself would have noticed it and recognized it.

Then Anthony's eyes gave a quick glance round the entire room to see if he could locate 'Charles Smith.' But to no avail. There was no sign. He was unable to pick out Smith anywhere. Although he had spotted him a moment or so previously. The Lord Chief Justice was now well in his stride and in his most sparkling form. Gusts of laughter attended his many *'bon mots'* and a chorus of 'hear hears' was the general garnish of the speech. As he listened, Anthony knew that Fifoot was rapidly approaching his peroration. Two more minutes passed and the Lord Chief Justice resumed his seat to a well-sustained accompaniment of applause. Anthony began to wonder. So far his anticipations had not been realized. Had he in any way been guilty of a miscalculation? As he turned the matter over in his mind, however, he remembered that although the Ides of March had come, they had not gone!

He sat down, therefore, to wait in patience and he couldn't help thinking that if he found the proceedings something of an ordeal what indeed must be the feelings of the Lord Chief Justice himself? The other speakers followed one by one. Hillman Horniman, Louis de Monterey, Sir Ashton Crawley, Sir Fane De Zoete, Lord Gramercy, Sir Waltham Ferrers, Sir Graham Preston until the time came for Sir Wardlaw Henderson to acknowledge the honour that had been accorded him. Anthony still watched. Chiefly—at this stage—Helen Repton. Every time he looked at her, his confidence was stimulated and fortified. She was alert, agile and seemed as cool as though she were watching a play from the stalls of a theatre.

Sir Wardlaw Henderson's reply to the various speeches came to a finish. By now, Anthony was definitely worried. All the plans he had made had been co-ordinated with the assumption that the attempt on the life of the Lord Chief Justice would have been made before now. And his worries were not minimized by the receipt of a hastily-pencilled note sent down to him by Sir Austin Kemble. Anthony read it from the corner of his eye and scrawled a reply (non-committal) across it. He then rose from his seat and walked up very quietly to the Commissioner to whom he handed the note.

The minor toasts were now being given and when Anthony resumed his seat, after his journey back from Sir Austin, no less a person than Keith Salt rose to propose a vote of thanks to the chairman. As Anthony sat down to listen, he saw MacMorran beckoning to him and the look on the inspector's face was very much akin to consternation. Anthony got up again quickly and tip-toed across the room to him. MacMorran pulled him to one side—behind one of the larger pillars.

"What's the trouble, Andrew?" he asked. He was unable to hide successfully the anxiety in his tone.

"Charles Smith," answered the inspector. "Your friend Charles Smith's the trouble. The worst thing possible has happened. He's disappeared. Darned well vanished. He can't be found on the building anywhere. Now what the heck are we going to do? It's a proper pills!"

The time was twenty-two minutes past nine.

6

At MacMorran's words, Anthony's heart sank. This was the very last contingency for which he had bargained.

"But damn it all, Andrew, I saw the chap here a matter of but minutes ago. Ten minutes at the outside. Where the blazes can he be? All my reason tells me that he can't be very far away. Besides—where's Helen Repton? If you find her—you find Smith—you can bank on that."

He had scarcely completed the sentence and MacMorran had no opportunity to reply, when Helen Repton skipped up behind them. Her face was white and distressed. Anthony saw at once that something was radically wrong.

"Oh—what will you think of me," she said, "but Smith's gone. And we had been at elbow's length all the evening. I carried out your instructions absolutely rigidly. About a quarter of an hour ago, Smith was standing just over there with a tankard of beer on a tray." She indicated where she meant. "I was there at his side. The next second, he had slipped behind me and I'd lost him. I told the inspector at once. Since then I've been everywhere—but there isn't a trace of him in the building anywhere. I've searched everywhere."

Anthony saw that Helen was on the verge of tears and had momentarily lost her nerve. To himself the news came as a severe blow, for he couldn't ignore the glaring fact that the Lord Chief Justice stood in deadly peril again. And then, to Anthony's horror, Viscount Fifoot showed signs of rising again to reply to Salt's vote of thanks. He stood to his full height—and the quarry had eluded the net!

7

Anthony turned and grabbed MacMorran by the arm. "We can't risk this, Andrew. We simply daren't. Use your authority and have all the lights put out. Then have an announcement made re the failure of the lighting. I'll get the L.C.J. at once. Don't wait, Andrew, for the love of Mike."

MacMorran nodded and dashed off. Anthony made his way silently and rapidly round the back of the tables to where Viscount Fifoot had just risen. Almost simultaneously with him reaching the chairman's seat and Fifoot's opening sentence, the room was plunged into darkness. MacMorran had done his stuff. Anthony leaned forward and caught the Lord Chief Justice by the sleeve.

"It's all right, sir," he whispered, "it's Bathurst here. Don't worry. There's nothing much to be alarmed about. And to oblige me stick close behind me and we'll make our way to the doors. I'll make all the arrangements about Lady Fifoot. It doesn't matter—the show's practically over and they'll have to forgive you not making that second speech. Take it as read."

The Lord Chief Justice, still cool and collected, took Anthony by the arm and obeyed the instruction. As they reached the door, they heard Monsieur Regnault apologizing for the lighting contretemps. MacMorran and three 'Yard' officers in evening dress joined forces with Anthony and shepherded Fifoot to the cloak-room and then to his car. Helen, on a word from Anthony, had gone off and found Lady Fifoot, and within five minutes Anthony and MacMorran, with Sir Austin Kemble fussing in the background, had the Lord Chief Justice and his wife seated safely in his car. His slightly built chauffeur had responded quickly to the summons sent along to him and they were all set for the homeward journey in an incredibly short space of time.

"The escort cars are ready," said MacMorran to Anthony. "I feel that they should do the return journey as they brought him up. Agree?"

"Every time," said Anthony, "and what's more, Andrew, you and I are travelling in this car all the way to Hart's Heath. Tell Evershed to get back to the 'Yard.' If *we* go, he won't be needed. Not only have I made a pills of things, but there are also many things which have cropped up that I don't like. But wait half a jiffy. I'll tell the Commissioner."

When Anthony got back to the car, after having spoken to Sir Austin, and the chauffeur shut the door on him, the time was twenty-two minutes to ten.

8

Neither Fifoot nor his wife spoke to Anthony or MacMorran until they were well clear of Kingsway. At least five minutes had elapsed. Eventually the Lord Chief Justice broke the silence.

"Don't think I'm critical for one moment, Inspector," he said, "but what happened? I feel that I'd like to know. My poor wife here nearly died of fright."

MacMorran wished that Fifoot hadn't addressed the question to him. But he put the best face on it that he could.

"The person whom we were shadowing (about a dozen of us—to be exact) unaccountably gave us the slip. Heaven knows how it was done. And it shows us all up in an extremely poor light. But rest assured, sir—no attempt was made on your life."

"That's a relief, Inspector. I've been wondering. I am truly thankful."

Anthony cut in. "Don't be, sir! But don't misunderstand me. I mean this. The danger's not averted. It's merely delayed. That's the position. The attempt will be made later. Where and how—I don't know! I'm baffled! Will you forgive me if I become violently anti-social for half an hour or so while I endeavour to sort things out?"

There came another awkward period of silence. Lady Fifoot eventually came to the rescue with her customary adroitness.

"We understand perfectly, Mr. Bathurst," she said, "so please don't worry about us or about anything. You carry on just as you want to. Just as though we weren't here. We still feel that we're in the hands of you and Inspector MacMorran here—and if it please you to know it, we're quite satisfied to be in them. So do just as you like and, as I said, we'll understand perfectly."

"Thank you so much," returned Anthony, "that's very charming of you. Now you keep your weather eye open, Andrew, and I'll do a spot of thinking."

MacMorran nodded. From where he was sitting, he could see one of the escort cars a few yards ahead of them, and the whole job on which he was occupied was far from his liking. Especially so now that things had gone awry. If only they hadn't let that fellow give them the slip! They were nothing more than a set of incompetent bunglers. Everyone of them—including himself.

Suddenly Anthony spoke. "Your house at Hart's Heath, my lord. Could anybody get in there easily while you're away from it?"

The Lord Chief Justice took a minute or so over his reply. He saw the extent of Anthony's meaning.

"That shouldn't happen, Bathurst. In anything like ordinary circumstances. The servants are all there. But you've set my mind to work with your question. I suppose—if I'm logical—that any determined person, who laid his plans cleverly enough, would be able to contrive entrance. Why? Do you think that it's a likely happening?"

"I've been considering it, sir. I've been forced to. Now that this has happened. I don't see how anybody can touch you while you're here with us in this car. Therefore, I'm bound to envisage all the other possibilities. And the next place you'll be in, will be in your own house."

Another period of silence followed—this time of longer duration. Tension, both individual and collective, was mounting rapidly. Anthony, through the window on the off-side, saw a landmark which told him that they were already through Lottingham. Twice the car lurched badly as it took corners.

"Searle's in a hurry to get you home, my dear," remarked Lady Fifoot with a smile—"and I can't find it in my heart to blame him."

Viscount Fifoot shook his head at the remark. "It's the road, my dear. That's the trouble. It's been raining recently and the moisture's lying on top. The surface is greasy. You know what that means."

Silence again—and Anthony still hammering and hacking at his problems—to save a man's life and to arrest a criminal. Any fragment of conversation that passed between the other occupants of the car, he heard and kept on hearing. But the repetition was repetition only because it meant nothing at all to him. All his senses save one rejected it. His ears heard it but his brain failed to register it. Because his brain dealt merely with his own thoughts and hammered away at them.

He had asked Fifoot about his house and the reply had been that the servants were on the premises. Which should mean no trouble. The servants—and then Anthony had a sudden flash of revelation. As it came to him, he muttered a sudden sharp exclamation. MacMorran turned to him almost quizzically.

"Thought of something?"

"By jove, yes, Andrew! I most certainly have thought of something! In a way I suppose it's fantastic, but I believe I've hit on the solution."

Fifoot and his wife looked across at him eagerly. Anthony leant across the car and spoke to the Lord Chief Justice.

"Your servants, sir—that you spoke of? Any one of them new to you or recently engaged?"

Fifoot shook his head "No. Not one, Bathurst. Every one of them has been with us years, and every one of them is thoroughly trustworthy. I would vouch for their honesty and loyalty. I'm afraid that if you're looking for treachery in that particular quarter, you're quite wrong. Sorry if I've upset any of your theories."

Anthony tried to see out of one of the windows. "Where are we now, Andrew? Any idea?"

MacMorran peered out as Anthony had but Lady Fifoot answered the question without the slightest hesitation.

"We're about a mile from the cross-roads that branch off to Cherry Vintner and Silken Courtway. If you notice, we're just coming to the rise."

"How long to go, Lady Fifoot?"

"Not more than twenty minutes," replied the lady, "and perhaps barely as much as that. Searle seems to have a clear road."

"Good," said Anthony; "now please will everybody listen very carefully. When the car stops outside the house, you get out first, Andrew—will you please? Then help Lady Fifoot to alight. By that time, probably Searle will be round to help you. I'll follow. But I want Viscount Fifoot to leave the car *last*. Behind the three of us. Directly he alights, I want you, Andrew, to place yourself on his *right*, where I shall be as well. Leave the rest to me. Now, is all that perfectly clear?"

The other heard him and nodded.

"Good," said Anthony again—"not a word now until we stop."

As he finished speaking, the car swerved to the left. "That's the turning to Hart's Heath that we've just taken," said Lady Fifoot, "we're now heading straight for home. We've only a couple of miles to go now."

Anthony's slight nod of acceptance was the only recognition given to her remark. He was silent, stern-eyed, and grim-lipped. The car passed the line of farm-houses and barns which Anthony remembered having seen before. Nobody spoke. The atmosphere of sharp tension had come back with aggravated acuteness and now maintained itself at the highest pitch. At last, Anthony heard the crunch of the car wheels on the gravel-drive and felt the car take the slope towards the house. MacMorran saw the apprehension on Anthony's face. The car gradually began to slow up. Anthony looked out and saw the escort cars just in front of them. He signalled to MacMorran. The inspector leant forward a little, bent his body and put his hand on the handle of the door. The car stopped. The escort had travelled a short distance further. MacMorran turned the handle back, crouched low and sprang out through the opened door.

Anthony saw Searle, the chauffeur, jump quickly from the driving-seat, and come round towards the door. MacMorran and the chauffeur helped Lady Fifoot from the car. As Anthony got out, the chauffeur fell back a little to give him room. Anthony, all his senses supremely alert, put his body across the doorway and half-turned, to assist the Lord Chief Justice to alight. Viscount Fifoot got up from his seat and bent from his height to come out. As he did so, MacMorran mindful of Anthony's request, came and ranged himself with Anthony on the Lord Chief Justice's right. The chauffeur moved silently behind them, to close the car door. MacMorran and the Lord Chief Justice began to move towards the door of the house, in the wake of Lady Fifoot who had already reached it. There was a moment when Fifoot's figure showed clearly away from the inspector. With swift and lightning-like instancy, Anthony flung himself upon the aggressor. He grasped the hand by the wrist, twisted it viciously and hurled the body violently down. The poisoned dart fell from the impotent fingers, and under the pressure of Anthony's weight, strength and swiftness, his opponent twisted to the ground and lay there panting.

MacMorran came running up as Anthony knelt on the prostrate body.

"Good work, Andrew," gasped Anthony, "and a very near thing—as I was afraid it would be. Let us thank the gods that be that I stumbled on the truth in time. But there's your prisoner and the Lord Chief Justice can sleep safely and soundly in his bed to-night."

MacMorran made no reply but pulled the prostrate figure from the ground. The peaked cap of the supposed chauffeur had fallen off in the struggle. He gazed open-mouthed at what he saw. But before he could put his amazement into words, Anthony spoke to him again.

"Allow me to present to you, Andrew, Miss Ada Rotherham Pemberton—twin sister of a certain Arthur Rotherham Pemberton whom you may or may not remember, but who was hanged by the neck until he was dead. Perhaps, though, you know her better as Paula Secretan."

9

Lady Fifoot edged herself a little nearer to the fire. The Lord Chief Justice observed that she was cold. She had shivered twice in quick succession.

"Shall I put another log on the fire, my dear?" he asked solicitously.

"Yes," she replied, "I think you might. I simply can't get warm this evening. When a May evening is cold, there are certainly no illusions about it. And I had been flattering myself for nearly a month now that we'd said good-bye to winter."

She leant forward and put her hands to the blaze. Fifoot brought the log and placed it carefully between the burning coals. His height did not seem so pronounced as it had been some little time back. The ordeal through which he had recently passed had undoubtedly taken its toll of him.

"Yes, my dear," he said, as he dusted his fingers with his handkerchief, "a cold wet evening in May is a thing of horror and a beast for ever. Still, I suppose one must expect it. The cricket season has started. That fact in itself is usually a most sinister happening." He looked at his watch.

"What is the time?" inquired Sybil.

"Just on half-past six. Our guests should be here in a very few minutes. That's a sobering thought, you know, my dear, in its way. Because if I live to be a hundred, which God forbid, I shall never be able to repay Bathurst for what he did for me. Especially at the very end of the affair. Dreadful!"

"How is Searle? Have you had news of him to-day?"

Fifoot nodded. "Oh—yes. I rang the hospital this morning. I meant to have mentioned it to you, but it slipped my mind. He's doing very well now. They seem to have cleansed his system of the poison pretty thoroughly. Excellent piece of work on somebody's part."

Sybil Fifoot again bent forward for warmth. "I shall never forget that drive home. And how I kept thinking that Searle was driving fast in order to get home quickly. Dear—dear—when I look back on it—how silly it was of me."

"Not at all, my dear. Who could blame you? It was a most natural assumption on your part. The idea was parented by the anxiety you were feeling on my behalf."

The Lord Chief Justice bent down and used the poker to keep a log in place on the top of the glowing coals. As he did so, there came a ring at the bell. Lady Fifoot's eyes met his.

"Our guests." She listened. "I can hear Sir Austin Kemble's voice."

"I'm afraid, my dear," said her husband mildly, "that you're destined to hear quite a lot of it before the evening's through." He smiled. The smile was devoid of malice or unkindness. His wife smiled back.

"Now, now," she said, "don't be catty. Leave that to the members of my sex."

She rose as there came a tap on the door. The manservant, who had met Sir Austin and Anthony on their first visit, opened the door and made an announcement.

"Sir Austin Kemble and Mr. Anthony Bathurst."

Lady Fifoot advanced to meet them.

10

When dinner was finished, Anthony and the Commissioner followed their host out of the door of the dining-room, across a low-ceilinged passage-way and into the lounge. The dinner, Anthony thought, had merited the mark of excellent. One of the best and one of the most comfortable meals which it had ever been his lot to eat and enjoy. The cooking had been beyond criticism, the sherry had been excellent, the claret of high quality and the port beyond reproach. The Lord Chief Justice and Lady Fifoot had been easy and charming all the time and not one word had been spoken by anybody with regard to the recent tragedies. The man who had ushered Anthony and Sir Austin in had been the only servant to wait at table.

The conversation had been as far away from crime and criminals as the poles are apart. It had gone from the Burnmarees of Billingsgate to the Fortunate Islands, from Magliabecchi the librarian, to Cosmo III, Grand Duke of Tuscany, to the ancient Greek school of medicine founded by Serapion of Alexandria and had finished up with an exceedingly witty description by the Lord Chief Justice of The Saliens, the priestly college of Mars in ancient Rome, traditionally instituted by Numa. It must be confessed that Sir Austin took but a humble part in the discussions. But Anthony had found the Lord Chief Justice a monument of erudition and Sybil Fifoot's pungent humour had found frequent opportunities for display.

As Anthony and Sir Austin followed Viscount Fifoot into the lounge, their hostess rose from a low chair by the blazing fire. She received Anthony with a charming smile. Her admiration for his powers of intellect, for his memory and for his amazing erudition had been growing all the evening.

"Coffee, Mr. Bathurst?" she inquired.

"Thank you."

"Black or white?"

"Black, if you please, Lady Fifoot."

She moved towards a table on the far side of the hearth which held cups, coffee-pot and spirit-lamp.

"What about you, Sir Austin?"

"Black for me, too, please," replied the Commissioner.

Lady Fifoot brought the coffee-cups and the Lord Chief Justice dispensed a liqueur brandy and cigars.

"Now make yourselves absolutely comfortable," he said, "while we all listen to Bathurst's explanation and summing-up. I'll confess I'm a little impatient to hear it. For once, I'll fulfil the role of listener."

They ranged themselves round the fire on which the logs were crackling merrily. Anthony lit his cigar carefully-before he embarked on his narrative. The others waited for him to start.

"Well," said Anthony, "the case that has just been concluded deserves to rank as one of the most extraordinary that has ever come my way. It was unusual in more than one respect. Instead of being called upon to deal with one clearly-defined crime, we encountered a series of rather shattering shocks. For instance, directly MacMorran and I arrived in Quiddington St. Philip to investigate the killing of Mr. Justice Flagon, we were brought almost to a standstill by the news of the murder of Mr. Justice Madrigal at Flagon's funeral. It was the effect of this that played such a large part in all my subsequent deliberations and investigations. Because, as is so obvious, every motive for killing Flagon that we might run up against, ceased to be a motive unless it could be proved satisfactorily that it was a motive also for removing Madrigal. And—although, as I just said, that fact was obvious and seems now to be *glaringly* obvious—it was really remarkable how, more than once, both MacMorran and I were prone to forget it.

"But anyhow, it all boiled down to this—we had to find a murderer who figured in both the Flagon and the Madrigal equations and who, afterwards, of course, had an integral connection also with the Lord Chief Justice here, himself."

Anthony paused to remove a length of ash from his cigar. "I was forced, therefore, to look for somebody who desired to remove from life all those three gentlemen whom I have just named. Who was near the scene of the crimes and who, in addition, was an extremely skilful darts-player. So I examined my circle of suspects one by one, bearing in mind at the same time, the actual conditions under which the two original murders had been committed.

"First of all, there was Maurice Fothergill. He was near Flagon when Flagon died, he might have attended Flagon's funeral *and* he was an expert with a dart. But where was his motive? I never found one and one was never suggested to me. *But* I retained him on my list as a possible. Number two was Fothergill's friend—Ronald Harcourt. In this particular instance, I ran into quite a healthy spot of bother. For Harcourt told a most extraordinary story. Instead of meeting

Fothergill at the Point-to-Point meeting, as they had mutually arranged to do, Harcourt, so the story went, had failed to put in an appearance. He had gone for a walk in the morning, been taken ill with some form of stomach trouble and had lain in a field until it was too late for him to keep his appointment with Fothergill. For some time, I must confess that I regarded this story as highly suspicious and I even toyed with the theory that Fothergill himself might have been responsible for his friend's sudden illness. But again, the death of Madrigal seemed to me to put Harcourt into very much the same category as I had placed Fothergill. Where was *his* motive to remove both Flagon and Madrigal? Neither Harcourt nor Fothergill seemed to belong to the normal criminal class, or even to have any connection with it, and another fact which told in Harcourt's favour was that, as far as I could reasonably judge, he was by no means so consistently skilful a darts-player as Fothergill was. Nevertheless and all the same, I decided to retain him on my possible list and to check up on him later in the same manner as I intended to do with Fothergill. After all, both these men were definitely eligible from one important point of view. Each was capable of having climbed the elm-tree. So you see," said Anthony with a smile at Sybil, "I wasn't making very much progress so far, was I?"

"One minute, Bathurst," interposed the Lord Chief Justice, "I didn't quite get your reference to an elm-tree. Should I have done, or am I—"

"No, sir," replied Anthony, "for the moment I was forgetting that you weren't 'in' on that. But I'll come back to it later and explain what I meant."

"Thank you, Bathurst."

Anthony sampled his old brandy. "I next turned my attention to a gentleman by the name of Michael Keegan. Here we had, from some angles, a highly promising suspect. But from some angles only! I'll explain. He fitted the Flagon murder. He had more than once publicly proclaimed his intense hatred of him. He had attended the Point-to-Point. *And* he had the reputation of being the finest darts-player in the district! But—and here was my mental barrier— if he hated the sight of Nicholas Flagon—there was no evidence or suggestion whatever, that he entertained similar feelings with regard to Justice Madrigal. It seemed to me, as I reviewed the possibility of Keegan's guilt, that although Flagon might have sent him down for a stretch at some time in the past, it was hardly likely, I argued, that his misdemeanour was of such an important nature as to merit the judicial attentions of both Flagon *and* Madrigal.

"After a time, I decided to eliminate Keegan from my list of suspects, and what finally decided me over that was this. Or rather these *two* factors. One—the fact that you, sir, received the third letter, and two—the fact of the Shakespearian allusion attached to the murderous darts. I simply could not fit Michael Keegan into this. My colleague—Inspector MacMorran—put forward the idea that the murders might well be the work of two people, but I wasn't particularly convinced by his arguments and I therefore eliminated Keegan from my list. I regarded this as the first real sign of progress that I had made and I now turned my attention to no less a person than the distinguished K.C., Mr. Keith Salt."

Anthony noticed the unmistakable look of surprise that showed in Viscount Fifoot's eyes. He hastened to justify himself.

"Here again, from the Flagon angle, we could point to definite motive. Perhaps even to two of them. Avarice and jealousy. Firstly, there was the matter of Flagon's estate. Salt had been Flagon's *fidus Achates*. Until Flagon had fallen in love and contemplated marriage with Paula Secretan. Flagon, without blood relations, had bequeathed his money to Salt. But his approaching marriage had caused him to alter his original intentions. Had he informed Salt of this, which from the point of view of their close friendship was a most likely happening, it would have certainly provided Salt with a motive for eliminating his best friend. But then, of course, and once again, the Madrigal murder made moonshine of all this and generally put paid to Salt as a suspect from the particular standpoint of Flagon's money. *Unless*—and here MacMorran entered the breach again—this second murder of Madrigal had been a pure blind committed simply to obscure the question of motive and to put the police authorities completely off the scent. So taking into consideration (a) the fact that Salt had been seen talking to Flagon not very long before the fatal race (I checked up on this), (6) that he seemed scarcely of the physical type for tree-climbing and that (c) there was no evidence that he could handle a dart with any unusual dexterity, I removed him from my list of possibles. Although, strangely enough, there came a time later when I was tempted to re-include him—for an entirely different reason. I'll talk about that, however, later."

Anthony bent forward and tossed the butt of his cigar into the fire. None of his companions spoke. Each was listening to him intently. He went on.

"I now found myself looking at Bentley. Here was a man who kept turning up in all sorts of odd places. He actually introduced himself to me one evening in a local pub called the 'Wheatsheaf' and when that happened the 'Wheatsheaf' had acquired a rather extraordinary significance. For the reason that the darts used by the murderer (or murderess as we now know) had been stolen from there and other darts substituted for them."

Sir Austin cut in. "I've often wondered about that, Bathurst. Why was that done, do you think?"

"In my opinion, Sir Austin, to throw suspicion on the skilled players who were known to use the house, and particularly on to one of them who had made no secret of his hatred for Nicholas Flagon."

"But why substitute? Why not have just stolen the three darts that were wanted?"

"Because I think, if that had happened, the loss might have been discovered before the murders were committed. Which, you will argue, mightn't have mattered much. But there you are, the substitution did take place and we can only conjecture as to the reason. But to return to Bentley. There was a curious feature about this man Bentley. He was frequently announcing *coram publico* that he couldn't play darts at all and drawing one's attention to the fact that he had an injured wrist. More than once, I found myself wondering whether 'the Bentley weren't protesting too much.' Anyhow, time went by, and despite the fact that I couldn't pin anything like a motive on to him, except that which eventually suggested itself to me, I kept him on my list of possibles. Of which I now had three— Fothergill, Harcourt and Bentley and to whom I was destined to add only one other. You can guess who that was.

"Now let me hark back a little. To the *fons et origo* of the whole wretched business. When Andrew MacMorran and I took our first look-see at the case, we were able to form certain very definite ideas as to the details of both the Flagon and Madrigal murders. In the first instance, the murderer had thrown the dart from the branches of a tree most admirably suited for the purpose, and escaped on a bicycle, and in the case of the killing of Madrigal, he had concealed himself in the thick greenery of the churchyard at Quiddington St. Philip. And as I looked at the churchyard and formed this idea, I couldn't resist thinking simultaneously how a woman, for instance, clad in a green mackintosh, and with a green scarf round her head, could have rendered herself almost invisible. Now listen to this. To a stroke of luck that came my way. When I called on Miss Secretan for the first time, she received me dressed almost identically with the image that I had conjured up in my mind. And when I thought of the proximity of her house to the gate which gave exit from the churchyard and the fact that she had deliberately invited me to lunch with her to discuss Flagon's murder—I began to grasp a really substantial thread. Which was not loosened in importance, believe me, when she made the surprising revelation as to the relations which existed between her and the dead man. I began to question her as to her movements on the day of Flagon's funeral. Arid as to climatic conditions. I felt certain that at least once she lied to me. So much so that when I left her, I was asking myself very seriously—'Can these things be—and, if they can—why?' Soon after that there came the third development. Your threatening letter, my lord. We'll call it that. I said to myself—Flagon, Madrigal and now the Lord Chief Justice himself. Three! Three in a row. And then—one day the trio position flashed into my mind and I deduced a court of appeal with the Lord Chief Justice presiding. Which, rather curiously, caused me to consider Keith Salt again and also Sir Claude de Monterey.

"It now seemed to me rather more than obvious that I must look for the guilty person amongst the more cultured section of the community, and that the crimes had definitely ranged themselves in what I will term 'the revenge class.' And revenge, too, for an injustice or a fancied injustice which had its probable genesis in a court of Law. The murderer or murderess had a knowledge of the poets and was endeavouring, according to his or her lights, to adjust a grievance which had arisen from a judgment delivered by the three Justices whom we now had very directly concerned.

"The significant phrase, 'the sharp quillet,' was only hazily familiar to me and it took me some appreciable time before I was able to identify it as Shakespearean in its origin. It was just about this time that I began to wonder again about Salt. Was I dealing with an instance of aggravated professional jealousy? These things, as you are all aware, *have* been known in the past. Had Salt been nurturing a hot and vicious resentment over a period of years under the guise of friendship which he had determined to end in wholesale murder? I asked you, my lord," Anthony turned to the Lord Chief Justice, "whether Salt was an unusually bad loser and when you told me that the description fitted him like a glove, I considered him very seriously. Eventually, chiefly, I think, by reason of the impressions I had formed of him at an interview we had, I discarded him and began to turn my attention towards Sir Claude de Monterey.

"He was close at hand, he was an athlete distinguished in many games, and also there were rumours that he had formed a strong attachment to Miss Secretan. I made it my business to go along and see him. As a result of that encounter, I was left with very little indeed to encourage my condition of suspicion. So I removed the name of de Monterey from my list."

Anthony paused and looked up at the assembled company. "Getting bored?" he asked. "I'm afraid all this is rather long-winded."

Sybil Fifoot was in like a flash to reassure him. "Mr. Bathurst," she exclaimed, "bored! Of all the ideas! Your story's most fascinating. Please go on and finish. I'm dying to hear how you fixed it all up at the end."

"That's very nice of you, Lady Fifoot. Thus encouraged, then, I'll proceed. I was now left with four main 'possibles,' one of whom I was compelled to regard as rather more like a 'probable'—Fothergill, Harcourt, Bentley and Paula Secretan. And as I turned the whole case over in my mind, I began to become convinced that one of these four—in all probability the lady—was not known to me by the name under which her entry into this world had been made. I realized that if I could find out and prove that one of these four suspects was moving under an assumed name and at the same time discover the real name, that real name might mean quite a lot to the Lord Chief Justice, and if so, would put the entire genesis of the crime in my hands.

"I resolved, therefore, to check up, if possible, on all four of them. The cases of Fothergill, Harcourt and Bentley I had to delegate owing to sheer urgency, but I reserved the Secretan angle for my own particular pigeon, for I was pretty certain in my own mind that here was my solution. I decided to employ a modest spot of burglary and my luck happened to be in. I argued to myself that there was quite a strong likelihood that, obsessed as she was by this campaign of revenge, she would keep her birth-certificate close to her, and that was what I desired to find.

"In this enterprise I had the invaluable assistance of a Miss Helen Repton, a lady attached to the 'Yard.' The Secretan house was unoccupied when I made my entry and, as I said just now, my luck went the right way. I discovered a birth-certificate made out in the name of Ada Rotherham Pemberton and I felt in my bones, when I made this find, that the name 'Pemberton' would prove the essential clue towards the solving of the problem. When I presented it to the Lord Chief Justice here, I was really thrilled to find that my surmise was proved to be one hundred per cent correct. He, supported by Justices Flagon and Madrigal, had dismissed an appeal against sentence of death which had been pronounced on a certain Arthur Rotherham Pemberton and then, you see, I had the main threads of the case in my hands. The lady whom we knew as Paula Secretan was this man's twin-sister.

"We have since learned that she went on the stage at a comparatively early age, taking the name of Paula Secretan, and was touring in the States at the time of her twin-brother's arrest, sentence and subsequent execution."

Viscount Fifoot intervened as Anthony paused. "A strange idea—visiting the revenge on the three judicial authorities whose sole responsibility rested in the dismissal of Pemberton's appeal?"

"Oh—undoubtedly, sir. But there was one really extraordinary feature of the affair which may, at the moment, be eluding your memory."

Sir Austin nodded. "I know what you're going to say, Bathurst. You mean with regard to the members of the jury who brought in the original verdict of guilty?"

"Yes, Sir Austin. They were all killed by a rocket-bomb. And in my opinion, for what it's worth, it was this elimination of the twelve jurors which planted this seed of mad revenge in Miss Pemberton's brain. Perhaps you get the idea? That these people had been destroyed by Divine intervention and that she, in her crazy way, would continue the fell work."

The Lord Chief Justice nodded. "Yes. I see what you mean. I think you may be on the right road there, Bathurst. But what about Mr. Justice Wilbraham who—oh, of course, he passed over in the autumn of last year."

"Well," went on Anthony, "there isn't a lot more to tell you. Except, perhaps, with regard to the inner details of those closing stages. You are as familiar with the main pattern as I am. Taking the murders of Flagon and Madrigal as precedents we felt fairly positive that the attempt on your life, sir, would be staged on the evening of your dinner. I actually followed Miss Secretan all the way from her house to a villa in Hammersmith. I wasn't expecting this. I had anticipated that she would drive direct to the 'Diadem' restaurant. But MacMorran has established since that she bribed one of the 'Diadem' waiters—and bribed him heavily—to take his place on that evening. She undoubtedly *intended* to murder you, sir, at the dinner. But thanks to the admirable way in which MacMorran placed his people—at her elbow all the time—the chance to do the job with certainty never came her way. So she fell back on her second plan which she had undoubtedly had in her mind, if the first fell through and for which she had come fully prepared. This second line of offence—I shudder to think of it—very nearly came off.

"Just as the show was finishing, she managed to elude Helen Repton's vigilance for the first time that evening, and went straight to the place where your car was parked and where, at that time of the evening, your chauffeur would be waiting. As a waiter, she was quite in the picture when she offered him the chink which, in all probability, she stated had been sent out to him by you. This drink she had 'doctored,' and when it had taken effect she rolled him into a corner and in his cap and jacket took his place. She reckoned that when you alighted here at Hart's Heath, you would be almost a sitting-bird. And if I hadn't tumbled to it just in time—thanks very largely to your mention of servants and Lady Fifoot's reference to Searle's taking on the mantle of Jehu—" Anthony broke off and shrugged his shoulders.

"Do you know, Mr. Bathurst," said Lady Fifoot, "that your saying that gives me an extraordinary sense of comfort. To think that I was able to help you just a little. I shall never forget that journey home. The responsibility was far too much for you to bear alone. That's what I was thinking all the time. Still—all's well that ends well—and we must leave it at that."

"I am still puzzled about one thing," said the Lord Chief Justice; "why did she have that love-affair with Nicholas Flagon? If all that she intended was murder?"

"My dear," said his wife, "with all your experience and erudition, how little you know women! What better way than that is there for an unscrupulous woman to get a man into her clutches? My dear—ask yourself!"

The Lord Chief Justice shrugged his shoulders at his wife's reply just as Sir Austin interposed.

"What baffles me," said the Commissioner, "is where she got her extraordinary skill at darts. A woman, you know."

"She had been a splendid player for many years, sir," said Anthony. "In fact—even in Quiddington St. Philip, her skill was well-known. Sir Claude de Monterey was in the habit of taking her round. And I think she was a little afraid with regard to that skill—from the point of view of possible suspicion being directed against her."

He turned to Sybil Fifoot. "If her ladyship will forgive me, I fancy that there we have, perhaps, another reason for the Flagon love-entanglement. As Flagon's fiancée, I suggest, she would be almost immune from casual suspicion."

Sybil Fifoot took up the challenge. "A minor—not the major reason. And please, Mr. Bathurst, allow me to know more about my sex than you do."

"Your ladyship," responded Anthony gallantly "in that respect, I am more than content to accept your infallible judgment."

"And I," said the Lord Chief Justice, with a twinkle in his eye, "to accept that of my dear old friend, Rudyard Kipling."

"And what exactly," retorted Lady Fifoot, "do you mean by that?"

"Something," replied Viscount Fifoot, "concerning the female of the species."

THE END

KINDRED SPIRITS . . .

Why not join the

**DEAN STREET PRESS
FACEBOOK GROUP**

for lively bookish chat
and more

Scan the QR code below

Or follow this link
**www.facebook.com/groups/
deanstreetpress**

CPSIA information can be obtained
at www.ICGtesting.com
Printed in the USA
LVHW030410150922
728386LV00004B/59

9 781915 393364